FOXHEAD BAY

MOONEY RIVER SERIES
BOOK 2

alicewoodlandauthor.com

Published by Alice Woodland 2025
Copyright © Alice Woodland 2025

Edited by Poppy Solomon & Emily Hunt
Typeset by Alice Woodland
Cover & Illustrations by Haylee Buswell

ISBN: 978-0-6455441-3-8
A catalogue record for this book is available from the National
Library of Australia

FOXHEAD BAY

ALICE WOODLAND

PART 1

NELLY

'I am powerful. I am capable. I am in control.'

I raise the white thread to my front teeth, plucking firmly to remove a small piece of spinach before repeating the three statements – which have been proven to improve individual success – after flossing each tooth on the top row of my mouth.

'I am powerful. I am capable. I am in control.'

Several tiny pieces of spinach and egg are scattered across the mirror, flecks resting on the reflected blue eyes, angular shoulders, and what my mum insists on referring to as a 'dignified nose'; she becomes quite impatient with my insistence that it is too large.

I step slightly to the left, away from the splatter, and refocus on the centre of my face. *Definitely* too large. Even if it weren't, I'm still far from conventionally attractive. I'm not supple or feminine like other girls. I'm never going to have the same impact as Abigail, whose mere presence can cause a frenzy, or Rain, who is so innocuously beautiful that although she manages to go unnoticed in a crowd is entrancing at close-range.

Meanwhile, here I am with my father's too-large nose, my grandpa's freckles, tiny breasts, and gangly arms that seem to have no genetic lineage whatsoever.

But there's no time to dwell on my physical inadequacies. There's simply too much work to do. I have to pack for camping, wrap Rain and Abigail's Christmas presents (which, thanks to an understaffed postal service only arrived the day before yesterday) and return an email to the chairperson of *Get Lost Gas* confirming my commitment to their grassroots movement. I'm excited to attend their next planning meeting in person; up until now, I've only been able to sit in on digital calls, and I find my contributions lack a certain gusto when delivered virtually. Next year I'll make a real difference.

In a clear, confident voice, *as if it is already done*, I announce: '*I have many talents, including perseverance, organisation and reverse-parallel-parking.*' I slide the minty string through the centremost gap in my bottom teeth, flossing out the omelettey debris.

Eye-contact, Eleanor. Sustained eye-contact.

'*I have many talents, including—*'

A knock at the bathroom door causes me to slip, grazing my thumb-knuckle on my lateral incisor. '*WHAT?*' I ask, running my thumb under the cool tap.

Erik answers in his morning voice, incompetent with drowsiness. I make out the word 'toilet.'

'Use Mum's ensuite! I still have five teeth left.'

I hear him grumbling, his bare feet slapping down the hall towards our Mum's room.

I re-coil the floss around my index finger. '*I have many talents, including perseverance, organisation and reverse-parallel-parking.*'

· · ·

Feeling significantly more buoyant after my morning routine, I proceed to Erik's room. 'I hope you're ready to help organise our supplies,' I say, pushing the door open and finding him lying on the floor staring at his phone.

'Now?'

'Yes, now! You agreed last night. I won't come if you're going to—'

'Jesus, Nelly. OK...' he rolls onto his stomach, presses himself up into a kneeling position and jumps lightly to his feet before following me to the garage.

I unfold the ladder in front of the ceiling-high shelves and my brother dashes to it. '*I* was going to climb!' I say, irritated by his flagrant disregard of proper ladder-climbing protocol; his feet are bare, and his hair, degenerately long at the moment, is hanging in loose white curtains.

He pauses, his left foot hovering in the purgatory between two rungs. 'You want me to climb back down?'

'Don't be ridiculous. You're *up* now. And don't forget to take down the butane stove,' I add, pointing to a shelf just above his shoulders. 'We can transport it in the dry-bag, thus ensuring it stays functional.'

He tips to the left slightly before steadying himself on the ladder. 'Exams are over, Nelly. Stop saying thus.'

I suggest he reposition his feet slightly to the right.

He responds with a crude gesture before wiping his forehead; the sun's only been up for a few hours and it's already *boiling*. 'Let's finish this later?' he says. 'New Year's is still a week away. I wanna call Rain, before she—'

'We've been *through* this! I want to be prepared. If you and the others *insist* we spend two nights sleeping on the sand while bugs gnaw at our flesh, I at least want to be organised. You know as well as I do how busy the next week is going to be, what with Christmas and the *Get Lost Gas* meeting — We need

5

to make sure we check the oil and water before the drive to the city, by the way. We only have a narrow window of opportunity to prepare for the camping trip.'

He sighs, taking the butane stove and thrusting the metal slab towards me — half-grill, half burner. I place it alongside the twelve-person tent and three sleeping bags (one for myself, one for Erik, one for Rain) which are already lined up precisely parallel to the front wheel of my car, facing the interior of the room.

Our garage, much larger than most, has changed over the last year. The space, much larger than an average garage, has changed over the last year. The square footage is still the same, as are the high horizontal windows, polished floor-coating, and the dozen surfboards arranged against the far wall; the paddle-board is still hanging next to the bikes and the built-in shelving units still hold all of Mum's art supplies and gardening tools, as well as all of our camping, hiking and emergency equipment. Dad's car is gone now, along with several other bulky and unnecessary items of his, including his jet-ski, kayak, snow-board, and three sets of gold-clubs. Erik set up a home gym in their place. It's hardly comprehensive, but does include a stationary bike, boxing bag, and a number of weights, ropes and bands. I use it too, though not at the same time as my brother. He becomes unreasonably irritated by my suggestions about proper form and post-workout nutrition.

I wonder whether Abigail is still planning to complete her Certificate in Fitness next year. There's no way for me to know. I haven't spoken to her in months. *No one* has. Which reminds me — 'Jenny said that Mia ran into Abigail at the supermarket in Bandler Beach the other day. Apparently she looked malnourished and she was wearing a hooded jumper. In the middle of *summer*.'

'So?'

'*So...* when have you ever known Abigail to optionally conceal herself? He could be *hurting* her. I think it's time we filed a report.'

Erik pinches the top of his nose. 'And say what? "This chick Abigail was wearing a jumper at the shops so we think her boyfriend's bashing her?" There's nothing you can do, Nelly.'

I roll my eyes. 'We've been *through* this. If she's a victim of domestic abuse, I for one—'

'You don't know that! You need to stop worrying about it. Abigail can stand up for herself. She was always pretty good at it when she was with me.'

'That's because you're not an abuser, Erik! Think about it *critically.* Forget your bias and examine the timeline. It's textbook! First, Abigail meets Harrison at that grotty club in Bandler Beach. The next day he love-bombs her with a dozen red roses. They become immediately obsessed with each other. On their second date, he says "I love you"! If *that* isn't a red flag, I don't know what is. Then they move in together after, oh, *a month*, and she steadily withdraws from her friends and family. Now she looks malnourished, wears suspicious clothing, and her own parents haven't seen her for months. She's not even speaking to her *sister*! It's time we formulated a rescue plan.'

'Nelly... you can't force someone out of something like this. You need to just wait it out and she'll come to you when... if she's ready. There's nothing else you can—'

'I won't go camping. I *won't*. Not unless you agree to help me get some answers. If I'm spending two nights with no access to wifi or running water, sweating in a tent, the least you could do is—'

'Fine,' Erik says, climbing down and pushing his hair out of his face. 'But you have to actually get into it. No talking about Uni or police-reports or gas-wells or anything. Just the group of us. One last time, before… you know.' He avoids my eyes, nudging a medicine ball with his foot. 'We've got two weeks left. Two weeks to just be us, before everything happens.'

He won't admit it, but my brother is feeling *emotional* about all of the changes imminent in our lives. Soon, I will be three hours away at Uni with Rain. Erik will be on tour, and Thatch will be doing God knows what – probably joining his dad on the mines to pillage the land of dwindling natural resources.

We'll never be able to return to how things are now.

Rain and Thatch and Erik and I have spent almost every day together for the last fourteen months, riding the bus and sitting under the big tree at school, staying out late at the oval and waking up early to get to the beach.

That's all in the past, now.

Which is perfectly fine, of course. Everything is going *exactly* as planned. *I am in control.*

'What time does Dad get here?' Erik asks, thrusting an elbow into his boxing bag.

I check my watch. 'Just over ten minutes, provided he's on time. He was extremely excited when I spoke to him last night.'

'I don't care, Nel. I'm not going for him. I'm going for you.' He pivots, kicking the bag with the front of his foot as a distant knocking echoes through the house. Mum's voice carries down the hall into the warm air of the garage, then Dad's. Erik grumbles something under his breath.

Before I can ask him to repeat himself more clearly, our dad appears in the doorway of the garage. 'Merry Chrissy!' he booms.

'It's Christmas *Eve*,' I answer, proceeding forward and allowing him to hug me briefly.

Erik exhales heavily before saying, 'Hey.'

'Are ya ready to go?' Dad asks, throwing his car keys up and catching them in his other hand.

I nod, briskly.

'I need a second,' Erik says.

Typical.

While we're in the kitchen, waiting for Erik to do whatever it is he needs to do in his room, Mum asks Dad if he'd like a coffee.

'I'd love one. Cheers, love. I mean... Cheers.'

'You're welcome.'

My parents have gradually become more civilised in their dealings with one another.

Initially, Dad called all the time, arriving at the door unannounced on more than one occasion. *Begging.* There was some yelling on Mum's part (in contrast to the sleepy, sombre state that would overcome her when left alone), a series of 'family meetings', and *six* sessions of couples' counselling. The proverbial damage, however, was already done. Mum simply could not get over the infidelity.

Lately, things between my parents have been less combustive. They now interact formally, like professional acquaintances. I suppose it's preferable to *kissing* all the time, like they used to. Though I *had* imagined a more exciting scenario in which Mum travelled to a series of exotic locations on her own, taking lovers of varied ethnicities and genders until finally realising that her true calling lay in something creative and/or entrepreneurial.

She *did* begin a glass-blowing class a few months ago, I suppose. Her instructor, Alexander (who wears open toed sandals and ties his ponytail with a leather strap) tells her that her work shows promise, though his motives for complimenting her art are murky; the few times I've encountered him, Alexander has seemed unable to take his eyes from my mother's most typically desirable features, and he showed up to our house unannounced last week to inform Mum of some new coloured glass that had just arrived from his supplier.

The following day, Erik dropped in on Alexander in the surf. He becomes quite agitated at the prospect of our mum engaging in new relationships. I initially noticed one morning last winter, when a barista in Bandler Bay poured a heart into the top of Mum's flat white. She pretended not to know him, even though she called him by his first name and her eyes lingered on his shoulders as he walked away from our table. Erik refuses to go back to that coffee shop, even though it's closest to the beach.

I, on the other hand, think it's excellent that our mother is enjoying the freedom forced upon her. I don't mind if she sleeps with glass-blowers and baristas. I think both men seem robust and athletic – if a little dull to be serious romantic contenders.

Dad is sipping his coffee when Erik reemerges, writing something on his phone that I can only imagine is a message to Rain. Sentimental correspondences like this are one of the by-products of his relationship. Others include smiling vapidly, going on *picnics*, and, occasionally, *humming*. It would be unbearable, if he weren't so happy.

'Forecast was thirty-five when I checked this morning,' Dad says cheerily.

Erik feigns a smile, passing through the front door and outside towards Dad's car.

For approximately three-quarters of the drive to Bandler Beach, Dad and Erik discuss the surf. Specifically, the unseasonably large swell that is predicted to hit our coast in a few days. Something to do with a tropical cyclone up north.

Dad continues to repeat the phrase, 'Once in a lifetime swell event!' smacking his steering wheel for emphasis. 'Next Tuesday n' Wednesday, they reckon...' He grins. 'Good practice for the big ones, eh? You've got Hawaii in—'

'I know,' Erik says. 'It's my schedule.'

Unperturbed, Dad changes the subject to a recent event in which Erik competed as a wildcard. He made it to the quarter-finals, which was quite impressive given the experience and notoriety of the other competitors. Dad maintains that Erik would have done even better on one of *his* surfboards, but Erik has refused to ride one for over a year.

'The boards I've got are fine. I like them.'

'Bullshit, Ricky. They're clunky and you know it. You're better on mine.'

I groan with impatience as the ocean becomes visible over the dunes and rooftops of Bandler Beach. Ignoring the fact that every parking space is taken, Dad heaves his Land Cruiser up a stiff verge and onto a patch of native fauna. It's absolutely pointless saying anything. He'll keep flagrantly injuring plants until he's a senile old man and a doctor takes his licence. I may report him myself when the time comes.

As we jostle along the busy track to the beach, I consider sending a letter to the council, encouraging them to put up some sort of fence or bollard, preventing people like my dad from destroying wildlife. Perhaps I could convince the Mooney River High School Eco-Club to spread awareness; although I'm not *President* anymore, I will *always* be a co-founder, and I have every right to remain involved in ongoing projects.

A bobtail lizard dashes across the track, centimetres from my toes, very quickly taking my mind off things, and I watch the ground more carefully as we pick our way through the crowded beach to a patch of unoccupied sand.

The water is warm. My muscles stretch and tighten as I

fight through the waves for thirty minutes, monitoring my heart rate occasionally. Then I swim past the breakers, past all of the tourists with their pink-skin and boogie-boards, and float, allowing my parasympathetic nervous system an opportunity to 'relax'. It turns out to be an extremely productive experience: I decide on my final elective for Uni next year and mentally organise my dry-bag for the camping trip next weekend.

Then I catch a perfect wave into shore, dodging a few idiotic teenagers as it breaks, and lie under the shade of the umbrella, which I've squeezed between a family's obnoxious marquee and a dense patch of vegetation. I block out the sounds of a mother fighting to apply sunscreen to her child's face (if you keep moving it'll go in your eyes!) and the screams of the idiotic teenagers I passed in the surf, finally managing to focus on my book.

Minutes later, Dad and Erik arrive, interrupting me before I can discover how technofeudalism influences individual identity. I'm so agitated by it that I dogear the page – a habit I swore off years ago.

Things become substantially more agitating when we arrive at Dad's unit.

It's on the industrial outskirts of town, behind an identical beige-brick dwelling. There are oil stains on the driveway and not so much as a cactus in any of the garden beds. And it's far worse on the inside. Despite living here for over a year, Dad hasn't bought himself any proper furniture or decor. An old sofa that used to reside in our games room slumps on one side of the room while a ridiculously large television, the first thing Dad bought after moving here, has been mounted on the opposite wall. A plastic Christmas tree sits unlit in a corner, two poorly-wrapped gifts waiting beneath it.

Dad must notice me examining them. 'Let's get the sand off before we crack into the pressies, eh? I cleaned the shower for yas. Then we can crack a drink! Can't believe you kids're *legal* now...'

Thirty minutes later, I'm drinking a can of vodka seltzer in what dad refers to as his 'courtyard'. The minuscule area is encased in a retaining wall made of the same beige bricks as the house, while the remaining space is occupied by a strip of sandy garden bed and a rusting black barbeque. In front of me, on a small wrought iron table, is a box of buttery white crackers. Dad is peeling the plastic lid from a tub of high-sodium supermarket dip, and Erik is taking long sips from a bottle of beer.

'Enjoy that, eh?' Dad says enthusiastically, gesturing at the dip before running back inside.

Erik takes a cracker, tentatively sliding it across the surface of the yellowish goo.

Dad returns, depositing a present into each of our laps. The gift-wrapping is shiny and tacky, with cartoon reindeers and children playing on it. At least my parcel is bigger than Erik's. He tears his open, letting its contents drop onto his lap.

'It's the newest model, mate! With the underwater housing and everything. Y'can get some POV shots in the surf, or ask a mate to film ya from the water.'

The box is visible now – an action camera with state of the art accessories.

Erik says, 'Thanks.'

Dad bobs above him, as if anticipating a hug, before rushing inside.

We wait, and Erik dunks another cracker into the revolting paste.

Dad reappears with a cold beer and a ridiculous grin, and I begin to open my own gift. I'm anticipating something useful for study or home. I've hinted that Rain and I need a microwave for the townhouse in the city, and this box seems to be a suitable size. Despite having no desire to preserve the paper, I untape and unfold the edges carefully.

What I find beneath the glossy reindeers is *not* what I predicted.

'Dad...' I start, through a mounting sense of confusion. 'Is this a... *drone?*'

'Yep!' he claps. 'A bloody good one too, love!'

Erik shifts. He eats another two crackers while I consider my response. I eventually ask, 'What *on earth* am *I* supposed to do with a *drone?*'

'Well...' Dad begins. 'Y'can film stuff, from the sky. Your eco-stuff, or uni, or—'

'Erik. You want me to capture aerial footage of *Erik*, don't you? That's my present.'

Judging by the tilt of his brows, Dad is beginning to realise his error. 'It's a bloody good one, love... I thought you'd be able to use it for lots of stuff...' His smile falters, and he uses the back of his forearm to wipe sweat from above his lip.

I consume the final sips of my seltzer before crushing the can into the bricks with my foot.

'I don't need you to film me,' says Erik. 'You'll be able to do other stuff with it. You'll think of something really good, like you always do...' He turns to Dad. 'Want me to do anything? For the barbie?' He's clearly trying to keep the peace.

'Sure, mate! Grab the stuff outa the fridge – I got some bloody great steaks from the butcher, and a coupla skewers. Even got prawns! I'll get the gas on.'

I cross my legs and type a message to the group chat, reminding everyone to check off communal items as they pack them: *It would be highly inconvenient to arrive with five fishing rods and no water.*

Erik deposits a fresh seltzer onto the table in front of me as

Dad groans, deeply, from behind the barbeque. It slowly turns into the word, 'Faaaaarkk...' and he kicks one of the barbeque's legs.

'What?' Erik asks.

In the beige-brick glare, Dad wipes his forehead with the crook of his elbow. 'No fucken gas left!' He kicks the barbeque's leg again, more forcefully, causing it to rock in an unpleasant, threatening way. 'Deano must've left the fucken nozzle on... Had a full bottle when he came round the other night...'

'We could just use the kitchen? Make everything in pans?' suggests Erik.

I fan myself with the cracker box, briefly considering eating one.

'I haven't got a bloody *pan*...' Dad answers. 'I usually just cook out here, or get something from town, or whack one of those heat-up things in the microwave...'

The thought of my dad eating microwave lasagne makes me forget, for a moment, about his horrifically insulting gift. 'We could get some more gas from town?'

'Nowhere's open, sweet'eart. Bloody Christmas. Spose we could go back out to Bandler — try grab a new bottle at the petrol station on the highway...'

Erik prods a raw chicken skewer through its plastic covering. 'Could we just microwave...?' He falls silent, registering my disgust.

Silently, the three of us sip our drinks, pretending not to consider the obvious: we have plenty of pans at *home*, as well as a barbeque, along with anything else we could ever need for a festive meal – including Mum. But our parents haven't eaten a meal together for at least eleven months and Christmas Eve is hardly the time to begin.

'...The pub's open?' Erik offers with a shrug.

·   ·   ·

The Mooney River Inn is an extraordinarily unpleasant place to spend Christmas Eve, only partially due to the fifteen percent surcharge on all food and beverages.

It's *extremely* busy – full of people who, like us, have absolutely nowhere else to go. The table closest to the entrance is occupied by intoxicated, sunburnt backpackers, calling out to one another in foreign languages, smoking cigarettes and spilling beer.

Clusters of city people pose for photos at smaller tables, recognisable from their ironed collars, matte lipstick and iPad babies.

The largest group of pub-goers, seated along three long bench tables, appear to be members of an outlaw motorcycle gang. At least twenty individuals in total. It's impossible to determine which club, as none of them are wearing specific insignia (I'm fairly certain they're not *permitted* to outwardly advertise their club, due to laws introduced recently) but they're all dressed in matching leather vests. Other aesthetic choices, including a number of bald heads, beards, and tattoos, seem closely coordinated.

I nudge my brother as we pass, asking if he knows which gang they belong to.

He hisses at me to stop pointing.

Inside, the fans, fridges, and icy beer taps have lowered the temperature.

We make our way to the bar. Two girls, approximately our age, step away from a pool table and directly into our path, leaving two muscular men in polo shirts. The girl holding the cue — a weak-jawed brunette — is staring at my brother. 'Are you Erik Everson?'

Erik startles, but recovers quickly. Smiling, he says, 'Yep. Yeah, I am.'

'That's me boy!' adds Dad, wrapping an arm around Erik and waiting eagerly for the same level of recognition.

I sigh, shifting my weight from one foot to the other, making sure neither are pronating. Aligning my stance has become a habit whenever I'm waiting.

The girl with the cue ignores both my shuffling and my dad's attention seeking. 'Can we get a photo?' she asks Erik.

'Sure,' he says.

With a revoltingly doe-eyed look, the girl passes a phone to my dad. 'Do you mind?'

Dad shakes his head, taking the offered device. His left eye twitches once. I think this is the first time Erik has been recognised in lieu of him. Erik, who must also be aware of this fact, does not seem concerned. He rests an arm around the shoulder of each girl as they squeeze his abdomen, smiling broadly.

When the interaction is finally over and we're walking away, I hear the cue girl snarl, '*It's out of focus!*' and smile at my Dad's act of petty revenge. He's quite a good photographer, when he wants to be.

We find a table covered in glasses and swipe a menu from the bar. On holidays like today, the Mooney River Inn is only equipped to prepare battered fish and chips, steak and chips, vege quiche and chips, or a *bowl* of chips. An *exceedingly* nutritious selection.

'Have you heard from Rain?' Erik asks, returning from the counter with our drinks.

I shake my head, squirting a dollop of sanitiser into my palm before taking my glass.

He sighs, checking his phone again. 'Thatch said Simpo loved her present.'

'Who's Simpo?' Dad asks, wiping beer foam from above his lip.

'Thatch's girlfriend,' Erik answers. 'Her name's not really Simpo. It's—'

'Good on him! Didn't know he had a chick.' Dad laughs, draining another quarter of his glass.

I don't respond. *I* hardly care if Thatch's girlfriend liked a cheap necklace from the Bandler Beach mall. I maintain that the heart-shaped pendant is cliched, but if Thatch wants to purchase his girlfriend inexpensive gifts, it's *hardly* any of my business. And if she's tasteless enough to appreciate it, I can't help *either* of them.

'What about that chick of yours?' Dad asks Erik. 'She around for Chrissy?'

Erik shakes his head. 'She's with her family. Marli and Doe's family.' He checks his phone, typing something quickly. 'It's a difficult day for her. She's seeing her mother for the first time in almost five years.'

'The junkie?' Dad asks.

'Not *junkie*, Dad. That's a disrespectful and outdated term. Rain's mother is living with opioid addiction. It's a very serious issue facing many people from all walks of life.'

'Sorry, love. Didn't mean to sound... Her mum's the kind of opioid addict that lives on the streets though, eh? The type that's a bit...' He scratches at his arms, contorting his face into a hungry, rodent-like expression.

Erik and I glance at each other, deciding to ignore him.

Dad clears his throat. 'Mind putin' your phone down for a sec, Ricky? I wanted to talk to you guys about something, 'fore the grub gets here...'

Erik finishes typing before placing his phone on the table.

'Look, kids...' Dad begins, before clearing his throat yet again. He gulps the remainder of his beer, covers his mouth with a clenched fist, burps, then recovers, adopting an air or solemnity before continuing. 'This is a bit bloody tricky for me, but I need ya both to know something. A *few* things. About the stuff I've been doin' and the stuff I've learned.'

The seltzer gurgles in my stomach. *What on earth* is he talking about?

'So... your mum and me saw a counsellor, you might know that already, and I've been doin' a bit of reading – for once, eh, Nel? Hah! Anyway. I reckon I owe you two another apology. I've figured out a bit more about meself, and the way I grew up, and my lousy fucken parents, and why I always feel like I need to *prove* something. And I'm not makin' excuses for what I did to your mum. It's unacceptable. There's no excuse.' He attempts to drain the final foamy droplets of beer from his glass and looks away towards the bar.

I look towards the bar, too, fixating on the barman, who seems to be pretending to look for a drink in order to hold his head inside the refrigerator.

Why is my Dad saying all of this now? He's *never* mentioned his parents. Every time I ask, he either changes the subject or leaves the room. I've accumulated information second hand, of course, through mum, but only vague adjectives, leading me to believe that Dad's childhood was violent and abusive.

'I'm bloody sorry, kids...' he concludes, placing his empty glass on the table before resuming eye-contact, first with me, then my brother.

Before either Erik or I can respond, we're intercepted by a girl. A *woman*, to be correct.

Lucy Buckingham.

A protective urge to shove her away from my brother rushes through me. I *also* want to tell her that the gaping rips in her denim shorts are not trendy, but completely contrived – much like the oversized glasses pushing back her artificially golden waves.

She must be back from the city, visiting her family over Christmas. They live a few houses down from us. *Unfortunately.*

'Hi!' Lucy beams. 'Merry Christmas, Eversons.'

I don't respond because I don't *want* Lucy to be merry.

I want her to get the *fluff* away from my brother.

Erik — like most of the boys at school — was once intoxicated by her charms. She paid little attention until he won his first state competition. A few weeks later, he'd lost his virginity to her. We had just turned fourteen, and Lucy was seventeen at the time. It was *quite* the controversy around school.

My dad booms back something about it being a 'Hot one.'

'Summer usually is, Dad,' Erik mumbles.

Lucy laughs far too enthusiastically, her thumb hooked casually in one of her belt loops. 'What are you guys doing for New Years?'

'Camping,' says Erik. 'Me and Nelly are going with some mates. And my girlfriend.'

'Oh?' Lucy asks. 'That sounds so fun! Is that the girl you were with at Easter when I bumped into you? She's so cute and quirky. I haven't been camping in *ages*. Who else are you—'

'It *will* be fun,' I intercept. 'And Rain is *extremely* cute. And smart, and artistic. What are *you* doing these days, Lucy? Still studying marketing?'

I know very well Lucy is no longer studying marketing. I have it on good authority that she failed her statistics unit not once but twice, leading to a tearful self-extraction from university. Her smile slips momentarily. 'Not anymore.' She bounces, unhooking her thumb from her belt loop and resting her hand on Erik's chair. He glances at it, flushing slightly before sipping his beer. 'It's a tough industry to crack, even in the city. I'm getting into real-estate now, working at my parents' agency over summer. It's crazy how much things are booming!'

'That's bloody great!' Dad announces, a waitperson arriving behind him.

Lucy simpers and moves out of the way so that the man — whose apron is absolutely filthy — can deposit our plates on the table. 'I'll leave you guys to your meal,' she announces. 'Great to see you, Erik. And you, Eleanor! Always a pleasure, Andy.' With a final smile, she turns back and walks towards the bar.

'*Rude.*'

'What was rude, sweet'eart?'

'It was *rude* of her. *Lucy*. Strolling over here and inter- rupting our festive meal...' I examine the contents of my plate: a plaid fish fillet, a mound of oil-slicked potatoes, and two wedges of tomato resting atop a bed of browning iceberg.

Erik glances over his shoulder to where Lucy and a few of her friends are laughing performatively. 'Don't worry, mate,' Dad says, clapping my brother on his shoulder. 'Nelly's just lookin' out for her friend. Girls've gotta stick together, eh darlin'?' He picks up his knife and fork, sawing through his overcooked steak. 'Must be tricky going out with your sister's best mate. 'Specially at your age.'

Erik dips a chip in tomato sauce slowly. 'It's not tricky. Not if you tell the truth.'

For a moment, I think my dad is choking. Then he swallows heavily, patting himself on the chest four times before coughing into his napkin.

'My dislike for Lucy has *nothing* to do with Erik,' I lie. 'There are other things about her which I find... unsavoury.'

'Well... she's a looker!' says Dad. 'But she's got nothing on my girl.'

'It's nothing to do with her looks!' My hand jerks in irrita- tion, knocking over the salt shaker. As Erik picks it up, I add, 'Women don't dislike other women based on appearance. There are plenty of other reasons. I happen to find Lucy extremely superficial and duplicitous. At times, I think she's even been quite... predatory.'

'Hey?' laughs Dad. 'What's she done that's so bloody predatory?'

Before I can answer, Erik demands, 'Drop it.'

Dad clears his throat before leaving to get another beer, and the three of us finish our meals in silence, checking our phones to avoid communicating. The group chat has been busy:

> Thatch:
> What's everyone doin tonite
>
> Clancy:
> Your mum
>
> Lara:
> Fishin the bay
>
> Thatch:
> catch anything?
>
> Lara:
> two skippy
>
> Jenny:
> I got a King George but it was too small
>
> Freddie:
> Anyone going out?
>
> Thatch:
> Me n Simpo will

Lara:
Oval?

Clancy:
Deadshit Brian's there

Freddie:
Thatch's?

Thatch:
Nah. It smells heaps bad at my place even with
    the windows open. Anyone know anythin
    about cleanin milk off carpet?

Zac:
Mum's got a steam vac thing if you wanna
    borrow it after Chrissy?

...

Erik:
We're at the pub. Come.

Clancy:
Fuck yous for bein 18

Zac:
Tell us if you end up at the oval

Well, I suppose that rules out my plan to organise the
drybag, drink two amaretto sours with Mum and get an early
night. Once everyone gets here we won't leave until after

twelve, then there'll be the trip home to worry about, and a very probable pit-stop at the oval.

Dejected, I poke at the thick batter encasing my fish.

Our plates are being cleared when Erik slides his phone across to me.

> Rain:
> Mum didn't show up
> I'm fine
> Hope you're having fun!

I look up at Erik, who has the expression of someone about to start running. Or fighting.

'That's *appalling!*'

'Didn't like your dinner, sweet'eart? You ate most of the —'

'It's something *else*, Dad. Rain's mum didn't arrive today. She couldn't manage a simple get together on Christmas Eve... It's absolutely... It's *completely*...'

Erik is already out of his seat and disappearing through the heavy wooden doors.

Dad shrugs. 'Don't worry about it, love. Nothing you can do.'

My nerves are bursting with rage. 'I'm so sick of hearing that. *There's nothing I can do.* Of course there's something I can do! *Anything* is better than nothing.' I clatter out of my own seat, following Erik's path across the sticky inn floor.

I expect to find him outside, but my brother is not in the beer garden.

He's not in the carpark either, or on the footpath running parallel to the main street.

He must be in the park *across* the street... or in the alley running between the pub and the post office.

I try the alley first — it's closer to my current position, so it makes more sense than the alternative.

When I arrive, I do not find my brother. Instead, leaning on the red bricks and smoking what appears to be a hand rolled cigarette, is a member of the outlaw motorcycle gang from the Inn.

I pause with one foot outstretched.

I have viewed hundreds of hours of crime drama, but none of them has prepared me for this moment. Alone in a dark alley with a criminal.

You should run, Eleanor.

Instead, I lower my foot and examine him. The man doesn't seem particularly threatening. He's alone. Not a *great* deal older than me. I would guess twenty-three – twenty-four, perhaps. He's dressed in a simple black t-shirt, jeans and black sneakers. It would be impossible to know he was a bikie if it weren't for the tattoos on his arms, neck, and face. A paw print, just below his eye. On his neck, '1%' in raised, black ink, surrounded by a red diamond. But most identifiable is the image on his arm: a bush-ranger in an iron suit; a Ned Kelly look-alike, with horns rising from the iron helmet and a forked tail flicking behind.

It's the logo for the Devil's Rangers – the most infamous gang operating in the region.

I take one step back.

'How's it going?' the outlaw asks. His eyes glint mischievously, an effect I'm sure is caused by reflected street-lights and not some innate devilry.

'I'm sorry,' I apologise unexpectedly.

The outlaw smiles as I inspect him. His hair is shaved almost to the skin, the tip of another tattoo visible on the skin above his ear, which seems to be bulging slightly. Generally, people would have asked what I was looking at by now; most people are uncomfortable being physically examined for such a long time. But his mouth simply curves around his cigarette. He breathes out smoothly. 'Do you want a drag?'

Thoughtlessly, I take three steps forward. 'No, thank you,' I say, realising my mistake. 'I'm looking for my brother.' I'm quite close to the outlaw now. Close enough to count three small cuts on his forehead.

'MMA.'

'Excuse me?'

'*Mixed Martial Arts*. I'm a fighter.'

Yes. The wiry muscles in his arms seem more than capable of inflicting damage. A biological advantage my eyes can't help but be drawn to. I focus myself with a swift shake of the head. 'I know what MMA is. It's been steadily rising in popularity in the last decade, thanks to ties to popular culture, and public figures like Joe—'

'You're clever, eh?' He pushes off the wall, tipping forward for a moment on his toes.

I tilt my chin up at him. 'My ATAR was ninety-eight-point-one.'

'Then we should celebrate,' he says, stubbing out his cigarette on the side of a huge red skip bin. 'Buy you a drink?'

'No. My dad's inside, and, as I told you, my brother's out here somewhere. Our friend – *his* girlfriend – is experiencing some significant personal issues. Her name's Rain. As in, precipitation. I'm Eleanor. *Nelly*. Everson.' I realise too late that this is probably more than I need to share.

'Sam,' says the outlaw. 'But my friends call me Pup.'

I swallow. 'It was very generous of you to offer your cigarette to me, Sam. I'd better be going now. I'm very busy with...'

He grins dangerously as I back out of the alley.

I walk somewhat dazedly through the courtyard, then inside and to our table.

The moment I sit down, Erik — safe, sound, and sipping his beer — tells me I smell like cigarettes.

'I smell like *cigarettes* because I had to fight my way through a crowd of *smokers* while I was looking for *you!*' I shuffle forward in my chair and sip the melted ice from my glass while he passes me a piece of spearmint chewing gum. I crack it with my teeth, applying a double-dose of hand sanitiser. 'Where's Dad? And what happened with Rain? Did you speak with her?'

'He's at the bar. And I spoke to her, yeah. Not for long. She was... OK. I heard Doe in the background. It's good she's got people there.' He leans over his shoulder, gazing northeasterly through the wall — roughly in the direction of Marli's aunt's house, where Rain and her foster family are spending Christmas.

'Don't get any ridiculous ideas, Erik. You're not *driving*. You've had *at least* five standard drinks in the last four hours, and you're still on your provisional licence! Besides. They're enjoying time as a family and probably preparing for dinner, and you know that Rain becomes anxious in social situations. It would be very inconsiderate of you to show up unannounced and—'

'I get it, Eleanor!'

'Get what?' asks Dad, appearing with three glasses squeezed precariously in his hands. Neither of us answer. We sit in silence, picking at our paper straws, tapping at our phones and glancing up at the bar from time to time. As he nears the end of his beer, Dad announces, 'This is me, guys! Too bloody old for this place.'

'Are you sure you're alright to drive? You've had—'

'I'm drinkin' *lights*, darlin'. They're only two-point-five-percent. And I had a bloody steak. I'll be right. But you two watch out tonight, eh? I don't want you gettin' in any cars with pissed deadshits later. Call me if ya need me, even if it's late, or walk to my place and spend the night. Just let me know if you're comin' round so I can leave a key out.'

In the darkening hour between seven and eight, the Inn becomes more crowded and Erik and I claim the last table outside. Sam the Pup smiles at me occasionally, sipping a honey-coloured beverage in a short glass.

When Freddie, Lara and Jenny arrive, I'm grateful for the distraction. 'I'm so glad you're here!' Judging by their frowns of confusion, my tone is quite out-of-character.

Lara shrugs. 'Better than babysitting all of my cousins while their parents get drunk.'

'Definitely beats my place.' Freddie nods. 'Mum's pretty out of it.' By *out of it*, Freddie is referring to the catatonic state his mother enters when online gambling. It upsets him quite a lot; he's shared some of his feelings on the matter with me privately.

I decide to change the subject. 'Who would like a drink?'

'Me!' Jenny answers.

Lara sighs. 'I'm driving. Fuck. Why did I say I'd drive?'

'You could get a fizzy or something...' suggests Erik. 'Lemon lime and bitters.'

'Yeah. That actually sounds *so* good. Get me one, Nelly?'

'I'll come,' Freddie says, smiling his gentle, covert smile.

There is a certain ease that comes over me in Freddie's company. We studied a lot together this year, having taken three of the same ATAR classes. His notes were always abysmal and he *consistently* made fun of my colour-coding, but other than that I found our sessions quite productive. He doesn't talk a great deal, which I appreciate. I'm a dominant conversationalist. He also has a delicate way of moving and speaking – of thinking – which tends to balance my approach. Freddie orders our drinks and I engage him in conversation about the future of the Mooney River High School Eco Club. '*Maddison Hargrove* is taking over, which is about the best we could have hoped for. I've promoted Zac — who was *reluctant*, but cooperative — to Vice President; he's no Rain Douglass, but I think he'll rein in some of Maddison's controlling tendencies.'

Freddie nods, accepting a black tray of drinks from the bartender. He taps his phone on the small machine, paying before I have a chance to offer.

Freddie's disposable income has increased since he began a part time job as a marijuana salesperson. His client base consists of around forty local residents – mostly kids from school; occasionally their parents.

Carrying two of the drinks, I lead him back through the now crowded space between the bar and the exit. We are *accosted* as soon as we're back outside.

'Merry bloody Chrissy!' Thatch screams as he spills a quarter of my seltzer and comes dangerously close to knocking me over completely with a rowdy half-embrace.

'Be serious, would you?'

He laughs, scrunching the collar of my shirt before throwing himself at Freddie.

'I can't wear nice things around him,' a meek voice says at my side. I glance, but there's really no need; I recognise the voice immediately as Thatch's girlfriend. Carissa Abarico. Also known as *Simpo*. 'It's a really nice shirt,' she adds. 'I love pinstripes.'

'Thank you. I like your... necklace. It's a flattering shape.'

There.

I only wish Rain heard my compliment. She thinks I need to be nicer to Carissa. She said it was rude of me not to invite her to our birthday gathering, though Erik ended up telling her to come anyway. I don't see why I should go out of my way to befriend someone I barely know, who will be out of our lives soon and, for the record, I have always made an effort to be polite to, despite her irrelevance to my life or future. She and Thatch have only been *together* since July, after all, and it's not like they're allowed to sleep in the same *bed*, or even see one another for lengthy periods of time. Besides: They're going to break up when she moves interstate.

She'll be studying *creative writing*.

I offer a rapport-building smile. 'Congratulations on your story. Being shortlisted is a strong achievement even if you didn't technically *win*. Thatch didn't sneak you out tonight, did he? I thought your parents had strict rules against going out after nine.'

Carissa giggles briefly as we stop to stand with the others, speaking so softly I have to bend slightly to hear her. 'I'm so excited to come camping!' In such a busy establishment, she really should raise her voice.

I'm about to respond that all the seats in our vehicle are taken when Lara interjects, 'You can come? That's awesome, Simpo! We're going to have the best time.'

The two of them embrace, and I cringe once more at Carissa's unfortunate nickname. It all began because Thatch thought her name was *Lisa*. It became fixed in his mind, as errors often seem to, and he continued to use it whenever he saw her, despite being constantly reminded by me, Rain, and Carissa. Thatch went on using the incorrect name and Carissa continued to answer to it, somehow completely unoffended. *I* would have been infuriated. Eventually, Thatch began experimenting with *Simpson*, instead, which evolved into *Simpo*.

This happened at around the same time he kissed her at an eco-club event by the river. The nickname stuck after that. According to Thatch, it works on multiple levels due to the fact that Carissa is always '*simping*' over him. It's disgusting.

'What do *you* think, Nelly?' Lara asks. 'Should Thatch bring the tinny? They could take some of the bigger stuff in dry-bags. It's not gunna be rough. And Thatch is a pretty good skipper when he's not pissed!'

I'm tempted to argue (I have witnessed Thatch capsize his dad's dinghy not once, but twice), however, I decide to simply nod. It's Christmas, after all.

'I wish I was coming!' Jenny moans.

'You're going to Bali, dickhead,' Lara replies. 'That's way better.'

'No it's not! It'll just be me and Dad. I'd rather be with you guys at the cove.'

'Hey — Let's go play pool,' Freddie offers.

Lara and Jenny nod and the three of them wander inside, knowing I won't follow. I find the thought of sharing slimy, pestilent pool cues absolutely nauseating — a fact I've never attempted to hide.

Observing my other friends, however, I briefly reconsider playing a round of pool.

Thatch and Carissa are whispering into one another's necks and Erik is so enraptured by his phone he doesn't notice half the beer garden stealing glances at him. Lucy included. She and her two comrades are so contrived, from the roots of their hair down to their toenails, they almost appear natural. I shoot her occasional accusatory glares as the night wears on, as the music bangs, and the beer spills, and the bikies and tourists and all of the others become steadily more intoxicated. I drink responsibly. I make sure to hydrate. I snack on peanuts from the vending machine in order to meet my protein targets.

Thus, the hours between 9pm and 11pm pass by.

The Inn becomes so busy in the hour before closing-time that I keep nudging Freddie in the ribs. To escape the fray, Erik leans over the fence and into the night air, tapping at his phone. Thatch screams nonsense about Carissa's mum's Christmas dinner, pausing between announcements to lean down and kiss his girlfriend.

'Yuck,' I say, accidentally aloud.

'You mean Thatch and Simpo?' Lara asks. I'm standing in a tight circle with her, Jenny and Freddie, thankfully too far away for Thatch or Carissa to hear us over the din.

I nod in answer.

'It's a bit gross,' Lara reluctantly agrees. 'Nobody wants to, like, *hear* it.'

'It's SO gross when you can hear it,' agrees Jenny. 'Abigail and Harrison were the same when they first met, remember?' She imitates the sound of vomiting. 'I told you Mia saw her at the shops the other day? She said she looked fucked. Like she's on meth. Really skinny.'

I sigh. 'We need to help her.'

Freddie nods sadly. 'She's definitely on something. She looked bad when I saw her at the servo a few weeks ago. Twitchy. She's getting something from Harrison. My brother told me some stuff about him... It's not good.'

A nauseated feeling enters my stomach, despite my sensible intake of alcohol. If Freddie's reprehensible brother *Steve* thinks Abigail's boyfriend is bad news, then Abigail is in worse trouble than I'd thought. 'We need to take immediate action,' I resolve.

Lara and Jenny share a glance, then Lara says, carefully, 'Harrison's a wanker, Nel. But there's nothing we can do. Abigail's got to leave on her own.'

Lara lunges forward, pushed by two strangers.

'Watch where you're going next time,' says one of the men.

Who is, on closer inspection, not a stranger at all. It's *him*. Harrison. He must have heard the entire conversation. He must have shoved Lara *on purpose*. Contempt obscures my vision momentarily before Harrison slowly comes back into focus. At first glance, he could be attractive. He is slightly taller than me, with thick hair gelled to stand in peaks. His lips are full and unsettlingly pink, his trapezoids too high – his shoulders too narrow to contain them. His jaw recedes slightly, which, coupled with his projected fringe, makes his side profile look like a cliff, jutting out over the world. Despite this (or perhaps because of the insecurity it causes) Harrison stands with exaggerated confidence. His jaw ticks from side-to-side as he stares at Lara.

The man beside him is staring with less confidence, but more relish. He has a long, pallid face and strips of lifeless hair hang over his eyes. I met him the year before last, on a traumatising voyage to get alcohol. Given the aroma of his house, the pills we found on the floor, and his association with Freddie's older brother Steve, I assume he's some middling-drug-supplier in the region. I don't know his name. I usually refer to him as *The Repulsive Fish Man*. With another surge of nausea, I recall the grey fish swimming hopelessly in an aquarium of green water in his living room. The Repulsive Fish Man looks from Lara to Harrison in eager anticipation.

'I... You...' Lara stutters.

Before I can think of a better response than her two mumbled words, Harrison turns, taking hold of the pallid older man by the shoulder and herding him through a knot of tourists. To my horror, though not entirely to my surprise, Harrison and his perverted friend join the bikies. They are greeted by Sam the Pup and the bearded man with friendly claps on the shoulder.

A growl at my side announces Thatch has joined us. 'Who let those fuckwits in?'

'He shoved me...' says Lara.

'I'll fucken smash him.'

'You'll do no such thing!' I admonish. 'This is a public place, Thatcher. You—'

'What's wrong?' asks Carissa. I hadn't noticed her nestled at Thatch's other side. 'Who are we looking at?'

Thatch sniffs aggressively. 'No one. Let's have a dance, eh?'

They begin to shimmy ridiculously. I look for my brother and find him resting against the wall, still on his phone. I approach him as a new song begins – heavy drums and a synthetic melody. Jostled by the dancing crowd, I'm thrown into bodies I have no desire to make contact with. Lucy and her friends, the bikies, and us, all merge into one throbbing mass. I squirm, trying to regain some personal space, but it's useless.

The next song is even more explosive. Freddie and Lara are back, laughing. Thatch appears to have forgotten all about his outrage. He whoops to the beat, his head bobbing over the rest of the group. He's dancing with three or four of the bikies, singing the lyrics proudly into their faces. As the song ends, with a sweep of his arm, Thatch gathers Sam the Pup and the older bearded man, shouting 'Meet my mates!' as he drags them toward us.

A moment later, almost sleekly, The Repulsive Fish Man squeezes his head through a gap of bodies. My fists clench. Smoothing back his thin hair, he worms his way into the circle, sunken eyes staring directly at me. Moments later, as if the universe were conspiring, Harrison appears at his side.

'Sup,' Harrison nods.

'Is Abigail with you?'

'She couldn't make it.'

'Why not? Where is she? I have a Christmas present for her and—'

Freddie clears his throat.

'She's at home. She wasn't feeling well.'

'Would you please tell her to call me or message me? I'm extremely worried.'

'*Worried?*' Harrison laughs – *laughs* – before nudging his revolting friend, as if they were sharing a private joke.

'I don't know why you're *laughing*. I've known Abigail my entire life and she's never been like this. Something is very obviously wrong and I'm going to find out what it—'

The Repulsive Fish Man makes a gesture with his right hand, snapping his fingers against his thumb to represent the yapping lips of a mouth. My blood boils.

'Don't get me started on you, *you*... you absolute—'

'Hey, hey, hey. It's Christmas Eve!' Sam the Pup says, clapping a hand on Harrison's upper back.

'Exactly!' I agree. 'It's *Christmas*. Which means people should be with their families and their loved ones. They shouldn't be in some hidden location where they're not even permitted to phone their own—'

Harrison steps forward, chest puffed threateningly. 'Abigail told me you do this. Get involved in everyone else's business. She doesn't want to be your friend anymore... so be careful,' he whispers, his irises a dirty shade of yellow-brown, the whites of his eyes a beige-pink.

Freddie steps closer.

'Why should I be careful?' I puff my chest right back at his. 'What will you do if I'm not? If you've done anything to my friend, I'll—'

'You're not her friend,' Harrison smiles smugly. 'You're a psychotic bitch.'

'How dare you!'

Erik rushes to my other side as more of the bikies look over at us.

Harrison's eyes remain fixed, hungrily, on my own. He attempts to move closer but my brother places a firm hand (still clasping his phone) on his chest.

'Fuck off, faggot.' Harrison throws his drink against the pavers and shoves Erik away. Glass smashes and rum and coke spray my ankles as my brother falls backwards, Freddie grabbing him clumsily, both of them crashing into a table.

Harrison lunges towards me, too quickly for Sam the Pup — who attempts to grab his arm — to restrain him.

For a moment, even as I'm realising how utterly cliched it is, my life's accomplishments flash before my eyes (*Head Girl / Dux / Environmental Warrior / Daughter / Friend*) before a shape appears like a battering ram and Harrison is forced back over a chair and into the retaining wall. A huge, instantly recognisable shape. Thatch pins my assailant, pressing with his legs, head down, as Harrison struggles against him.

Astronomically late, a bouncer emerges from the crowd, interjecting with a loud, 'OI!' Thatch looks up and back, notices the bouncer, and draws away from Harrison's struggling body, hands raised in surrender. 'Out!' the bouncer yells. 'Last straw, Thatch. You're banned.' Sam the Pup slides an arm around the bouncer's shoulders, causing a slight flinch. He says something inaudible and the bouncer nods. 'Out, Harrison. You've got one more straw, Thatcher,' he adds, holding up an index finger.

Thatch, attempting to fix his torn shirt, nods schoolboyishly. 'Righto, mate. No worries.'

Sam the Pup, along with the bearded bikie and another Devil's Ranger, escort Harrison off the premises.

I'm completely nauseated. Moving away from the others to a dark section of railing facing the dimly lit street, I barely speak to anyone for the next forty-five minutes. When Erik and Freddie appear, both slightly shell-shocked, I tell them I need a moment. They retreat to a table with Lara and Jenny, pursued by Lucy and her friends.

Sam the Pup seems to have taken a particular liking to Thatch. Despite glares from his friends — particularly the man with the beard and thousand-mile-stare — the outlaw claps Thatch on the back, complimenting his grappling. I even over-hear him offer to buy Thatch and Carissa, who stands meekly under her boyfriend's arm, a drink. He brushes past me on his way to the bar, smelling of cigarettes and something metallic.

Once he's gone, Carissa mumbles that she has to get home to her parents, as it's almost midnight. Who does she think she is, *Cinderella*? Her sundress practically screams, *I still enjoy Disney movies and will continue to do so until a ridiculously inappropriate age.* As soon as Sam the Pup returns with the drinks, Carissa begins to say her goodbyes. I smile and wave as Thatch walks her out of the Inn to her parents' car.

'How's your night going?'

I startle slightly. Sam the Pup is unexpectedly close. Hope-fully he didn't notice his effect on my nervous system. 'Per-fectly fine. Yours?'

'Best night I've had since I got this...' He rubs the scab on his cheekbone lightly.

I feel a pleasant tug in the muscles around my perineum and speak without thinking. 'You're extremely attractive for someone in your line of work.'

Sam leans forward and clicks his tongue once between his teeth. 'You're going to get me in trouble, Eleanor Everson.'

I don't blush exactly. I never *blush*. But there is rather a lot of heat on my face.

Something buzzes against my hip. My phone.

Missed Call: Rain.

'I have to leave now.'

'Probably a good idea,' Sam says, extracting a bag of tobacco from his jeans.

I dial Rain as I walk down the steps onto the slightly quieter footpath.

'Nelly?' she answers.

'Of *course* it's me. I was going to call you, but I was... distracted. I'm extremely sorry your mum didn't show up. It is *extremely* inconsiderate. I hope you're not having a horrible time. Perhaps I should ask you some more positive questions. Is the food pleasant? Are you having fun with Marli and her cousins?'

'They were a lot of fun, yeah. I've tried to get through to Erik a few times... Are you still at the pub?'

'For approximately five more minutes. The night has definitely passed its climax.'

'You're heading home tonight though? You're not staying in town?'

'I'm *hardly* about to sleep on Dad's sad sofa. Lara's driving us.'

Glancing towards Lara, I notice Lucy is still sitting next to Erik, leaning in to whisper something in his ear.

I scramble. 'I'd better get off the phone now! It's far too noisy to focus on a conversation. Perhaps we could talk in the morning instead, when we're both rested and alert.' I say all this frantically as I barge my way back up the steps.

I barely make out Rain's faltering 'OK' before forcing myself between Erik and Lucy. I spend the next few minutes ensuring that her hands stay out of his personal space, only relaxing when the bouncers begin herding us off the premises. As we make our way through the exit, Lucy asks Lara for a lift to her house, to which Lara unfortunately agrees. She's driving her dad's van, so there are seven seats.

The carpark is completely empty, save the van, a discarded shopping trolley, and one broken thong.

Freddie's house is farthest from everyone else's, past the dog beach and near the sewage treatment facility, so Lara drops him off first. He exits at a familiar cul-de-sac, walking without urgency towards the back of the house where he often leaves the door open, while Jenny scrambles into the front seat, kicking Lara in the mouth as she falls into it. 'Sorry, Lar!'

Lara leans away from her best friend, pressing a hand to her jaw and indicating to turn onto Thatch's street. 'Nah!' Thatch objects. 'Dad's still gone. Pretty sad waking up alone on Chrissy. I'll go to the twins' place. If that's orright with you guys?' He repositions himself, seeking permission.

My brother responds, 'No shit, dude. Mum's making pancakes in the morning.'

'I love pancakes...' Lucy says, leaning around me to fawn at my brother as if expecting an invitation.

'Yeah.' Erik smiles, shifting in his seat. 'They're pretty good.'

'*Pretty* good? His mum makes the BEST ones! Heaps fluffy.' Thatch points towards our house as Lara turns onto our street. 'Nita's the best chef in town.'

'How *is* Anita?' Lucy asks. 'It's been so long since I've seen her.'

'She's perfectly fine, Lucy. In fact, she made quite an impressive paper weight last week — for Rain, Erik's *girlfriend*. She's going to give it to her for Christmas.' I make very little eye contact with Lucy during the sentence, preferring to examine the side mirror.

'That's so nice! Your mum is so talented,' she simpers. 'I'll get out here too, Lara — I'd love to say hi to her!'

Thatch winks at Erik, who runs his hand through his hair.

Lara nods, yawning as she pulls into our driveway. 'Night, guys,' she groans as we exit the vehicle.

'Night, fuckwits!' says Jenny, with a small hiccup.

I unlock our front door, shushing Thatch more than the other two. 'If Mum *is* asleep, she won't be for long. Keep your voices down.'

I needn't have shushed them quite so forcefully. Mum is in the kitchen, listening to music too loudly and laughing at something obscured from view by the open fridge door. I worry for a moment that it's a glass-blowing barista before Rain steps out, a bottle of grapefruit juice dangling from her fingertips. Of course she flinches (a trauma-response, I've researched) and of course the bottle goes flying towards the glass cabinet.

The next few moments are a silly mess: Rain tries to catch the juice bottle and sends it hurtling towards Mum, who manages to catch it in two hands, bringing it to her chest like a football. Rain swivels, unsure whether to press the glass cabinet shut or cover her head with her hands. She does a combination of both. Meanwhile, the cabinet shudders. Thankfully, it doesn't break. Rain recovers, straightening and tucking her hair behind her ears.

She smiles, bashfully, at Erik.

Thatch misreads the tone of the moment and moves across the kitchen in a slow-motion mockery of martial-arts, landing a karate chop in the air an inch from her face. It's progress, I suppose. 'You came outa bloody nowhere, Spooks!'

'Merry Christmas,' Rain says, nudging the hand out of her personal space with a florally-clad arm. Ever since she started *working* at the vintage store (I'm quite sure she holds a record for lowest sales ever made), she has been prone to alarming mismatchery. She is standing on the toes of a pair of dark-green, thick-strapped sandals, which she paired with a red and grey plaid miniskirt and top covered in pastel flowers.

Thatch gives her a thick-armed squeeze and adds, 'Sorry about your mum.'

'Thanks...' She squeezes him back.

'How'd ya get here?'

'Marli. She was going into town to get her projector, so she only had to detour a little. I thought I'd surprise... everyone.'

Erik overcomes his initial shock and closes the gap between them, gripping her shoulders and pressing his lips to her forehead.

Lucy animatedly approaches my mum. 'Anita! Your hair looks amazing short. I'd love to just chop all of mine off one day.'

'I said that too!' Thatch jumps in, tousling my mother's new bob and provoking a brief glare from Lucy. 'Are you staying up for a bit, Nita, or...'

'I'm not cooking, Michael. You can have the rum-balls Regina gave us. No more than four. They're strong. Rain and I already had a few, didn't we, baby?'

I roll my eyes. She's been referring to Rain as an infant for at least six months now, and she's not even her *daughter*.

Thatch dives for a rum-ball, but pauses to prod a stack of presents wrapped in painted paper and vines. 'These from you, Rain?' he inquires, poking the top-most parcel.

'Mmhmm,' she replies, standing on her toes and smiling over Erik's shoulder.

'Can we—'

'*Tomorrow*, Thatcher.'

Thatch rolls his eyes at me. He shoves a thumb behind his head in the direction of the clock. 'It *is* tomorrow!'

'When the sun is up, obviously. Everyone knows those are the rul—'

'Break the fucken rules for once!' Thatch cries. 'The *bloody* rules I mean. Sorry, Nita. Who cares, anyway? I've gone to church with Simpo about eight times, and I reckon Jesus'd be fine with it. He doesn't give a shit if we open pressies before the sun's up. He probably never got a pressie in his whole fucken life — it was the olden days.'

His reasoning is infuriating, if somewhat accurate. 'We'll talk about it *later*.' I nudge my head in Lucy's direction, perhaps a little aggressively.

She seems to notice, her smile slipping for a moment. 'Well!' she chimes. 'It's really late, so I'm going to hit the road... for like, twenty steps!'

Mum is the only one who laughs.

The others say polite goodbyes while I check the weather, hoping for a sudden unexpected downpour but seeing only clear skies. A shame.

If Lucy is offended by me ignoring her departure, she doesn't let on. Finally, she leaves. Mum goes to bed shortly after that, telling us all to make sure we get some sleep tonight and not to touch our presents, as they may be fragile.

Thatch continues to push the matter of present opening. 'C'mon,' he says. 'We've gotta do it when it's just us four! It'll be special.'

'Mum's asleep, Thatcher. We'll make too much noise.'

'We'll go to my place! Or the oval! One last late night mission to the oval. C'mon! You guys're so fucken bor—'

'Fine! Bring the rum-balls. Erik — go and get the lamp from the camping supplies. Rain — you know where the picnic blanket is. If we're going to do this, we can at least be comfortable.'

· · ·

It's almost two o'clock by the time we arrive at the obsolete football oval, the five-minute walk from our house illuminated by approximately three blinking street lights and a half-full moon.

We're going to be severely sleep-deprived tomorrow.

I settle myself into the only remaining camping chair in the old canteen, the others having been stolen by the likes of Brian Decker. Erik throws the blanket across the ground for himself and Rain, while Thatch draws up the tiny plastic chair and switches on the lamp.

'I'm goin' first!' he announces from his comically under-sized seat, reaching into the pillowcase — which he just retrieved by jumping over his back fence (which marks the boundary of the oval) and into his unlocked house — before haphazardly throwing each of us a parcel wrapped in newspaper.

Erik and Rain, settling themselves on the picnic blanket, are hit in the head and back respectively. They *oof* and we unwrap Thatch's gifts together, peeling ragged strips of masking tape from the newspaper before opening the crumpled sheets. Inside mine is a large bag of potato chips, a packet of chewing gum (for after the chips, I presume), and two ten dollar scratch cards. Glancing at Rain and Erik on the old blanket, it becomes instantly clear that all three presents are identical.

'Cheers,' Erik says, scratching his own card with his thumb nail while Thatch leans across silently, taking his packet of chips.

'Youse've gotta give me half if you win,' he orders through a spray of potato starch. 'It's the rules.'

I examine the square of plastic-coated paper. 'You know, data has revealed that scratch cards to be particularly harmful gateways to serious gambling addictions.'

'Data's revealed you're heaps uptight, more like it,' says

Thatch, dusting several chip crumbs from his chest. 'Ya haven't even said *thanks* yet!'

'Well – what am I supposed to scratch it with? *I'm* not using my nails, and you haven't provided me with any—'

'*Bloody princess.*' Thatch rolls his eyes, taking the top off a fresh beer bottle and flicking it at me.

I catch the small piece of metal and scratch both cards, despite the problems caused by the gaps in the ridges of the lid. After revealing their worthlessness, I fold the newspaper closed over the remainder of my bundle. I'm not going to eat the chips, but I'm hardly going to give Thatch the satisfaction of consuming my bag as well as my brother's. Not that Erik could care less; he's currently staring at Rain's *wrists*, running his fingers over her skin in a way that looks so ticklish and unpleasant I almost slap him off myself. With her free hand, Rain slides both of her scratch cards into her skirt pocket and smiles. 'Thanks, Michael.'

If she appreciates a bag of chips wrapped in an old piece of newspaper, she is going to be absolutely thrilled with my gift. Unlike Thatch's, my choices have been curated for each individual. To Rain, I hand a carefully-wrapped rectangular package, watching impatiently as she reveals a new hard-back copy of Aldous Huxley's *Island*.

A curiously blank expression comes over her face as she holds the book up, inspecting the cover and reading my inscription. She continues to stare blankly at my handwriting on the inner page. I almost interpret her silence as disappointment, before she lifts her gaze to mine and I realise that her eyes are shining.

'You said you wanted to read it,' I say. 'Remember? We were watching the others at Jumprock and you specifically stated that you'd like to. It wasn't difficult to source. I did have *some* difficulty with shipping – the total cost would have exceeded our agreed upon twenty-five dollar spending cap, but I bought myself a few legal texts to qualify for free postage.'

Rain directs a dewy smile at me, says, 'Thank you, Nelly,' and places the novel face-up on the blanket at her side.

The boys' reactions to my gifts are far less satisfying. When Erik opens the parcel containing his new organic hypoallergenic travel pillow, all he can muster is: 'This'll be good... for my neck.'

Thatch, upon receiving an extremely useful pair of labourers gloves for his new job, flips them over to see if anything else is underneath. He's still searching when Erik hands him another present — a gift-bag containing a new pair of orange and black flippers. 'Jonesy gave me a discount,' he says as Thatch whoops with approval.

Erik hands *me* a shoebox. Hoping vehemently that he hasn't purchased me distasteful footwear, I lift the lid. There is far more colour inside than I anticipated — foamy, squishy balls in a variety of patterns and themes. One is shaped like a unicorn's head. Another is covered in stars. I tilt the box, watching them roll, and estimate that there are at least fifteen.

'For uni.' My brother grins.

'*Stress-balls?* I don't *use* stress-balls. I have other methods of stress-management which work perfectly—'

''Member that time you chucked a stapler at that bird on the other side of the window? Ya cracked that window pretty good, for someone who manages their—'

'Stress balls are highly processed and completely unsustainable, Thatcher! What even *is* this material? Rubber? Polyurethane?'

'That one's silicone, I think,' Erik says, pointing at the box.

'Honestly, Erik...'

He grins, unabashed, and reaches for a small bag, pearly white, with a pale blue flower outlined on the face — the logo of

Mooney River's jewellery store. 'Um. Yeah...' he announces pointlessly, handing Rain the bag. She opens it, extracts a small case, lifts the soft-shelled lid and stares at the glimmering bracelet inside. 'You lost the other one, with the shells... I thought you'd like the colour. Jade. I've still got the receipt if you don't.'

Rain shakes her head and, after at least four seconds, responds, 'This cost more than twenty-five—'

'He sought our permission first!' I answer. I nudge Erik, eyeing the bracelet, then Rain's wrist.

He takes the bracelet lightly from its case. Attempting to close the tiny clasp around her, he fumbles; the bracelet dangles in the air, pinned to Rain's skin by Erik's thumb. 'Shit! Sorry.' He attempts a second time, successfully.

Rain turns her wrist. She looks up at my brother and the two of them engage in at least seven seconds of off-puttingly saccharine eye contact.

I avert my gaze, assuming they're on the verge of an intimate moment, before Thatch screams, 'Where's our pressies, Rain?'

She startles slightly. 'Um, I think I need to change mine. They're nothing like...' Her eyes fall to her wrist, then the book on her blanket.

'As if, Spooks! I'm gettin' *three* pressies tonight, or there's gunna be fucken hell to pay. Don't be bloody *embarrassed*. Whatever you got me's gotta be better than *gloves*.' Thatch leans back on the faded legs of the plastic chair, out of my reach, grinning intolerably. I can only hope the plastic cracks beneath him. Rain sighs heavily, passing him a small rectangular gift, approximately thirty centimetres in diameter. He yanks on the jute string bow and tears off the paper. 'Fucken hell...' he breathes.

'*What is it?*' I rush to his back, leaning over his shoulder to see for myself.

'It's a bloody...'

'Painting,' Rain has painted a remarkable likeness of Thatch, standing on a stretch of the oval, rocks dropping from his hand. The style is soft; watercolour, I believe. 'This is *very* good,' I advise her.

'I'm a bit more shredded in real life, but.' Thatch winks at Rain.

In a brisk movement she passes Erik and I each a package, her cheeks, already mildly sunburnt, reddening.

Erik and I open our gifts in unison.

I don't instantly recognise the vibrant female figure. Then I notice the sharp cupid's bow, the slightly too-large nose, the way her elbows stick out a little too much. She has depicted me sitting under a pink sky, looking off into the distance. I'm quite sure she used a picture of me she took in front of the museum as a reference; the angle of the head is the same.

'There's a mistake in the corner,' Rain says, pointing to a smudge. 'It was too late to fix it, but I can do it now.'

I shake my head vehemently. 'It's absolutely perfect.' Looking more closely at the smudge, I add, 'I suppose, if, at some point, while we're in the city...'

'I'll touch it up for you.' She smiles.

My brother clears his throat and we all wait. And wait. He goes on staring until I'm forced to say, 'Turn it so that we can see!' I try not to sound impatient, but I've always had difficulty managing that particular emotion.

Erik turns the painting.

There are blues and golds. White and silver. My brother — unmistakably, my brother — grins, half-submerged in water. His hair fades into the sun and his chest blends into the ocean. The bay, I assume. There is a sparkling quality to the paint which isn't present on either mine or Thatch's. Perhaps some kind of metallic dust.

'I dunno what to say,' my brother mumbles.

'That's pretty fucken unusual!' laughs Thatch.

Erik clears his throat again. 'This really means a lot. I've never... You're so...' He looks up from the painting, into her eyes, and they slip into another off-putting moment of requited adoration.

I'm grateful when I hear the staccato vibrations of my phone against the leather of my satchel and alarmed when I see who is calling me. 'Abigail!'

The others stare at me for a few moments while the buzzing continues. Then Rain advises me, 'Pick it up.'

I do, pressing my phone firmly, as if precision will ensure it really is Abigail on the other end of the line. 'Hello?'

Rapid, heavy breathing emits from the top of my phone. Then a frightened voice breathes, 'Nelly...?'

'Yes. Of course. I've been so worried about you! Please tell me where you are, and that you're alright. I have a present here when you...' On her end of the line, it sounds as if she's been running. 'Abigail? Are you al—'

'I don't know what to do. He's so angry.'

'Who? *Harrison?*'

More breathing.

'Are you alright? Are you safe?'

'... I don't know.'

Turn it on speaker! Thatch mouths, propeller-like arms rotating widely. I do so, and Abigail's voice echoes through the destroyed canteen — the concrete and the ceiling of stars — as she emits bursts of panicking sobs.

'Where are you?' I mime a writing gesture and Rain takes out her phone. 'The *exact* address.'

'I'm at the new place. Fuck. I don't know the exact address.

48

RMB... three... *something*. It used to be a farm. There's a dam... *two dams*...' Something crashes on her end of the phone and she screams.

'Abigail! Are you there? Erik, call triple zero!'

'No!' she whispers urgently. 'No. It's not that bad. He's been so stressed lately. Pressure... Everything.'

'Abigail! If you're in danger, this is an *emergency*. We have to get you help right—'

'It's OK. He's gone. I just heard the front door. He's gone.'

'Abi—'

'I miss you, Nelly. I miss you guys. I'll talk to you soon. I'm sorry.' I hear a motion, like cloth running over the speaker, and Abigail ends the call.

'Well, what are you waiting for?' I say to the group. 'We have to call the police!'

'You can't!' says Thatcher, knocking the phone from my hand.

'Hey! What do you—'

'You can't do it if she doesn't want ya to. She'd *never* fucken talk to ya then.'

I retrieve my phone from the concrete, dusting off the sand. 'If it's a matter of life and death, what choice do we have?'

'We don't even have an address,' says Erik.

'We can't just do nothing!' I argue, typing the three numbers and moving out of Thatch's reach. Erik's hands move to his head while Rain watches me sadly.

A female voice sounds from the top of my phone, assuringly serious and bureaucratic. 'Police, Fire or Ambulance?'

'Police!' I say. 'Police please. We're in Foxhead Bay, so the closest station would be—'

'Patching you through.'

A dial tone, followed by another voice. Male this time. 'Bandler Beach Police Department.'

'Hello. My friend is in trouble. We have reason to believe she's under threat by her boyfriend – there have been various signs of domestic abuse, and she just phoned me. I'm hoping you can send a squad car to check on her, or a—'

'How old is your friend?'

'Eighteen.'

'Is she being held against her will?'

'Well... not *against*. There's been some evidence of coercive control, but—'

'Has she reported her partner to the police before?'

'No. But as I said—'

'Has the partner been violent to your friend in any way?'

'... I'm not sure. The word violent can have a number of meanings in today's context. What I mean to say is—'

'Listen. It's Christmas Eve. We're very busy, and I'm not authorised to send officers to check on people who aren't in any danger. If your friend files a report, she can get a restraining order in place. But she's an adult. It has to be her choice.'

'She's barely *eighteen*! Her birthday was only four months ago. Please. You could say you had a noise report and simply pop by, just to make absolutely sure.'

The officer sighs. 'Alright... If a squad car becomes available, we'll see what we can do. The address?'

'Oh. Well, it's... ah... RMB three... something.'

A long silence answers. 'You know there are fines for wasting police time. If this is a prank call, we can trace it. Now do you have an address, or should we end the call now?'

'I... I know there are *two* dams.'

A click, followed by a long, drawn out dial-tone, followed by successive beeps.

I stamp one foot and consider throwing my phone through the gap that was once a roller-door. I consider saying *fuck* but only manage the 'Ffffff!'.

It's still enough to get the others' attention.

Rain is at my side, patting my arm consolingly. 'Who else could we call? Is there anyone who might know where she is, who could check on her?'

I shake my head, fighting the urge to cry. I feel completely impotent. One of my oldest friends needs me and I can't help. I don't know where she is. I don't know anyone who knows where she is.

Think, Eleanor.

No problem is insurmountable.

Think.

I fight to clear my mind; to rifle through its contents for anything or anyone that might know of Abigail's location. I pull a thread of thought from Abigail to Harrison to — 'Sam!'

Thatch's face twists into a confused wince. 'The *bikie*? Why d'you wanna—'

'Shh!' I tell him, opening my contacts and scrolling down to the newest number.

I've never slept so late on Christmas Day. Nor have I felt so exhausted.

By the time we contacted The Pup, returned home and

waited for his response (an unsatisfying message that included two words: 'she's alright'), it was well after three in the morning. I phoned to confirm, obviously, and his voice was thick with tiredness. It was quite attractive, if I'm being honest. An outlaw like him could never be a viable sexual partner, but there's no reason I shouldn't appreciate an attractive voice, or a steady gaze, or a capable, combatant figure. I'm quite sure he was juggling stress-balls in my dreams.

A pounding on my door pushes the memory further into my subconscious as Erik's voice carries into my room. 'It's almost eleven. Mum says you have to come out for brekkie.'

Thatch yawns, swatting a fly from his pancakes with half-closed eyes, killing it on contact. Erik brushes the fly's carcass off the table, only for it to land on Rain's lap. He swears an apology, but she only smiles, standing to let the tiny black body fall under the table.

'Everything's really delicious,' Rain says, returning to her seat. 'Thanks, Anita.'

'You're welcome! It's so nice to have you. What are you and Barry up to tonight?'

I cut my pancake into eight equal pieces while Rain answers – something about a roast chicken and a Christmas episode of a ridiculously outdated TV drama. I spear a slice of strawberry, then a piece of pancake, wiping them both through a generous lake of ice-cream and maple syrup.

My normal rules about caloric intake don't apply on Christmas, or birthdays, or Easter weekend, or Halloween – most major holidays – as well as four-to-two days before the beginning of my period, which, thankfully, isn't today. I eat five pancakes. I'm about to ask if anyone else would like another coffee when an offensively irritating ringtone emits from

Thatch's phone, which is on full volume, despite being an inch from his hand. Thatch stands up, his chair scraping across the decking, and rips his phone from his pocket.

'Hey, Simpo! What's up, Babe?'

Of course Carissa would choose this moment to phone. She always has terribly inconsiderate timing. 'Unbelievable,' I mutter.

'What's unbelievable?' Mum asks, as Thatch stomps off to the edge of the deck. 'Is it the gas wells again?'

I blink. 'Of course! Of course it's the gas wells. Do you have any idea how many species will be annihilated if the new projects go ahead? It's absolutely disgusting. I can't wait to get to the city and make a real difference in the fight. Starting with the meeting next week! I was thinking – while we're in the city – we should try to pick up a few things for the townhouse. Perhaps we could even pop in and do a walk through. You haven't seen it yet, Erik, and I'm sure you'll be spending quite a lot of time there next year. We could pick up the keys from Arthur before we... Rain? Are you *listening*?'

Rain's cheeks redden and she dives in for another pancake, gaze averted.

'Douglass,' I press. 'When you've finished chewing that ludicrously large mouthful, please tell me that you're still coming to the meeting.'

She swallows slowly. 'I'm so sorry, Nelly... You know how busy it's been. Kathy's short staffed at the moment, and I need the money. I promise I'll be at the next one. We'll be in the city, so it'll be so much closer.'

'*Unbelievable!* So Erik and I will be perched in the hotel alone?'

My brother is moving a grape across his plate with his index finger while scratching the back of his head with his fork.

'No,' I say, alarm rising in my voice. '*No!*'

'I don't know for sure yet, Nel. It's just, the surf report says it'll be good. Perfect, maybe.'

I fold my napkin through the centre, then do so again, and again. I slam it onto my plate and rise, pushing back my chair so furiously it tips over. 'That's it. That is it. I'm not going camping. I'm not. If you can't even...' I clench and unclench a fist. 'Merry Christmas and a happy New Year, Everyone!' Slamming down my knife and fork, I stand tall. I have no idea why I'm getting up or where I'm going. I march to the north edge of the balcony, then realise Thatch is there, giggling with his feeble little *girlfriend,* so I turn and march in the opposite direction, stopping and leaning over the rail. I scream into the trees for approximately three seconds. When I stop and turn, Thatch has ended his phone call. Erik has one hand over his eyes, and the turn of Rain's brows indicates either confusion or guilt.

Mum puts down her fork gently. As if approaching a cornered animal, she walks to me, laying a hand on my upper arm. 'I'll go with you, baby,' she whispers, moving between me and the others while I wipe my eyes. 'The others wish they could come. Life's just like this sometimes. But I would love to go with you. We'll have a girls' night in the city! Go shopping... Come on, Nelly-Tot. Let's have one more pancake and go to the beach with your friends.'

What has your life become, Eleanor?

I eat my final pancake self-critically; it is spread with a choc-hazelnut-palm oil concoction responsible for destroying the rainforest, which is the least of my problems, I suppose. My best friend and my brother have abandoned me. I have committed to two nights of sensory torture also known as *camping.* Abigail is in danger. The last twelve months were the driest on record, and our fire-plan is in desperate need of an update. Dirty gas is going to leak into one of the most biodiverse ocean regions in the world.

And there is absolutely nothing I can do about any of it.

You're out of control, Eleanor.

As evening falls, Erik and I help Mum prepare for our annual dinner with her parents. We lay out the creamy linen tablecloth first, then the plates, glasses, cutlery, Christmas crackers and a chilled bottle of sparkling wine, followed conclusively by the food — free-range turkey, Dutch potatoes, nectarine salad, buttered green beans and freshly-baked rolls.

Lastly, I place my open laptop at one end of the table, ready for our video-call.

Grandma and Grandpa are as prompt as always. It's only noon in Cape Town, so the sun is shining through the windows in the background of the video feed, haloing their aging faces. Erik and Mum and I fill our plates and feign cheerfulness as we listen to the same five stories our grandparents tell us every Christmas.

It takes Mum a full forty-five minutes to mention my ATAR results. When she does, she says 'ninety-eight', instead of 'ninety-eight-point-one'.

I correct her.

'Excellent work, Eleanor,' Grandpa says from the screen.

'I was pleased with the result.' I smile.

'She was Dux for our whole year, too,' Erik explains. 'The principal said at graduation it's the first time the Head Girl's been Dux since the eighties.'

My gaze snaps to Erik. I wouldn't say I give him an approving look, but I do make eye contact for the first time since breakfast. I look away swiftly.

Grandma and Grandpa are both chewing gammon, nodding. 'Very good…' Grandpa says.

'Absolutely outstanding,' Grandma adds, after swallowing.

And you, Erik? Did you do well in all of your subjects?'

'Most of them,' he answers.

'He did very well, Grandma,' Mum corrects. He scored a seventy-four, and passed everything with a clear margin, *despite* all of the time off school.'

'And the surfing...' Grandpa grunts suddenly. 'You're touring?'

'Yeah. I'm starting on the qualifier series, so I'm mostly competing in Australian events next year. Maybe a few over-seas. But I have a few sponsored trips planned, too. The first one's in a few weeks. My mate Lara's going too — she just got a deal. We've got a comp a few weeks after that, so there's no point coming home in between. I'll be gone for a while. I'm just, kind of, taking a bit of a break till then. Enjoying home.'

'He's worked *very* hard this year,' Mum says. 'They *both* have.'

'Well, I always say the effort is the reward! Let's toast to that.' Grandma holds out her glass of brandy to the camera, followed by Grandpa. We pick up our own glasses and gesture forward, as if to 'clink'.

My grandma lowers her glass and, with a businesslike turn of her head, says, 'Tell us about your recent pursuits, Anita. Are you putting your two years of tertiary education to use?'

I'm grateful the focus has shifted to my mum. I'm exhausted, slightly sunburnt, completely betrayed, and fed up. The air conditioning is making me drowsy, as is the white wine. Mum tells Grandma about her freelance bookkeeping work and her investments, before segueing into a long anecdote about her attempt to blow a flower into glass. 'When the last one broke, I threw up my hands. I swear, Alexander, the teacher, makes it look so easy. I keep telling Erik he needs to come along. He's always been so creative.'

'Not really, Mum... Not like Rain or someone.'

'How *is* your young friend?' asks Grandma.

'She's good.'

Mum sighs thoughtfully, her champagne glass hovering near her lips. 'She's such a sweet girl. It's just *not* fair about her own parents.'

'It's a pity,' Grandma says, dabbing the corners of her mouth with a white napkin. 'But we can't choose these things. Nor can we change them. That young lady is very lucky to have you all in her life. Isn't that right, Grandpa?'

My grandpa nods, swallowing quickly. 'Yes, yes. Cut your hair though, son. It's not good for a man to have such long hair. Sends the wrong message. Your sister will tell you. Whatever gentleman's caught her eye doesn't have such long hair.'

I wince.

There are a *number* of flaws in my grandpa's comment.

Firstly, he is assuming my sexual preferences are heteronormative. What makes him think I'm interested in gentlemen, and not *gentlewomen*? I happen to be open to sexual interactions with any genders; though, statistically, all of my interactions have thus far been with men. Boys, really.

Secondly, I have an issue with the word 'caught'. It's far too consumptive.

My *third* issue is with his final two words, where he implied that I select male partners based on their *hair* – an extremely superficial method. In actual fact, my sexual partners are selected through a rigorous and unbiased collection of academic, social and economic data.

Following a considerable silence, I answer, 'I have absolutely no time for *gentlemen*.'

My comment is followed by a stretch of silence, before Mum asks my grandparents if they can hear the waves in the distance. This prompts Erik to discuss the surfing conditions for approximately six minutes — cyclone predictions, then something about a Southwest swell combining with an offshore wind from the East-northeast. There are a few topographical words, which I'm quite confident he pronounces incorrectly.

Grandma and Grandpa look almost as disinterested as me by the time it's over.

'So, it's pretty rare,' Erik continues. 'My sponsors want me to take a camera out. Hold it in my mouth. I can't do it though. I tried once and couldn't focus.'

Mum nods sympathetically.

'Dessert anyone?' Grandma asks.

Even with my white noise machine set to maximum, I can hear Erik on the phone.

I can't sleep, listening to him go *on* and *on*. He's never talked as much in his life as he has in the last year with Rain. '... Mmhmm... Yeah... That's right... Was it good? Did it fit and everything? That's good. Haha. Fuck. Yeah. Classic Barry... Is he asleep? Should I...? Yeah...?' A stifled laugh, then, 'See you soon.'

My brother moves around his room. I hear the unmistakable click of his bedroom door, followed by dull footsteps through the house.

Finally, the front door closes.

PART 2

ERIK

She's breathing out of her mouth. Nose twitching. Not awake yet. She's lying a little on her side and a little on her stomach, her legs bare, blanket curled around her feet. Her cheeks are kind of tanned. Like apricots.

My mouth is dry.

I reach across her for the glass on the bedside table and feel her breath on my arm as she rolls half onto her back, t-shirt snagging under her, wrapping tight around her middle.

I have a long sip of water.

Barry's house isn't that well insulated, and the upright fan in the corner moves slowly. You can barely feel it on 'high', even though it rattles the little pieces of paper on the walls.

When I first came here, to her Pop's house, this was like a room no one lived in. Almost empty. Then, after us, she started to stay here more often. As much as she could. She'd still sleep at Doe's most weeknights, but she'd spend some Thursdays here. Mondays, too.

Now the room's full of her. On the wall above her dresser are a wide circle of pictures – drawings, photos, illustrations from old books. Around them, feathers and paper flowers. The Blu Tack must be sweating, cause the corners of a few clippings are sagging and there's a little blue feather on the ground.

I put the glass back. Wipe my mouth. Shuffle down. Press my body into the back of hers, as soft as I can. I cup her hip in my hand. Slowly. I don't want to wake her up. Still, there's a soft movement. A tilt of her lower-back. A breath in.

My fingers move across her skin.

She rolls over to face me, chin tipping up, drunk with sleep, kissing me haltingly, like a question. More awake now, mouth softening.

Then we're water.

It's like the middle of a wave, but slower. Easier.

Even if Barry was awake, he wouldn't hear us.

The first thing she says to me afterwards is, 'I had a dream I was a cloud.' A little more warmth in her skin now, she's lying with her cheek on my chest, arm draped over me, hand in mine. The hairs closest to her face are stuck down with sweat, curving like ripples.

I swallow. 'Like, floating on one?'

'No. I was one. I was made of tiny drops of water and I was trying to decide whether to let go of them... On the one hand, I'd fall apart, but then I would have been a river. Or a lake. Or a puddle.'

'You could've landed in Rodney's water tank. He never cleans it. Got giardia a few years ago – it was pretty heavy.'

She laughs in that sudden way she sometimes does, like a burst of light. Then she claps her hand over her mouth. Barry doesn't know I'm here. Dimming her voice, she says, 'Yeah. I guess I could have turned into giardia water. Win some, lose some.' She stretches away from me towards the edge of the bed, putting her face right up against the fan.

'Do you want to come over?'

She sits up, fanning her stomach with the bottom of her shirt. 'You said you needed to workout before fishing. And post those photos, in the boardshorts.'

'I don't care. I mean... I can do both. You can watch me, or wait for me, or hang out with Nelly, if she lets you. I'll turn the air-con up. I'll make you a Ribena with so many ice-cubes—'

There's a knock on the door and Rain's pop's voice. I think he's saying good morning. Before I can hide — cover myself up or anything — the door's opening. I jerk back, grabbing a pillow and clutching it to my undies, my back slamming into the wall as Barry's head pushes through the gap. He makes a face like he's just seen a dead body. Covers his eyes with his forearm and slams the door.

'Fuck...' Rain whispers. '*Fuck!*' She scrambles off the bed and starts looking around on her floor. Picks up a pair of shorts.

'Whado I do?' I ask, holding the pillow like my guts are falling out. 'He saw me, yeah? Is he gunna...? Should I...?'

'I don't know!'

'Do you want to go talk to him first, before I...'

She stops pulling on her shorts, sitting down on the edge of the bed with them halfway up her thighs. 'I don't think I can ever speak to him again.'

I breathe in. Out. Nod. 'We'll go out there together. We'll go out there and I'll tell him I'm sorry. I'll tell him it was all me. And if he never lets me over again... there's always my place. The oval. The lookout. The car.'

She hides a smile in the corner of her mouth.

'Should I... Do you want me to go out first?'

'No. That would be... No. Thank you, but... he's my pop.'

We finish getting dressed. Then she opens the door and slips down the hallway, a few steps ahead of me.

Most of the walls in Barry's bungalow are covered in light wallpaper with pictures of some type of bird. A stalk, I think.

The centre of the house is taken up by a little living room, connected to the kitchen by a bar-window. Barry's sitting in his big armchair, facing away from the kitchen towards the black TV screen. The hat I got him for Christmas is sitting on a little table next to the chair.

'Pop...' Rain says. 'I'm so sorry I didn't tell you that... I hope it's OK that—'

'It's not my first day on earth,' Barry grunts. 'You don't need to explain. Just... put a flamin' sock on the door next time. And... You make sure you do right by her and be... smart. Both of you.' He turns in his chair and his eyes flick up to mine for a second before he starts coughing.

When he stops, I say, 'Sorry, Barry. I should have... Merry Christmas. For yesterday.'

He waves his hand in front of his face and grunts, like he couldnt give a fuck about Christmas.

Rain shifts her weight from one foot to the other. 'I think we're just going to... I'll see you this afternoon. We'll have a shandy, before Doe picks me up.'

Barry turns the TV on. 'Don't do anything I wouldn't do,' he says, sinking back onto the upholstery.

Our house is empty when we get there.

I dunno where Nelly and Mum are.

Rain lets go of my sweaty hand once we're inside, taking two glasses from their shelf and filling them with ice. I pour the dark purple syrup over the cubes and add cold water. She stirs the Ribenas with a butter knife. Quietly. The lightest little clinks. Neither of us have said anything for a while. Sometimes it's like that. We sink into these pockets of silence that make me feel like we're the same person, just going about our day. I don't even have to try.

We flow through the motions, down the hallway, into my room.

She walks to my bed, rolling her icy glass across her neck. 'I can't believe you're going out on the boat in this heat.' The glass keeps rolling, wet, on her skin, and I sit down next to her. Kind of stare for a second or two. She stares back. Runs a thumb over the rash on my neck. The tip of her finger's dewy. Then she's sipping her Ribena again. The ice-cubes collide with each other in frozen little drumbeats.

I'm about to kiss her, but her phone starts ringing.

When she looks at it her face drops. Her eyes are wide. She holds the screen like it's about to blow up. Shows it to me. White letters spell out:

Mum

For a fraction of a second, I think she means my mum. But of course it isn't. It's *her*

mum. Which is... better? Worse? She swallows. Taps the green button. In a faded voice, she says, 'Hello?'

On the other end, a muffled, urgent sound.

As her mum talks, Rain shrinks. Like a little pebble, sinking. I take her free hand. Press the fleshy part between her thumb and forefinger, lightly, so she knows I'm here.

Her head tilts. Eyelids flutter. When she taps the speaker symbol, her mum's voice echoes up the walls. She drops the phone face up on the bed, leaning back, away from it, then takes a breath. A hopeless smile. Her mum sounds dreamy and angry all at once. It makes me think of the witches from The Wizard of Oz. Both the witches.

'... and you never do know what's in a cat's saliva. I said that, after it bit me. And I would have gone straight to the doctor but I wanted to make you a cake – with orange icing. I had your presents all ready – and then my ride fell through. I should have never trusted that guy; I knew he was shady the second I saw his facial hair – you remember what I said about handlebars, don't you? Never trust someone with a handlebar moustache when they say they'll lend you their car. Then the train got stalled on the line. Some capitalist drone threw themselves on the tracks again. That's what consumerism does to people, you know? I tried to call, but there's something wrong with my phone. I have to call the phone company about it, but the phone doesn't work, so I can't, can I? Fucking 5G. But I finally borrowed a phone from Mitsy, to put my sim-card in — she has the smallest feet you've ever seen, Mitsy. You'll meet her one day and see. Tiny. Her hands, too,' she laughs. Then, when Rain doesn't, she says, 'I knew you'd be angry...'

'You were right.'

Rain's mum lets out a staggered sigh. Three notes, like a song. 'I've got a new roommate with a car. I'm going to borrow it and come to the Bay.'

'You said you never wanted to come back to the Bay. You said we'd have to meet somewhere else. That's why—'

'Mooney River then. I always liked it there. I like being around all that canopy. Green's my favourite colour, you know? Green like your eyes. My baby girl's eyes. I'll have the car next week while my roommate's at work. It's completely legal and everything, Rain – I have permission to borrow it. It's going to be fun like the old days. Maybe we can go for a walk? Remember our walks? Remember what we used to sing? *"It's such a perfect day, I'm glad I spent it with you..."'* Her voice is clear and anchored – more stable than when she's talking. It's rough. Beautiful.

Rain swallows. Her eyes are kind of glassy, but not like when someone cries. It's more like falling asleep. She's pulling back, into herself. Then she says, 'OK.'

'Great! I'll come on Wednesday. Is the little cafe still open? The one with the scones and the birdbath?'

'Claire's?'

'Claire's! That's the place. I'll meet you there at eleven.'

'...OK.'

'Perfect. Eleven at Claire's. I'll see you then, honey-girl.'

Rain's tiny. Only half there. When she looks at me, her eyes say something I can't understand. Something between *sorry* and *help*. 'See you, Mum,' she says. Then she taps the red button. She looks like she's about to cry, which takes me aback for a second. Scares me. I've never seen her cry before.

Say something, Erik.

'I don't know what to say.'

Fucking useless.

Try again.

'I'll go with you. I can drive. I'll...'

'You can't. You said the surf was going to be good on Wednesday. You should do that. I'll be fine on my own.'

'I can do both! I'll just go out for a few hours in the morning. I can do both, Rain. I want to be there.'

She nods, still only half there. Then smiles. 'So... you've met my mum, now.'

Thatch cups a bowl of seawater and splashes it over his face. 'It's too fucken hot for this shit! I should've stayed at Simpo's. They were doing board games – her mum n' her dad n' her. Drinkin' ice tea. Or I could be at home, watchin' the Boxing Day Test.'

'I would've stayed at home.' I lean over the edge of Thatch's dad's dinghy, hot metal almost burning my arm, and let the whole body of my fishing rod fall into the water. 'I left Rain with Nelly – she's been a psycho since yesterday. You're the one who said we wouldn't get another chance till at least—'

'It fucken IS our last bloody chance, dickhead! The swell's

gunna be way too big after today and then we're gunna be campin' and then I'm startin' work – *thanks for fucken asking about it, by the way* – and then you're off to the other sidea the world. So don't be a pussy.'

I close my eyes for a second. Breathe.

Thatch is sad about Carissa leaving. I don't think *he* really knows yet. When I try to ask him about it, he says stuff like, 'That's the way the bickie crumbles,' and, 'I miss bein' single anyway.' Then I'll catch him smiling in this dumb way, looking at her, and I know he's sad.

I take my hat off and wipe the top against my forehead, soaking up some of the sweat. 'Let's just catch something and go home.'

Thatch winds his reel a few times. 'Gimme another icy-pole.'

I pass him a Zooper-Dooper from his dad's Esky, then cast out and wait.

The shore's busier than last year and the year before. People moving in and out of the water like ants around a puddle. The tide's high, so there's barely any beach – bodies lie close together, reddening flesh spreading up the rocks.

'How's Nel goin'?' Thatch asks after a while.

'Good. Rain and her are doing stuff for their new place in the city – researching vacuum cleaners or something. And she's obsessed with figuring out where Abigail's living. Said she wanted to "discuss some theories" with Rain.'

'What theories?'

'No idea.'

Thatch cracks up. 'Weird that Harrison's hanging with the bikie's eh? And Decker's uncle. Wonder what that's all about.'

'What?'

'Decker's uncle. That fish bloke.'

'You mean the guy from the pub? The one that nearly

murdered us in his crack-den last year? And Brian Decker? *What?*'

'Yeah.' He tips his Zooper-Dooper wrapper upside down, pouring the melted juice into his open mouth and wiping his chin. 'Yeah. The fish-feeler – he's Decker's uncle. I told ya, didn't I? I saw 'em at the shops the other day. A coupla months ago. Heard Brian call him Uncle Fred. Or Frank it mighta been.'

'You didn't tell me that!'

'Well... tellin' ya now, aren't I?' He reels in his line as fast as he can, tongue squeezed between his teeth. 'It sorta makes sense a creep like that'd be related to Decker. You can tell Nelly, if ya want? Might cheer her up. She likes findin' shit out. Oi – did I tell ya Clancy saw a massive hammerhead out here the other day?'

'Clancy's full of shit.'

Thatch scrunches the wrapper in his fist and pockets it. 'He *said* he saw one. With his dad and Lara. Ask her, if ya wanna know for sure. I reckon it was true.' He runs his arm through the water, splashing hard like a kid. Like he's trying to tempt a hammerhead with raspberry flavouring. 'That sorta reminds me...' he stops punching the water and dried his hands on his shirt. 'Clancy said other stuff. About your dad.'

I feel sick straight away.

'I don't have to tell ya, if you don't wanna—'

'You can't do that, Thatcher. You can't tell someone the start of something then ask them if they want to know. It's too late.'

Thatch pulls the sleeves of his old flanno down his arms, squinting angrily at the sun like he wants to fight it. 'We could just pretend I didn't say nothing? Have another icy-pole?'

'Thatch.'

'Clancy reckons he saw a chick leaving your dad's place when he was driving past, getting his hours.'

'What chick? Who?'

'Someone "hot as balls", Clancy said. She had a massive hat on and she definitely went into the back unit.'

I swallow. 'Bound to happen.'

'It's still fucked, mate.'

'Yeah. Thanks.' I lift my rod and start reeling hard, trying to get the image out of my mind. 'Tell me about the job with Rodney. When do you start?'

'Monday after New Years. Gunna be *rakin'* it in. I'm gunna get the best bloody car. Way better than yours n' Nelly's. The chicks'll be all over me! Maybe Lucy'll start tryna root *me* too, eh?' He kicks my ankle, rocking the boat.

'Lucy's not trying to root me, Thatcher.'

'Yeah right. She wants to get in on the action before you're proper famous.'

'No she doesn't. And I'm not.'

'Not *yet*. But you smashed that wildcard back in winter, and the junior pro last year.'

'I came fifth, Thatcher. Fifth's not that good.'

'Yeah, but ya got robbed those couple times. And ya kooked it in that one round – a nine and a zero. It was bloody hard to watch, mate. You're too picky – you wait too long. Everyone knows you could've won it. You're just about on top of your game. Look at ya! Fucken muscles n' everything! Spooks'd better learn how to fight.'

He winks in slow motion and I let myself laugh.

'Dead serious. Bet you're getting nudes on Instagram and not tellin' anyone. You are, aren't ya? And Hot Lucy was FANGIN' for it the other night.'

'No I'm not. And she wasn't.'

'Fuck off! You KNOW she was. And she sent ya that message yesterday. Did ya tell your girlfriend about that one?'

'I didn't write back.'

'Not what I asked, mate. I dunno how you handle it, honestly. Hot Lucy's pretty bloody hot. I remember the first time she DM'd ya, back when you only had about three pubes. *Remember?* She said "hee-eey" or some shit. And you came in your pants!'

'*Jesus*, Thatch. No I didn't. Can we stop talking about Hot —. *Fuck!* Lucy. Stop talking about her.'

'Orright! Calm down. I just wanna know what you're gunna do if she tries to root ya.'

'You don't know what you're talking about.'

'Don't I? You've got Hot Lucy droolin' all over ya, and you reckon everything's gunna be—'

An urgent tug.

I almost drop my rod, then scramble to get a better hold, wedging it between my legs, winding the reel. There's a kick at the end of the line and I wind faster. The fish turns. I feel its energy shiver up the line into my fingers and through my arm as I bring it in.

When it's out of the water, dangling over the lip of Thatch's dad's dinghy, it's just a little one. A whiting. Nowhere near full size. And I've hooked it through the gill.

Something clenches in my chest.

You've killed it, Erik.

It's dying.

'I reckon it's fucked, mate,' Thatch says, leaning over me so the fish is shaded. 'See how it's breathing?'

'It's fine.' Holding it tight in one hand, I start to pull the little silver hook back, through the silver folds. A millimetre. Then another.

Then it bucks, tiny and silver.

A spray of blood and the slick body is thrashing on the boat floor in a dirty pool, trying to breathe through the gash. Flailing through the dirt and the chip crumbs and the drips of icy-pole. I dive, fumbling, missing, then get my hand around it and hold it tight while it squirms and bleeds.

It's dying.

'Better put it out of its misery, eh?'

But I can't.

I should give it to Thatch. Let him do it.

I don't, though. I put it back in the water and it flaps off in a dizzy circle, bright red swirling a trail behind it, until the trail thins and it disappears.

There's blood on the Esky, on the floor, and on Thatch's shin. He's rubbing it off with my towel. 'Ya should've held it tighter, dickhead.'

I stare at the blood on my fingers. 'Let's just go in.'

Thatch calls me a princess, but he shifts around to start the motor.

When we get home, Rain and Nelly are planning the layout for their living room. Or, Nelly's planning it. Rain's nodding and answering, 'Sounds great!' to every question.

Thatch watches the cricket on his phone while I do a lazy workout; some resistance stuff and a handful of sprints on the bike. I keep seeing the fish in everything metallic – the rims of my car, the shelves, the end of a weeder.

I need to stop thinking about a dead fucking fish and get serious.

I need to market myself. That's what my sponsor keeps saying.

It's all about marketability. It's not just about contests. You've got to build a brand.

A brand. It makes me feel sick, thinking about it. Some of the other guys I've competed with love social media. It's so easy for them. They've got filmers who follow them everywhere and they post whatever they want without thinking about it too much. They've got tens of thousands of followers. Lara's been all over it, ever since she got her deal and they told her the same thing they told me. Film as much as you can. Share as much as you can. And she did. Meanwhile, I haven't posted in weeks. If I lose my sponsor, I won't be able to afford the flights, or the trips. I'll blow my chance. I need to figure it out somehow. Figure out what my brand is. How to market myself. Then I need to win.

I clear my throat. 'Thatch?'

'Yeah?'

'Can you take a photo of me? I need to post those shorts.'

Thatch laughs his head off, then takes a pretty good photo.

I post it with a stupid line about comfort in the water being important to me. Then I check the surf report, notifications buzzing in the background, and get lost for a while in the green arrows and dark lines, feeling a rush through my centre – like popping candy going off, one vertebra at a time.

It's going to be good.

Really good.

Rain taps on the internal garage door at the top of the stairs and Thatch makes himself busy with the punching bag. 'Did you catch anything?' she asks, the silver links on her bracelet sparkling like scales.

'I got a little one, but I... put it back.'

'Oh. Next time.'

'Yeah. Hope so. What time are you working tomorrow?'

'Eight to four-thirty. The same the next day.'

The pillowy thump of Thatch's fists. Carabiners straining.

She steps down, one, two, three steps, looking at me the

way she used to look at her Maths book. Like I'm a puzzle to figure out. When she reaches me, she takes hold of my fingers.

I lock my arms tight around her and say 'I love you,' too low for Thatch to hear. I won't see her for a few days. She'll be working, and I have to work too. Get some waves, even if they're shitty. Build a brand. 'I'll see you on Wednesday,' I tell her. 'I'll pick you up and we'll go to the cafe.'

She pushes back a little bit, looking up at me. 'You don't have to. I don't know what Mum's going to be like. She might not even come. Just... see how you go.'

I pull her back, closer. I tell her, 'I'll be there,' and kiss the top of her head. Then I let her go.

The second she's out of earshot, Thatch collapses forwards onto the red leather, clutching the bag like he's about to pass out. 'Yous're fucken painful. I swear to bloody god, I'm puttin' in headphones next time.'

I tell him to fuck off.

I'm balancing on top of a wave. Just my bare feet against the foam. There's a breeze. Jellyfish dressed in white bubbles. Jumping. Slapping against me. Slap. Slap. Tap. Slap. Tap. Tap. Tap.

I flinch hard, waking up all at once, registering a person on the end of my bed. 'Nelly?'

She's sitting down there on her laptop again. 'I'm *not* apologising!' she erupts. 'While you've been resting, I've successfully narrowed our search to three properties, so I should be saying *you're welcome* if anything.'

'What're you talking ab—'

'Abigail! I know where she is. We have a thirty-three-point-three chance of finding her on our first try!'

'How...'

She smiles like one of those girls at a pageant. 'Real-estate listings! I searched all sold properties from here to Bandler Beach. Five in the last year. Perused Google Maps for aerial footage and counted the dams. Only *three* had *two* dams. There were twelve properties with zero dams, two with one, and three with two! Then there were the rentals; that took even longer, and didn't result in any positive results. Don't you see? I've *done* it!'

I try to make sense of it. Properties. Rentals. Dams. Abigail. Nelly, trying to be a detective again. When she gets like this, you can't stop her. You can only slow her down. 'What about private rentals? Lots of people don't trust real-estate agents, especially out on farms. They'd rather just figure it out with each other.'

She blinks. 'Obviously I'd thought about that, Erik. Obviously I'd thought about private rentals...'

'So?'

'I don't have *all* of the answers, you know. I'm only *one* person. We're going to *start* by trying any leads we *do* have, so that we can at least rule out the—'

'I'm not going. I can't knock on random strangers' doors. What if they're a psycho? What if they have a dog? Or a gun?'

What if it's actually Harrison and his mates? No way. You haven't thought this through. You always do this.'

'What if the others come too? What if we have back-up?'

'I'm not asking them to risk their—'

'*I'll* ask them! I'll ask them later, at the oval, when they're in a state of... relaxation.'

It's hot mid-morning when we get to the oval, away from the crowds of burning tourists. We spent an hour or so trying to surf shit waves with city people, wishing they'd fuck off and leave us alone, before I couldn't take it anymore and paddled in. The others followed and our bodies took us here. Automatic.

Now Thatch is running back from his house, a bag of bright icy-poles swinging like a trophy from his hand. He falls onto the blanket next to Lara and Jenny, who're talking about the swell. Nelly's on the big seat next to Freddie, who's on the small one. I think she's telling him about the origins of Santa Claus. Zac and Clancy are reaching into the hole in the wall, throwing warm beers to us.

I drink one. Listen to the others talk. Close my eyes against the heat.

I say 'Nah,' when Freddie offers his peace-pipe. I need to workout today. Analyse some footage. I take a bite of my icy-pole and stand up. 'I'd better go.'

Clancy's ears prick and he stares at me, like a dog who just heard *walk*. 'Where're you goin?' he asks.

'Just home. I've got to do a workout and stuff.'

'Need a spotter? Zaccy can come too. We could grab one end each.'

Thatch stands up. Stretches. 'I'll go. Erik doesn't need you little shits askin' him dumb questions the whole time. And you're not strong enough.' Walking past, he flexes at them.

Nelly hesitates, but follows us out.

The whole way home, she tells me how rude it was not to wait for her to say goodbye, let alone ask the others for help with Abigail.

'Nelly,' I say, as we're coming through the front door. I want to tell her I don't give a shit about Abigail, and she needs to stop talking about her every five seconds. But then she won't come camping. She'll be in a shitty mood for our last weeks together. So all I say is, 'Sorry.'

She's satisfied. She even says 'Thank you,' when I hold the front door open. Mum's smiling at something in a basket on the bench when Nelly gets to her. 'What are these? Peaches?' Nelly asks, picking up a piece of yellow-red fruit.

'Hello to you too, baby.'

My sister rolls her eyes. 'Yes, hello Mum, it's excellent to see you. Might I enquire as to whether—'

'Nectarines,' Mum says. 'Lucy popped by. Bev's tree is going absolutely berserk – more fruit than they know what to do with! Isn't that lovely of them?'

Something swims in my gut.

Lucy came over?

'Would've been even better if she'd brought round some *cherries*, eh, Erik?' Thatch winks, picking up a nectarine and throwing it up and down to himself.

'I don't think they have a cherry tree,' Mum says, scratching a spot on the window above the sink.

Thatch cracks up.

Nelly pushes the basket away from herself so hard one of the nectarines rolls across the kitchen bench, then storms off to her room, muttering the whole way.

Mum catches the piece of fruit before it can roll onto the floor. She looks at me like an X-Ray. 'What was that all about?'

'Nothing.'

'Nothing? It was clearly something, Erik.'

'Just drop it, Mum. Please. She's just... angry. About the gas wells.'

I'm not sure, but I think Mum mutters, 'Those fucking gas wells,' before grabbing her keys. 'I'm going. To town. I've got to pick up something. Milk. I'll see you kids later.'

Nelly avoids us until she's hungry.

I knew she would be. I heated up a lasagne from the freezer — the one mum makes with the mushrooms — knowing she'd smell it. I heard her feet in the hallways a second after I took it out of the oven. She barges into the pantry, pretending she doesn't know I'm already in here. 'Oh. It's *you...*'

I try not to ruffle. 'Yeah. It's me.'

'Well could you *move*? I need to take my multivitamin.'

'Just a second.' I reach for the bottle of hot sauce. She shoves her way past me, jabbing me with her pointy fucking elbow, and I crack. 'I dunno why you're angry at me, Eleanor. I didn't... It's not like I asked Lucy to come over. I dunno why she—'

'You know *exactly* why, Erik. You know *precisely* what she wants.'

'I can't help what other people do. She knows Mum likes cooking. They had too many nectarines. It was nice, Nelly. Sometimes people do nice stuff.'

'I can't believe how utterly NAIVE you are!' she yells so loud Thatch comes running into the kitchen.

'Naive?' I say.

'Yes! You don't understand the subtlety of these *personalities*. When you have a relationship as rare as yours is with Rain, you need to—'

'You don't know anything about relationships, Nelly. You've never had a boyfriend.'

There's a flash of rage on her face. Thatch, who's been listening, starts driving spoonfuls of lasagne into his mouth, banging his spoon against his plate, chewing like a horse. Nelly whispers, 'I don't *want* a boyfriend, Erik.' Then she hacks off a bit of lasagne and takes it to her room.

Her door slams.

A second later, when Thatch is going in for seconds, my phone buzzes.

Of course it's Lucy.

I hope you like the fruit x

I click on her picture and scroll down her profile. Lots of beach photos at the top. Then a lot of pictures at night, in clubs and bars, in the city. Her hand on her hip. Dresses that show her tits. Heels with straps that lace up her calves. There are other photos with her friends in front of laneway murals or at the beach in the city. In one, she's lying on a towel, on her side, bending around to look at the camera.

I start typing a reply without letting myself think.

Yeah. Thanks heaps

Like a gunshot, she responds:

See u soon I hope. I always
have the best time with u ;)

Guilt plugs up my throat when I tap on the words and a little blue thumb pops up in the corner.

'What the fuck're you doin'?' Thatch asks.

I swallow. Click the side of my phone so that the screen darkens. 'Checking the report. Looks good for Wednesday.'

He scrapes the last bit of sauce from his plate and sucks it off the spoon. 'Are you gunna check on your sister? That was a bit harsh, roasting her for not havin' a boyfriend.'

'I wasn't... I didn't mean to... I'll check on her later.'

'Whatever, dickhead. Finish your bloody dinner and I'll go see how she's doin'. Save the fucken day as usual.'

He puts his spoon down in the middle of his dirty plate. Scrapes his stool across the hardwood and leaves it there, a metre away from the bench. Then he goes to check on my sister, and I stay where I am, my phone hot in my hand.

I re-read Lucy's messages.

What the fuck are you doing, Erik?

Whatever Thatch said must have worked. When I get to Nelly's room, they're both laughing. She even smiles at me.

'Hey,' I say. 'About before. I—'

'Let's not waste our final days together talking about *Lucy Buckingham*,' Nelly says. 'You know my thoughts on the matter. I expect you to do the right thing.'

I nod.

'We were just gunna go to your room,' Thatch tells me. 'Wanna come?'

I'm so stoked that Nelly's OK — that things finally feel normal again — I follow them to my room without asking questions. It's not until Thatch starts opening drawers I realise what's happening. 'Why are you going through my shit?' I ask him.

'I'm lookin' for socks.'

'What about looking for a pair that actually belong to you?'

'No can do, mate. Holes. Dirty. Buried in the backyard.

You name it. Haven't worn socks for months, have I? But I need some now. I said I'd help Simpo's dad in the garden tomorrow, and I've got bloody *work* next week. I've gotta borrow some. Just two pairs.'

By borrow, he means obliterate and leave to stink under his bed for two years.

I take the three biggest pairs out of my top drawer and throw them at him.

'What're you so shitty about?' he says, picking up the pair that dropped on the floor.

'Nothing! Just thinking. About the tour and stuff. Everything else is fine, with Rain and everything.'

My sister lets out a long sigh, like she's fed up. 'What's going on with Rain, Erik?'

Thatch sits down on my bed, trying on the socks, the bottoms of his feet dark brown.

'Nothing,' I say again. 'Everything's good. Really good. I just need to see her I think.'

'You see her every five bloody seconds!' says Thatch. 'I have to go the whole week sometimes without seeing Simpo. All ya do is bloody whinge, mate.' He wiggles his now-socked foot then rips the cotton back off, kind of snarling at me. 'Just drive into town and take your chick on a fucken date. It's what I'd do, if I had my own car. And if Carissa was allowed out after dark.'

'So it's *Carissa* now, is it? What happened to *Simpo*?'

'Nel...' Thatch looks at me, lifting his eyebrows. 'I'm not sure if ya know how nicknames work, but it's not a rule that you've gotta use 'em every fucken time. I know my girlfriend's name.'

For some reason, Nelly's angry again. She crosses her arms. Walks to my window. Opens the curtains, then closes them, hard.

Thatch must realise the energy's shifted. Again. He shoves

my socks in his pocket and leaves, rubbing his knuckles over both our heads on the way out. He gets me harder than Nelly. So hard it burns for a couple of seconds.

'I dunno if I'll miss that,' I say to Nelly's back.

She turns around, rigid. 'Miss *what*?'

'Thatch. Grinding the skin off the top of my head. Feels like getting scalped.'

Nelly tuts. 'Go and see your girlfriend, Erik. You're absolutely no help to me in this state.'

I park close enough to the shop to see Rain inside. She's talking to Kathy, the owner, who likes her too much to fire her even though she barely ever sells anything. Kathy puts up the CLOSED sign and starts to count the till while Rain disappears for a second to get the vacuum, which she pushes around the shop for a few minutes. When she's done, she gives her boss a little wave. Kathy says something that makes Rain laugh.

She's still smiling as she walks up the pavement towards my car.

A few metres away, she notices me. Lights up.

I say, 'Hey,' through the open window. 'Um... Sorry to bother you but... Do you live here?'

She's taken aback for half a second. 'I'm as local as they come,' she says, leaning up against my car door.

'I could tell.' I nod, liking the way her chest looks from this angle, brushing against the hard metal. I lick my lips before I talk. 'Can I get directions to the tourist centre? I'm pretty lost.'

Rain leans a hand against the window frame and the gems on her bracelet catch the sun. She points with her other hand, looking off into the bush at the back of town. 'You just need to make a right, up there, and keep driving for twenty minutes. A *good* twenty minutes. Then you'll get to a fire trail. You'll need to hop out and walk another thirty minutes or so, past the pine plantation and over the dried-up creek. You want to take the hidden tunnel under the fallen log – left at the lichen. Then you're there.'

'Sorry... I've got, um, maplexia. I can't remember directions. Do you wanna... show me?' I kind of forget it's a joke for a second. My heart starts racing, waiting for her to answer.

'I don't usually get into cars with strangers.' Her gaze lingers on the picnic basket and six-pack of beer on the passenger's seat. 'But you seem OK.'

When she gets in, she kisses me. Soft and excited.

She doesn't ask me why I came.

As I drive to her house, she tells me Doe and Marli aren't home. They're staying an extra night with their family.

I drive a little bit faster.

'So... they're not coming home tonight?' I ask as I jump out of the car. 'Not at all?'

She smiles over her shoulder, walking to the front door. She doesn't answer.

I try not to grin too wide.

Inside, Rain walks around for a little while watering plants with a spray bottle. Soft leaves, pale green, falling from pots. 'I'm glad you're here,' she says, spraying her own face and arms with water. 'I don't know what I'm going to do next year, when you're... and I'm... It's going to be strange, not seeing you all the time.' She wanders over to the picnic basket and peeks inside.

'Mum packed it,' I explain. 'She thought we might want to go for a walk or something. Said something about quality time, but...'

'We've got the place to ourselves.'

I kiss her. Her mouth, then the silk of her collarbone, then her neck, then her mouth again. I lift her up onto the bench next to the microwave. Take her knees in my hands and shift them aside, pressing against her. She's warm and soft and so good.

The picnic basket turns out to be pretty full. Cheese and bread and homemade relish. Beetroot and sweet potato chips. Two pieces of lemon cake and three of Lucy's nectarines. Rain reaches straight for one, cracking the gold-red skin then pressing her chin forward to slow down the juice. It doesn't really work. It runs down her neck, and she catches it with the edge of her finger. Sucks it off, sideways. 'Is this from the farmer's market? I swear, your mum has a sixth sense for choosing fruit.'

I'm about to say, *Yeah. The farmer's market.* She gave me the perfect out. Then I tell her, 'It's from one of the neighbours.'

'Which neighbour?' she asks, taking a bite. Juice bursts out like blood from an open wound.

'Um... Lucy.'

She wipes her mouth and puts the nectarine down, slowly, like it might bite her if she's too quick. 'The girl I met the other night?'

'Yeah.'

'Oh. Is she...'

'Yeah?'

'Is there — did something happen there?' she asks, in a way that makes me think she already knows.

'We used to...' My voice sounds high and boyish so I clear my throat. 'We hooked up. A few times. Over the years, or whatever. But we were never *together* or anything.'

Rain looks at me hard. I don't think she's ever looked at me this hard before. 'Did you hook up with her while you were with Abigail?' I feel the blood fall out of my face as she turns on the tap, rubbing the yellow juice from her skin. When I'm not brave enough to answer, she admits, 'Nelly told me you lost your... that you had sex, for the first time, with her. And that you cheated on Abigail with her.'

Jesus Christ, Eleanor.

What the fuck do I say? I was young. Lucy wasn't. She wore pleated Catholic skirts and those shiny black shoes with the straps. White socks. Everyone wanted her and then all of a sudden I had her.

Say something, Erik.

'It didn't mean anything.'

Rain dries her hands before picking up her beer. She hooks her fingernail under the corner of the label, peeling it up, pressing it back down. 'You had sex for the first time with someone who looks like *her*, when you were *fourteen*, and it didn't mean anything?'

'Yeah. OK. I had a crush on her. But I was just a kid. Honestly, she was kind of mean. She... played with me. Like a cat or something. She didn't care, and I don't care about her. It was just f—'

Fuck.

'Fucking?'

'I'm sorry, Rain. I didn't know Mum was going to pack the nectarines.'

She picks the bitten one up. Throws it hard into the sink, so that pulp flicks up onto the backsplash. She turns and I watch the breath rise and fall in her delicate shoulders. Then she spins to face me. 'How many girls have you fucked? Don't answer that. I'm sorry. That was... I don't know how to talk about any of this. I don't know what it's like to fuck a bunch of people or get followed by them on Instagram or get delicious fucking nectarine deliveries from Foxhead Bay's Wet Dream. I only know *us*. I think about you with Lucy, or anyone, the way you are with me, and—'

'Don't think about it.'

Useless, Erik.

I put my beer down in the puddle of juice and take her face in my hands. The jade green of her eyes. Peace. I breathe in. 'I'll tell you what it's like to fuck a bunch of people. It's good. Friction in the right places. But it's nothing like what we do. I don't know what you do to me, Rain. I don't know what's going on between me and you. But nothing's ever come close.'

We're frozen there for a second, her face in my hands.

Then I'm tasting her, the fruit still staining her lips and tongue. Tangy. Sticky. Sweet.

My thumbs press into the creases of her hips and she moves, like the lip of a tiny wave.

A lick of foam.

We eat bread and cheese under the bamboo ceiling fan in Doe's living room and watch a documentary series about a shipwreck. I hold her. I can feel how tired she is. When I make her a cup of tea, she doesn't finish it. She falls asleep with her head in my lap.

I look at the surf report for a while. It doesn't change, but I can't stop checking it, my breath catching every time. The predictions can't be real. If they are, Dad's right. It's the swell of a lifetime. Rising tomorrow afternoon, peaking the next morning. I should wake up early and do some callisthenics. Breathing exercises. Film myself talking about it, maybe.

It's all about marketing, Erik.

Rain's head shifts, eyes opening. 'Did I fall asleep?' Her voice is the purest thing I've ever heard. Slow and light. She sits up, pressing down on my lap with her elbows.

'Nah. Just for a second.'

She stretches. Stands up. 'Can you stay?'

I shouldn't.

I should get a good sleep. Get ready. Focus.

Rain's pulling her hair up into a bundle on top of her head. I love it when she does that. The sudden slope of her jaw and the way it eases into her neck, shoulders, back. Nothing else comes close.

'Yeah,' I say. 'I'll stay.'

PART 3

THATCH

I grab the avocado round the bottom, twist and yank.

It comes off easy. I'm heaps good at getting 'em off, even when they're real high. It hurts my neck a bit, but. I hold on to the top of the ladder and lean my head from side to side to give it a bit of a stretch.

Simpo's down at the bottom of the ladder holding a sack. She lifts it up over her head, waitin' for me to drop the avo into it. I don't, but. I chuck it from one hand to the other for a bit. Leave her hangin'.

She's got on a dress with flowers that looks real cute in the garden. She's so good lookin', sometimes I've gotta pinch myself cause I can't believe I scored such a good lookin' girlfriend. Maybe I should just grab her, chuck her in Dad's ute, do a massive burnout and run off with her. She's heaps nice all the bloody time. Even when she told me she wanted to go to Uni a million kilometres away in the middle of a massive city. She broke it to me real nice, made me choc-chip cookies and said she was so glad we got to spend our last year of high-school together, and I could always come visit after she moved.

I know I won't, but. I can't stand cities.

Carissa drops the sack a bit. 'Are you planning to hold on to that all afternoon?'

'Nah. Just till you tell me you'll come back on the holidays. If we're both still single we can hook up. Be a temporary couple.'

'A temp—'

We both hear her dad's voice over near the house and our ears flinch like rabbits. He's calling her name. He says something else but I can't make it out. Carissa drops the sack a bit more, lookin' past the other avocado tree and around the property where the tomato patch is. I mulched it last week with her dad – Emong. He reckons I did a heaps good job. Not too thick, not too thin, he reckons. He'd be over there watering it.

She says, 'Five minutes,' so that must be what Emong yelled. They'd be used to screamin' at each other from the other sidea the property.

It's a decent bit of land. Only an acre, but there's heaps of old trees here and they've packed it even fuller. It makes me think of the farm where Mum grew up. The smell of the sun on the dirt. The feel of it under your nails. Carissa's folks don't have sheep or nothing so there's none of that oily shitty sheep smell, but still.

I keep chucking the avo from one hand to the other. 'Look how fast I can go... See that? *Hand-eye cordanation*, that's called. I don't even—'

My foot slips on the ladder.

Fuck.

I'm gunna fall.

I lean forward over the top rung, grabbin' on like a dickhead, till it steadies.

Then I stand up. 'All good,' I tell Simpo, chucking the avo up one more time to prove it.

'*Michael*,' she giggles 'You're going to break your skull open if you keep—'

'This thing?' I knock my head a couple times with my knuckles. 'It's like a lead ball. *Un-fucken-crackable*. Drop me head-first from a light pole and I'd probly be right.' I give her a wink.

She shakes her head, smilin' heaps cute.

I drop the avo in the sack.

Simpo sings a little song to herself while I keep yanking fruit off the tree and droppin' it to her for a couple more minutes. Then I get down and take the sack off her. The bastard weighs about a hundred fucken kilos and I'm already sweating all over the place, even before walking it back to the house.

It's an old place. Been done up a few times, the kitchen and the bathroom and all that, but it's still got old bones. Colourful glass in the top windows and massive timber beams.

I put down the sack just outside the door and Simpo reminds me I needa take my shoes off, so I tug 'em off one at a time while she gets out of her little welly boots. Once we're inside, me in just Erik's socks, she puts on these heaps cute fuzzy slides and starts padding round the kitchen, washing her hands and pouring us waters.

Her mum n' dad're talkin' bout something to do with salination. They're dirt doctors. Soil scientists, Carissa says. But dirt doctors sounds heaps better. They met at Uni in Manila and fell for each other on the spot, which seems like a pretty stupid thing to do if you ask me. To not even talk or nothing. Just fall in fucken love, at the drop of a hat. If everyone went round doin' that, it'd be a disaster. What if I was drivin' through Hendo's one day and fell in love with the pimply chick in the window? Or some old lady, or fucken *Clancy* or someone. It'd be alright with Clancy, I spose. If I liked blokes and if he loved me back. He's pretty fucken funny.

The thing I like the most about Carissa's place – even more than her fuzzy slippers or her singin' little songs or me getting to do stuff in the garden so much – is every time I come over I leave full as a goog. I eat so much I dunno why they don't charge me.

And her folks seem to love it more than I do. Emong's fillin' up my plate now, loadin' on fresh-baked white rolls and eggs and tomatoes and capsicum from the garden just out the window, and I pour on heaps of banana ketchup from a glass bottle. Tala – Simpo's mum – starts pourin' me juice and tellin' me how tall of a guy I am and how I'm gunna hit my head on the fan.

'I got heaps of avos,' I tell her. 'Right off the top.'

Tala pinches my cheek. 'So strong, too!'

She's kinda takin' the piss outa me but I reckon she sorta means it too. I *am* pretty fucken strong. I bring my arm up, flex my muscles a bit and wink at her so she knows I'm sorta takin' the piss too, even though I *am* heaps fucken strong.

'*Stop*,' says Simpo, rollin' her eyes. I give her a squeeze with my other arm and keep on eating.

I try ignore her and Tala and Emong while they talk about Carissa goin' to uni. Next fucken week. It came so quick. I feel like she just told me yesterday how she got into her dream course. I was heaps stoked for her. I still *am* heaps stoked for her.

But now it keeps makin' me sad every time I think about it. I'm gunna miss hangin' out here with her n' her folks all the time. Maybe they'll let me keep comin' over even though she's gone... Both her brothers went and studied on the other sidea the country, so it's just gunna be them. They'll probly be heaps lonely and need someone to help 'em in the garden and eat all the extra food and that.

They're all lookin' at me all of a sudden so I swallow the stuff in my mouth and say 'Huh?' Then, 'Beg your pardon I mean?'

Emong leans back. 'There is a tarpaulin in our shed. For the camping trip?'

I think about it for a sec. We could probly use another one under the tent or down at the beach. I dunno what I'm gunna cover the stuff on the boat with, either, now I think about it. 'Yeah,' I say to Emong. 'Yeah, cheers. I'll come grab it in a sec.'

'And you're sure we don't need the tent?' asks Simpo. 'Nelly said something about there being limited space in theirs. I don't want to impose.'

'Nelly's off her fu—' I stop myself just in time. 'Their tent's *heaps* big. And Lara's bringin' one too. Trust me. You'll be able to spread *right* out.'

I go to wink at Tala again but stop myself pretty quick. She's got this look on her face like she's heaps worried. She's lookin' at Emong who's thinkin' pretty hard. I only realise what's goin' on when Carissa says, 'It's *alright*, Mum!' She adds something in Tagalog real fast.

Tala shakes her head. 'I want you to make the right choices, Carissa.'

In other words, she doesn't want her heaps smart, heaps pretty, heaps nice daughter rooting some no-hoper in a tent, getting preggo and having some big stupid kid like me to take care of.

Carissa's giving her mum a pretty scary look now. She says a few more words I can't understand, heaps slow. Then, in English – 'I'll be *leaving* next week. What are you going to do then?'

'Carissa is her own woman now, Nay...'

Tala shakes her head at Emong. She puts another four rolls on my plate, pushes the jam over to me, then goes to her room.

Emong sighs. 'It's not you, Michael. Carissa has always been the baby.' He shakes his head, pretty sad-lookin'. Carissa's hand closes round her butter knife, resting next to her plate. Emong reaches out and gives it a squeeze.

I don't stay too long after that. I get the feelin' they needa hang out as a family, and the surf'll be pumpin' in the bay soon — I don't wanna miss it. So after me n' Emong grab the tarp, and I have a bit more of a chat with Simpo, I tell 'em I'll see 'em soon.

It's gettin' on now, just before four and still stinkin' fucken hot. I've gotta leave all the doors of dad's car open for a bit before I can even drive off. Tala comes out with more food in containers and bags. Heaps of stuff for the freezer. Bolognese sauce and spring rolls and brownies. The dried mangoes I like, and these coconut bickies that taste like heaven on fucken earth. A few boxes of cereal, just cause. I reckon Tala likes feedin' me even more than Anita.

Before she goes back in the house, she says, 'I'll see you at the party.'

She means Simpo's goin' away party on Saturday. The day we get back from camping. She's havin' a party, then she's off the next day. I won't see her again for ages after that.

It came so bloody fast.

The car gets cool enough that I can touch the wheel and I drive off, waving out the window. I do a couple honks at the gate, then head down the track. It's dusty as. Gets all in my eyes and throat. I'm pretty stoked when I hit the main road, not just cause the dust gets better but cause there's reception again and the music comes on.

My phone starts ringin' through the speakers. I tap the

answer button on Dad's steering wheel. 'Whadya want, Spooks?'

Rain does a massive sigh. I hear it, even though I'm goin' ninety on the highway. 'Nelly said you were at Carissa's. Are you still around?'

I know what she's after. She wants a lift out to Foxhead to see Erik. I swear, those two can't go a bloody day without seeing each other. She's nowhere near getting her licence – too much of a pussy. 'You at work?' I ask her.

'I just have to do the front windows, then I'm done.'

'Do we needa go past your place on the way?'

'It'll take one minute.'

'It'd better,' I tell her, slowing down to sixty and having a look at the fire risk chart at the top of town. *EXTREME.* ' You owe me fish n' chips. And a drink. And maybe one of them apple crumble slices Tilda sells at the counter.'

Rain tells me she'll get me fish n chips but I've gotta get my own drink and slice. She's gotta save for uni, she reckons. 'Thanks, Thatch,' she says. 'See you soon.'

I see her two minutes later when I get to the shop. She's spraying windows with some orangey smelling stuff and wiping 'em in circles with a blue cloth. I go on my phone for a bit. Check the cricket scores. That pisses me off a fair bit, so I check Instagram.

Jenny's posted a shot of Lara struggling in an ice-bath. Nelly's done a story talking about her meeting tomorrow. She made me go to a couple back when we were doin' her eco-stuff and it was the most boring bloody shit I've ever had to sit through including Miss Jones's lectures about respect. Thank fuck school's done.

Nelly's next story's her talking about trucks going too fast on the highway. There's a picnic bench and some trees in the background so I reckon she must've pulled over for a dunny break. Maybe she's waiting for her mum to have a piss. I feel bad she had to go to the city with just her mum. She's been lookin' forward to it for a while.

I click on Abigail's page but there's nothing new on her grid. The last thing she posted was months ago on her birthday. Her and Harrison went out for dinner.

Zac's shared some shots from the beach. Bright blue fucken barrels. Massive and messy. Clancy shared the same ones, then a shot of Erik puttin' on his arm rope and about ten of his own head reacting. One blurry one of a wave.

Hot Lucy pops up next. A shot of her sittin' on a towel with some heaps hot mate then a bit of writing that says – *Perfect views, perfect company, perfect life. So grateful to live in paradise. Can't wait for the show!* She's tagged @erikeverson and her mate @fifimckay. It's a pretty good thing Rain doesn't have Instagram. Usually I reckon she's missin' out, but this'd probly piss her off or make her heaps sad or somethin'.

Spooks is still wiping, so I check my bank account. It's not fucken good. Twenty-eight bucks and seventy-five cents. Dad left cash when he went away, but I spent it all already and I can't ask him for more cause he's all fucken pissed off about working over Chrissy, plus he's savin' up for a fishing trip with Snapper after New Year's. I could ask Erik for a loan I spose, but it'd go to his bloody head.

Thank fuck I'm starting work soon. It's gunna be sick. Heaps of cash, and chicks love a tradie. They go fucken crazy for a guy in high-vis gear. Abigail always used to say so.

I think about Abigail a fair bit.

Nelly reckons her boyfriend's more than just a dickhead and that he's keeping her home and not letting her talk to her mates. Nelly reckons he could even be hurting her.

I don't wanna think about that.

The sound of her voice on the phone the other night scared

the shit outa me. But like the cops said, there's nothin' we can do. I can't go fucken rescue her. She doesn't wanna leave her boyfriend and I've got Simpo and my new job to think about.

Out of the blue, Rain's there. 'Done,' she says. 'I'll just get my bag.' She heads to the back of the shop into a little room for a sec, coming back out with her bag and no spray bottle or cloth.

Rain barely talks the whole bloody drive to the bay. She turns the radio down while they're doin' the news. All I hear is 'Tuesday the 28th...' then nothing for a coupla minutes. It's fucken boring, but I spose the news'd be even worse. When she turns it up, the music's back on and she's fucking round with her seatbelt. I dunno what she's doin' with it. She's turning the band over in her hands, heaps serious lookin'. It makes it hard to watch the road with her twistin' her bloody seatbelt like a psycho.

I ask her what she's so worried about.

She starts twistin' the fucken seatbelt again. Then she goes, 'That guy from the surfshop... Jonesy? I heard him at the super-market this morning, talking about the waves. He said you wouldn't catch him dead out there. That it was dangerous.'

'Course it's fucken dangerous. Anything could happen. Sometimes the lip breaks guys' backs or their leash'll get trapped in the reef – they get held under, ya know? Drown.' It's not till I see how dead white she goes I realise – she's worried about him. 'Erik's pretty good at readin' that sorta stuff but. It's not too dangerous for the pros. He should be right.'

Rain looks a bit like she's gunna spew.

We roll over the crest into the bay and it hits us all at once. The cars, bumper to bumper, all the way down the hill, crammed into the carpark, then all the way up the street.

People're everywhere, all over the rocks, right up to the edge of the big cliff, on the beach and standing waist deep in the pounding foam. Heaps of clean-lookin' city people. One guy's on top of his car, phone held out.

I turn quick and park on the verge outside the caravan park and me n' Rain walk down the rest of the hill in total quiet. We're both pretty busy watching. Even from my car, you could see the massive explosions where the water's hitting the rocks, roaring, and the sun's getting lower so the spray lights up, yellow-green, and the bodies out there're just silhouettes. The wind's hot, blowing hard from the desert, and everything smells briney and hard like seaweed on hot rocks. It makes me think of fishing up north with my dad.

Rain goes, 'Shit,' and I couldn't agree more.

I don't reckon I've ever seen it this big or this busy.

We've gotta muscle through the crowd. Rain follows close to my back and we push through a mob of kids, then a mob of tourists, then some more serious guys with tripods, all the way to the edge of the cliffs where you get the best view. I see Clancy first cause he's jumpin' up and down like a dickhead. A few other guys are around him – Duke n' Liam n' Toby. It's not till I'm through 'em that I see Freddie n' Zac, sittin' right up near the edge.

Zac's got his camera on a tripod so close to the edge it could tumble easy and smack on the wet rocks down below. Freddie's a bit further back with his phone in Nelly's drone controller. Rain n' me squeeze into a bit of rock behind Freddie n' Zac. I've got a pretty decent view over the back of Zac's head. I'll be able to grab him if he gets too close to the edge.

Next to us, hogging the best spot, there's a filmer from the city or somewhere. He's got a black cap on and heaps good equipment. Worth thousands, the stuff he's got. I reckon a few of the black shapes in the water must be pros. The waves're big enough to bring 'em in. There's even a jet-ski buzzin' round in front.

It's closing out, but it's sposed to be heaps cleaner tomorrow.

I can make out Erik now, cause of his hair and the shape of him. He stands up on his board to see the ragged lines coming in. I reckon that's Lara next to him.

The rich filmer takes out a muesli bar and I wish *I'd* brought bloody muesli bars. I've got all that food in my car I spose. Maybe Clancy or someone'd run and grab the cereal, or the frozen brownies. I sigh pretty hard.

I don't recognise any of the other guys but they must be good to be out there. Or fucken crazy. Clancy tells me, from pretty much under my armpit, that he would've been in the water but he's still crook from when he got glandular fever a few months ago. He keeps tellin' me n' Rain stuff even though we're not answerin'.

We're tryna watch.

Slowly but surely, it gets unsurfable. Just about every wave starts to close out. There's no entry points. Lara goes to drop in, but changes her mind. Good thing, too. She would've got *pummelled*.

In the carpark after, we talk to the city guys for a bit. Erik seems to know 'em. Maybe from comps, or through his dad.

It's a bit past eight and the rest of the carpark's empty except me n' Rain n' Erik and these blokes he's talkin' to. Rain's got her arms wrapped round her shoulders, but Erik's so bloody focused on what he can see of the waves in the dark and what these city blokes are sayin' he doesn't even notice his chick's cold. 'Come sit in my car if you want?' I tell her.

She does a nod.

We only have to wait in there for a sec before Erik rocks up, dustin' off his feet a bit before gettin' in the back seat. 'Sorry,' he says. 'Lost track of time.'

Anita left dinner.

Two big salads, thick bits of Chrissy ham, crusty white bread and butter. She's left plates and knifes and forks and all that next to the note so we barely even needa lift a finger.

I have a bit of bread with some ham while I wait for Erik to get outa the shower and Rain to get outa her work clothes. I'm already pretty comfy so I just eat and go on my phone. I'm on some pro's page, watching some ad he's done for perfume or some shit, when there's a knock. I reckon it's nothing at first – maybe Rain knockin' on the bathroom.

Then it goes off again and I turn round to the front door. That's definitely where it came from. Probly Clancy or Zac or Lara or Jenny – or all of 'em – here to talk about the surf. I open the door, ready to grab Clancy in a headlock.

It's not him but.

It's Hot Lucy.

What the fuck's Hot Lucy doin' here?

I go – 'What're you doin' here?'

Lucy sorta cracks up. She's got a dress on that looks like a net, bathers showing underneath. 'Hey... What's your name again?'

'Michael bloody Thatcher. Who're you lookin' for? Nelly n' Nita're in the city.'

'Oh... Well... Is Erik home?'

'How come?'

She cracks up. 'Are you, like, drunk or something?' She looks round my side, tryna get a glimpse into the kitchen.

'We're just about to have dinner.'

'What are you having?' Hot Lucy says, pushing round me pretty hard for a chick and marchin' in like she owns the joint.

A sec later, Rain comes back in from the shower. She's changed into some PJ shorts that look like old man boxers and one of Erik's old t-shirts. She stops dead. Big eyes like a roo. She looks at me like it's my fucken fault Lucy's here.

'Hey!' says Lucy. She waits for Rain to answer for a sec. When she doesn't, she goes – 'Have you guys *taken* something?'

Erik comes out holding his towel and grabs it tight at the middle when he sees who's here.

I crack up a bit. I can't fucken help it. Erik looks at me the same as Rain did, like it's *my* bloody fault she got in. I could'nt've stopped her if I tried. She pretty much jumped *through* me. She'd be good at footy, Hot Lucy.

'I got locked out!' she tells Erik. 'Mum and Dad went into town while I was at the beach and I got home and the whole place was locked. I didn't take my key! I've been sitting in the backyard with Polly for the last two hours.'

Polly must be a dog I reckon. I don't ask but. Instead I go, 'That was a bit fucken dumb. When're your parents back then?'

'Soon, I hope. I know. So stupid. But I can just go back if you guys are in the middle of something. It's not *that* cold in the backyard...' She wraps her arms round the net dress and hugs herself.

I try tellin' Erik with just my eyes that it's bullshit. She's puttin' it on cause she wants him to ask her to stay. Rain knows too. She's lookin' at Lucy how people look at me when I eat something off the floor. Not very fucken impressed. Erik doesn't get it but. He's always been a soft touch. 'If you need to, you can hang out here for an hour or whatever.'

'Great!' says Lucy. She stops huggin' herself and strolls

straight up to the bench, grabbing a plate off the top of the stack.

I push in front of Lucy and grab a bit of ham. She doesn't say nothing. She knows I know what she's up to even if Erik doesn't. For someone who did ATAR, Erik's pretty fucken dumb. He looks down at his towel then heads for his room at a bit of a run.

Lucy starts puttin' salad on her plate like a fucken psycho and Rain's still standin' there like a stunned roo. I make a sound in my throat at her – a *get your shit together* noise. She snaps out of it and goes to the glass cupboard, taking out two of the big ones. I hear her filling it up with ice and some kinda drink while I pile my plate up with bread and butter and a big pasta salad and a big green salad.

Erik comes out just when I'm finishing up.

'Here,' Rain says, giving him one of the glasses. Ribena, it looks like.

Erik does a massive smile and says, 'Cheers.'

We eat at the big table for some bloody reason. Erik asks Rain about work and she asks him about the surf. Lucy keeps saying how amazing he was. I go on my phone. Nelly's just shared a reel to her stories. Something from a profile called *Get Lost Gas*. I'm about to skip past cause it's some boring climate shit again, but then I see her. Nel. And Anita. Someone's interviewing 'em.

'We're joined now by a mother and daughter Anita and Eleanor Everson, who drove all the way from Foxhead Bay to attend the planning session.'

I turn the volume up and Erik looks over my shoulder. Rain leans over him to look too and we all listen.

'Anita, how important was it for you to come along with your daughter today?'

'Oh, it means the world to me. I'm so glad I can share these things with my baby, before she's all grown up. It's very special, and very important.'

'And Eleanor – what advice would you give to young people like yourself wanting to get involved?'

Nelly gives the camera one of her serious looks. 'At the risk of sounding cliched, Martino, young people need to act *locally* while thinking *globally*. While the online fight is important, studies have proven that we have most success when functioning as part of a physical collective or group. Form an eco-club and act in your immediate environment while thinking about greater threats, the largest of which being fossil fuel companies like Wooltide. This is why it's so important for people my age to prioritise groups like this. It grounds the fight in humanity. Real people with real lives, who are making the *effort* to be here.'

'Some say activism is hypocritical when you have, say, a mobile phone in your pocket. What would you say to those people?'

Nelly laughs in the way you never want to. The scary way, like a bad guy in a movie who's just caught someone in a trap. 'What would I say?' she says, still smiling. 'I would *say*: how dare you conflate the impact of an average teenager's smart phone with an industry predicated on the destruction of our environment? Secondly, it is hideous to first create a problem only to judge those suffering from it. People my age did not design the technology that made mobile phones. We were merely *given* them – at extraordinarily young ages, considering the unknown impact on our bodies and minds.'

The reel ends and we all stare at it for a sec.

'I should have gone,' Rain says. She's staring at her plate, lookin' pretty sad. 'I should have just taken work off. I should have been there with her.'

'We all should have,' Erik says.

I make a noise that means the same as 'Yep.'

Lucy says, 'No way! You couldn't have missed the surf. This could be, like, your big break.'

'He could break his neck, more like it!' I say.

That makes Rain look even more uncomfy.

Lucy only eats half her plate. She must get a pretty good sense of how things're going, cause she holds up her phone and says her folks're home. Pretty sure they've been there the whole time. 'Thanks for having me!' Lucy goes. 'Catch up again soon, OK?' She gives Erik a heaps tight hug and says a quick bye to me n' Rain.

Rain goes to bed after that. Erik only stays up long enough to wax up a coupla boards. We don't talk much cause he's got his earphones in. When he finally takes 'em out, I tell him I'm stayin' in Nelly's room.

He tells me I've gotta leave the door open. 'Don't touch anything, Thatcher. And don't wank in her bed.'

I knock him a salute. I'd never risk wanking in Nelly's bed. She'd know for sure. She's got a bloody radar for that stuff.

I hear Erik n' Rain have a bit of a fight through the wall. She reckons he didn't need to ask Lucy to stay and he says it just came out and he didn't mean to. Then she says Lucy was flirting with him and he says that's just how she is. Rain says, 'I can't believe I ate the fucking nectarine.'

They're quiet for heaps long.

I reckon she's giving him the silent treatment.

Then I hear a coupla moans and the word '*Erik*', real soft.

For such a rich house, these walls're thin as flyscreen.

Erik and Lara are in the water at 4:30. It's heaps dark still, but I can already tell it's ripping. One set after another, coming in in perfect lines, like someone drew 'em with a ruler. We get the best spot on the rocks, cause we're early.

Then the others start rocking up – Jenny, Zac, Clancy, Freddie, some of the older guys, Jonesy from town and Andy Everson. He brings a whole bag full of pies from the general store and hands 'em out. The out-of-towners fill up the rocks all around us, and the beach, and the carpark.

I keep forgetting it's the bay, it's so fucken busy. And the waves are SO fucken good. Looking out there, you'd think we were in Pipeline or somewhere – massive slabs, clear blue and shaped perfect, one after another, no pause, just bloody savage. *Too* big. The calibre of talent's pretty unbelievable. Even my favourite bodyboarder's here. He grew up in Bandler but he's lived overseas for ages. Must be back for the summer. He could've flown in just for this — it's worth it.

Erik gets lucky straight away. He catches one of the best waves I've ever seen — movies included. It's bloody huge. Andy lets out a roar when he sees his kid paddling to the top, dropping in deep. The wave throws real wide and starts to drive down the line like a train, wrapping 'round the reef, Erik there, in the barrel. The wind comes in hot and powerful — exactly what the wave needs. It spits and blows and Erik comes flying out a second later and the whole fucken beach cheers, like everyone just blew their load at the same time.

Erik n' Lara get three barrels each before the sun's even properly up. Zac gets some pretty good shots by the look of it.

And my mate's the best one. No fucken kidding. It's like the waves're choosing him. Lara's holdin' her own too. She's better since school ended — even ballsier than she was before.

Every time someone takes off, Rain asks who it is. Except Erik. Every time *he* goes, she gets heaps still and stares at him like he's a carcrash.

'This next one's gunna be good!' Clancy says, squeezing in between Rain and me. 'Can you see that, Zaccy?!'

Zac nods, but doesn't turn away from his lens.

I see what's comin' and groan. 'Jesus fucken Christ...'

It's the biggest one so far. And I reckon it's Erik's. I see his little head and his arms paddlin' for their lives up to the lip. He drops in smooth and heavy, levelling out on the face, speedin', and it's almondy and perfect like on a fucken poster. He's racing the section, flyin' along, out of sight for a whole second then there again.

Fuck.

I blink and the wave bottoms out. He's falling. The whole beach does a massive gasp. I see his board go over, and him, like some kinda toy, black wetty and white hair. Rain's got hold of my arm. I tell her, 'It's all good,' but Erik could be in a bit of trouble – there's his board, tombstoning. I hold my breath. The next wave's getting closer.

Then his little fucken head's there, his arms scrambling, still in the impact zone, looking for his board.

The next wave crashes right in front of him and there's nothing but white for ages.

He comes up again, a bit closer to shore, moving slow but

managing to get onto his board. He flops over it like he's going to bed and doesn't try paddling or nothing, just gets pushed along.

Rain's let go of my arm. She's practically legging it through the crowd to the beach. I catch up to her in the shallows where Erik's coming out of the foam.

He's heaps white.

I go, 'Fucken hell!' cause I reckon someone's got to.

He dry retches then spews a bit, sitting down hard on the sand.

He looks out of it. 'How's your head?' I ask him. 'Did you hit it on the—'

'Just held under.' He holds his eyes shut for a sec then rubs 'em with the inside of his elbow. Rain passes him his bottle. 'It's OK,' he says. 'I'm OK.' After a couple sips of water, he goes, 'Stupid. *So fucking stupid.*'

'Erik.' Rain pushes back his wet hair, looking into his face. 'You were amazing. You don't have anything to be a—'

'You don't know what you're talking about.' He shrugs her off just as Andy skids up to us, kickin' sand everywhere. He's got a board under his arm but he drops it straight away and gets down on his knees.

'You right, Ricky?' He grabs his kid's shoulders and gives them a bit of a shake. Then he gives Erik a little punch on the arm and says, 'Happens to the best of 'em, mate. You just needa—'

'I know what I'm doing, Dad. I just...' He spits into the sand then leans back with his eyes closed for a big breath. 'Need a minute.'

We all leave him to it for a minute. He stares at the sand, hair dripping, back moving with big breaths. Then he puts his leash back on.

'You're going out again?' Rain asks him. She bites her lip,

white as a fucken ghost. She gives me a look, like she wants me to stop him.

I give her a shrug. *I* can't fucken stop him. It's his life.

Erik has another big sip of water. As it's going down his throat, he flinches, like he's remembered something all of a sudden. 'Shit. I'm sorry, Rain. You're meeting your mum. I said I'd come.' He stares out at a fresh set, his eyes real hungry. 'I can't miss this. I'm sorry... Could you get Doe to—'

'I can give ya a ride,' I tell Rain. I dunno why. I'm bloody spewing I'm gunna miss all the action – the last thing I wanna do is sit around with Spooks and her druggie mum while this is goin' on. But she's a mate, and I've got dad's car for a couple more days. 'You've gotta get me a milkshake, but. And *two* muffins.'

She laughs a bit.

Andy clicks his tongue a couple times. 'Maybe ya *should* stay in, mate. If your mum was here, you know what she'd tell ya.'

Erik heaves himself up and grabs his dad's board from the sand instead of going for the spare he brought. He starts dusting the sand off and I catch Andy's cheeky side smile — I reckon he's pretty chuffed about the board change. Erik ignores him, walking backwards into the surf. 'I'll come see you as soon as I'm done.'

Rain gives him a bit of a smile. Tells him to be safe.

On the way to town, to see her crazy fucken mum, Rain looks outa the window and Bluetooths her playlist. Some boring shit with too many words and no beat. I let her play it but. I reckon she's a bit stressed out and I dunno what to say to her. Erik's acting like a dickhead. I can't say *that* to her cause it'd be heaps snakey, but he is. So I give her a bit of a nudge on the head with my free hand. 'I'm startin' to feel like we're best fucken mates.'

Rain cracks up. She doesn't usually crack up when I do jokes but this time she's just about crying.

'Is it that fucken funny?' I ask her.

She gives her eyes a wipe. 'If you'd told me that when we were in year nine, I might have left school. Gone back to the city and lived on the street.'

'Now you love my bloody guts. Ya painted a picture of me n' everything.' I wink at her.

'I've done something for Carissa, too. I thought I'd give it to her at her going away party.'

'Yeah? She'll like that heaps I reckon. Have ya done anyone else, other than us?'

'Just Doe and Marli.'

'Not your mum or nothing?' I turn the music down a bit.

'No.'

'... Ever paint your dad?'

She shifts round in her seat. 'I don't know what he looks like. So...'

I shoulda probably guessed she didn't know her dad cause she's never talked about him or nothing. Still. It'd be weird to not even know what they looked like. If ya got their chin or their eyes or their shithouse temper. 'Ya never even met him?'

'I did when I was a baby. Apparently.'

'Ya don't have any photos?'

She shakes her head.

'And your mum didn't tell ya about him? What he looks like? Didn't even give ya a bit of a lead?'

She laughs a bit out the window. 'When I was six she told me my dad was a circus performer named *Constantine Geronimo*. And when I was eight, after figuring out that Constantine Geronimo was probably not a real person, I asked her again.' Rain gives the seatbelt another twist. 'She told me my dad was the drummer from Silverchair. I think I knew deep down that wasn't true, but I still went through this whole Silverchair phase. I mentioned it to her a year later and she had no idea what I was talking about.' She stops twistin' and stares straight ahead. 'When I was about ten, I heard her on the phone, asking someone for money. She thought I was asleep. I think it was my dad's parents on the other end. She kept saying, "Don't you care about his daughter? Don't you care about your *granddaughter*?" Apparently they didn't.' She blinks a couple times – sorta shakes herself awake. 'At least, they didn't care enough to give her money. I get it. She wouldn't have spent it on me.'

I don't reckon I ever really got the full gist of how it was for Rain growing up. She's got her shit together and she did good at school and everything. The song finishes and I say, 'Fuuuck...' I dunno what else to say to her. *I'd* probably want someone to just say, *fuck*, if it was me. What else is there?

She nods and does a swallow.

'When's the last time you saw her? Your mum?'

'Years ago. Before she went to jail.'

'She did time eh? For drugs?'

'Not drugs. Criminal neglect.'

I puff my cheeks full of air and let it out real loud. 'How long?'

'Ten months.'

'And you haven't seen her since then? Since you were a kid?'

'No. I've had some letters, and a few phone calls. But I haven't seen her.'

'Bloody hell. You must be pretty nervous then, eh?'

'Mmhmm. Not because I'm worried she's going to be bad... I know she's going to be bad. I'm nervous about how she's going to make me feel. How I'm going to act around her, and how I'm going to...' She does a shrug.

I remember *my* mum always made *me* feel heaps good about myself. She reckoned everything I did was fucken genius. Always goin' 'wow' and givin' me high-fives. It'd be shit, not havin' that at all. My dad can be a waste of bloody space, always pissin' up the second he gets home, but he works hard and I can count on him for stuff. Not every-fucken-thing, but some stuff. Rain's got no one.

'What's your mum's name, then? I should probly know before I meet her.'

'It's Rachel. And you don't have to. Meet her. Just stay in the car and I'll get you takeaway.'

'And leave my best fucken mate to meet her druggo mum all alone? Nah, dude. I'm comin'.'

She goes to say somethin', then stops. She picks up her bag and checks her phone. 'Thanks, Michael.'

I tell her I'm gunna get a thickshake instead of a milkshake. 'It's two bucks for an extra scoop.'

Rain's mum's sposed to get to the place at eleven.

She doesn't, but.

Me n' Rain sit in the outside part of the old cafe, waiting for ages. The tables're a bit wobbly and there's flies fucken every-where, but there's heaps of shade outside and it's not too busy.

'Just a few more minutes...' says Rain, havin' another look at the time on her phone, bitin' her lip. 'Do you want another thickshake?'

I *go* to say *Yeah – a banana one this time*, but it doesn't come outa my mouth. I don't say it, cause I'm watchin' a trippy-lookin' lady walk in through the cafe door. Rachel Douglass, I reckon. I point with my thumb and Rain turns round.

The lady sees her straight away. She doesn't walk over to us but. She stops next to a little table with water bottles on it and turns round, pullin' down on her jacket. It's fucken boiling, but she's wearing this big brown jacket with tangly-lookin' furry bits round the neck and the bottoms of the arms, and she's pulling it down over a denim skirt. There's big white boots on her feet, with black scuffs round the heels — she's like a banged-up mannequin from the shop Rain works at.

This lady, Rachel, I'm dead fucken sure, pours a water, takes a couple sips, and puts it down on the table with the bottles. She turns round and heads over in one move then starts talking about a metre away. 'I've never seen so many Teslas in my life. There aren't this many Teslas in the city! Amazing how much changes when the yuppies learn about a place. Never the same again, hey?' She sits down on a wobbly seat across from Rain. 'Is it always like this, or just on the holidays?'

Rain closes her mouth, then opens it again. 'Mostly on the holidays,' she says back.

Rain's mum looks heaps like Rain, but if all the life got sucked out of her and if she got sprayed with grey paint and rubbed it in, but not fully, and if ya could see bits of scalp between her hair. Rachel wipes her nose, talking fast again. 'You're completely stunning. You're a woman now, apparently. When did that happen?' She takes a hold of Rain's hand and has a good look at the bracelet Erik got her. 'This place isn't turning you into a *plutocrat* is it?'

I go to ask what the fuck a plutocrat is but Rain's mum talks first. 'I didn't know you had a boyfriend,' she says, nudging her head at me.

'No. *No*,' Rain says. 'This is Michael. A friend.'

I stretch my hand out for a shake. 'One "no" would've been enough eh? I'm one of her *best* mates, actually. Real nice to meet you, Rachel.'

Rachel grabs my hand with her skinny fingers. I reckon she's decent lookin', even though her skin and her teeth're fucked. She's got this way of holding her shoulders and lookin' ya right in the eye – like she owns the fucken world. She pulls a pack of ciggies out of her pocket. The pocket turns inside out when she does it, and a few bits of tobacco and a button fall on the ground. She shrugs, takin' out a lighter and sparking up.

'You're not supposed to smoke here,' says Rain. She's looking over her mum's shoulder at the waitress picking up plates a couple tables away.

Rachel blows smoke up into the air over her head. 'Better to ask forgiveness than permission sometimes.' She takes another big puff and blows it just about onto Rain's head then puts the ciggie out on the table. 'They used to let you do whatever you want here. The guy that used to own this place would smoke behind the counter. He grew the best weed in town.'

'No way?' I ask. 'Ya mean the bloke with the massive glasses? I remember him from when I was a kid. D'ya know what he's up to these—'

'I don't do drugs,' Rain says, putting her muffin down real hard, so her plate makes a noise on the table.

'Hope I didn't put you off!' Rachel laughs. She wipes her nose with the fluff on her sleeve then keeps talkin', telling us all about how she's been goin' for swims in the harbour and she always sees these same dolphins — a mum and a baby. She tells us how she's going to have her own place soon, in the hills, and Rain'll be able to come visit.

Rain's sorta shrivelled up into herself, starin' at her muffin. She only looks up from it when Rachel goes to the dunny. 'I'm sorry,' she says. 'You should have stayed in the car.'

'Nah! It's fine. Your mum's alright, Spooks... She's got the dolphin swimming and all that. The herb-garden on the verandah.'

Rain picks a berry out of her muffin, chews it heaps slow and swallows. 'She doesn't go swimming with dolphins, Thatch. You should take everything she says with a grain of salt, OK?'

The first thing Rachel says when she gets back from the dunny is, 'The toilet paper's all wrapped up like Christmas presents in there. What the fuck's that all about? It said *good for you* or some bullshit. Yuppies with too much time on their hands. Like rich people don't already think they're better than everyone else, they've gotta put a massive congratulations on their toilet roll — make everyone else feel shit for buying the cheap stuff.'

I go to tell her I couldn't agree more, but she keeps on talkin'. She's like a fucken steam-roller. She goes on about how kid shows are all subliminal messages making zombies and then about some show she played about twenty years ago where some bloke called Nick Cave told her he liked her single. She just keeps goin' on and on, wipin' her nose every now n' then.

She hasn't asked Rain a single fucken thing about herself.

She hasn't even technically said *hi* to her yet.

When she starts talkin' about some time she chained herself to a bloody bulldozer, I barge my way into the convo. 'Did Rain tell ya 'bout our eco-club? She helped start it with our mate Nelly and her brother Erik. *That's* Rain's boyfriend. He's my best mate too. Last year, we did this whole thing at the Bandler Beach Junior where Rain told everyone the town was on fire and we got heaps of signatures on a petition. Stopped Hendo's coming to town and everything. And we did heaps of clean-ups, and started this whole compost thing at school, and Nelly got the canteen to ban plastic forks and shit. *Stuff*, I mean.'

Rain's mum lifts her eyebrows up at Rain. She picks a choccie chip out of her muffin and flicks it onto the brick paving. Then she sucks her fingernail, glancing back at her kid.

'So you *do* have a boyfriend?' She takes another choccie chip out and holds it in her fingers. 'Who is he?'

Rain picks up a sugar packet and tears the tip off, then shakes about two grains into her cuppa tea. 'We went to school together, and the club. He's really nice, Mum. He's so smart. Funny. And just...'

'A heaps good surfer don't forget! He'll qualify for the world tour soon – I bloody know it. The year after next, I reck —'

'A *surfer?*' Rachel says, looking hard at Rain. 'Not a fan of surfers. I didn't think you were either, but I haven't seen you in a while I guess. You love him, don't you? I can tell. Mums can always tell. You have to be careful with young love. It gets into your bones and stays there, and you can never really move on.'

Rain's got hold of the sugar again. She has a good stare at it, but doesn't pour any. 'Is that how it was for you?' she says. 'With my dad?'

Rachel nods and has a massive sip of her coffee, swallows it slow. 'Your grandparents, too. Your nan and pop loved each other more than anything. Did everything together and I never once heard them argue. They were good to each other no matter how miserably they failed in other *duties*... No matter how much they failed me.'

'Pop's only ever been good to me. I haven't seen you in... And he...' Rain closes her eyes and starts to breathe real deep.

I fill up her water.

'Yeah, yeah,' her mum says. 'Your Pop's a bloody saint on the surface. Just don't expect him to protect you. Don't expect him to *believe* you, when things happen to you, when people do things to you, and you need your dad. Cause he'll tell you your skirt was too short and you were out too late and then he'll pretend you never told him.'

It goes heaps quiet. Rachel drinks a few mouthfuls of coffee.

'I...' says Rain. 'I didn't...'

Rachel waves her away. 'Forget it! Ancient history. Let's focus on you. Tell me something about yourself. You've changed, I can tell.'

'Oh. Um. Well... I wanted to talk about... My dad. I wanted to ask...'

Rachel licks her cracked lips a couple times before she answers, 'What about him?'

'Who was he?'

Rachel leans back in her chair. 'Just a boy. Overdosed when you were six months old. Fucking bastard. He'd been so good. We'd both been off everything, even ciggies, since we found out. He didn't have any tolerance anymore. So when he used again, it hit him too hard.'

I'm pretty bloody gobsmacked.

'So he's dead?' Rain says, in a real small voice.

Rachel takes out another ciggie and lights it up.

'What was his name?'

Rain's mum shakes her head. 'He hated his name.'

'I have a right to know, Mum. Do you have any idea how... I have a right to know.'

Rachel gets up, dusting a couple crumbs off her lap. 'You're better off. Leave the past where it is and keep doing what you're doing. You're glowing, girl.' Then she's off, stomping a bit in her boots and dragging the jacket by a fistful of ratty fur.

Rain looks up at the bald branch of the cherry tree and takes a massive breath out. I barely hear her say, 'Bye, Mum.'

She's quiet the whole drive back. Then at the very end, just as I pull the handbrake, she goes – 'Don't tell anyone about my dad.

Especially him. Please.'

It's a pretty bloody hectic thing to have to keep secret, but I'll do my best.

I drop Rain off at Erik's but I don't go in cause I'm too worried I'll say something about her dad. I spose I should head home anyway — it's pretty late arvo and I've still gotta clean up a bit and sort my stuff out for camping. Dad's back tonight and the house is pretty bloody dirty and I still haven't packed a single thing.

When I get to my street, Clancy's on the corner tryna do tricks on his skatey and stacking it. He reckons Zac kicked him out cause he wouldn't stop talking when he was trying to focus on editing photos. I tell him he can talk all he wants at my place if he helps me clean up and pack. We can chuck the cricket on in the background, I tell him.

You'd think I'd asked Clancy over for somethin' good, he's so fucken excited. He pretty much jogs next to me the whole way, balancing on the gutter like a primary-school kid. 'Is it so good, getting a whole house all to yourself so much? You can just do whatever ya want, eh? Like a full grown up.'

I give him a nod. 'You can even have a beer if ya don't break any more of my chairs.'

I can't believe little Clancy's in year *eleven* soon.

Time fucken flies.

PART 4

RAIN

Fixed to the roof like a stalactite, the shower head is a huge chrome circle of eyes crying warm and hard. Pristine tiles cover the floor and walls, and even the grout sparkles. I don't think I'll ever get used to it. I don't think I'll ever get used to the white shine, the wood accents, the cream labels on black glass bottles.

I wonder what my mum would say about the Eversons. About the way they live. The word *yuppie* would be there. She blames yuppies for everything. *Stepford Wives* and *Suits*. Like it's the direct fault of every upper-middle class person that she's killing herself with opioids. That she nearly killed me.

I remember people used to call her pretty. A music reviewer once described her as 'a fragile yet rugged grunge-pixie'. One stranger in the library – an aging lady in a cheese-cloth smock and a pink beret – called her 'transfixing beyond man's ability to be transfixed'. I think she was a poet.

I don't want to know what she'd think of my mum now.

Dying isn't poetic. Not in real life. There's no buttery renaissance glow. It's just fucked.

And my dad...

I step forward, leaning under the downpour, and a ribbon of hair blocks my left eye.

Half the world gone.

Half of me gone.

He's been dead all along.

I move my hand under the little black tap at the top of the soap bottle, pump twice, and stare at the bubbles.

When I was a kid, we were always leaving places so fast we'd never have soap or shampoo or anything. We'd shower at friends houses, or use the basins at public bathrooms. We went to one particular recreation centre a lot, before I got tinea on my feet from the spongy shared mats. To get rid of it, Mum made me distract the pharmacist by pretending to vomit while she stole the antifungal cream. I felt like actually vomiting, I was so guilty. It made me never want to lie again.

I think my mum's so used to lying, she doesn't even notice she's doing it anymore. It's like breathing to her now.

She could have been lying about my dad; he could be unlocking a door or tying his shoes or spreading his favourite mustard. He might laugh like me. He might be a painter. I might find him one day.

But there was no sparkle in Mum's voice when she told me about him.

I'll be an orphan soon.

Wet shrapnel bounces off my back and I fight the urge to sit on the shining tiles and fall apart. I turn off the shower and immediately step, dripping, onto the plush bathmat. I take a clean white towel from the cupboard under the sink and wrap it around myself before slipping across the hallway into Erik's bedroom.

He's leaning against his pillows looking at his phone, sort of frowning. When he notices me he shoves it aside, stretching his arms and smiling at the ceiling. He smiles, and the world is entirely beautiful.

I have to turn away from him.

I rub my ribs with the heel of my hand, trying to unblock whatever's stuck inside me. Whatever it is I don't want him to see. Now I'm facing his mirror and the little photos he looks at every day. A tiny Erik and Nelly at the beach, stripes of zinc on their cheeks. Him and me at the ball, laughing under fairy lights.

I look back at him on the bed, real, sublime, and, for some reason, waiting for me.

Heat creeps into my cheeks. The knot in my chest loosens. I move to the bed, on my knees like I'm praying, and maybe I am.

The mattress shivers as he comes to me, his eyes blue and clear.

'If you want to talk, about your mum and stuff...'

I shake my head and take a steadying breath. Salt, zinc, cotton. Something ancient and peaceful underneath it all.

He tries again, soft and low. 'You can talk to me, Rain.'

Part of me drifts away while another part starts speaking in a voice that's scared and small. 'I don't know who... I can't... I feel like, maybe, I shouldn't exist...' I'm dizzy from pushing back the tears. Swallowing them down, down, down. I lean against him, my head in the cradle of his shoulder, breathing out slowly as the fluffy white towel falls over my hip.

He runs his thumb slowly over the revealed skin — the line where a gentle tan meets pale white. 'If you didn't exist... I'd spin off into space. Like a lost satellite or something.'

That's all it takes.

My fingers tangle in his saltburned hair and I surrender, completely, to his lure.

· · ·

We're cutting watermelon at the kitchen bench when Nelly and her mum get home. I think Anita knows how we spent the morning; she drops her bags and pinches back a smile before hugging us both. 'Did the two of you have a nice time?' she asks innocently.

'Don't ask them *that*, Mum. We hardly want them to answer. Besides: *We're* the ones who've done something interesting. *They* should be asking *us* about the meeting.'

'Ugh,' Anita sighs. 'It was great. Such a wonderful sense of community and purpose.'

'It's a pity the community wasn't *larger*... but I suppose people have *things* to do. I bought us a microwave, Rain. We can discuss compensation later.'

I rush to the box Nelly left by the front door. 'Oh. Wow! This looks great. Thank you. We'll need this for... warming up our... food.'

Nelly raises an eyebrow.

'How was the hotel?' Erik asks.

'Adequate.'

'Did you guys do much in the city?' he asks, offering her a dewy pink triangle of fruit.

Nelly looks at the watermelon sceptically before taking it. After a few bites, she answers, 'Nothing notable. I had a brief visit to the state archives to conduct some research, and Mum and I went for a mediocre dinner at the Greek restaurant Regina recommended. Other than that — and the lifechanging meeting you both missed — it was uneventful.'

Somehow, Erik smiles. 'We were just talking about camping. Everyone's really excited.'

She sighs. 'Yes. *Camping*. I suppose I'll have to get started unpacking and repacking.'

Erik and I follow her to her room, watching as she methodically empties her backpack, refilling it with carefully folded clothing and underwear. She digs through her closet and rips out a long-sleeved yellow dress. 'Will this do for New Year's Eve?' she asks, waving it around like she's trying to swat a fly.

'Might be too hot,' Erik answers.

Nelly slams her closet door. 'If you don't have anything nice to say, Erik, keep your mouth closed. Have you finished packing yet, or are you going to make us all late?'

'Yeah. No. I did it last night. It's done.'

She levels a glare at me.

'I'm almost done,' I say. 'I need to pick up a few things in town.'

'I'll come with you. *Just* me. You've been with her all night, Erik, and I need to pick up something from the chemist. A feminine hygiene product.'

'You can say tampons or whatever, Nel,' he laughs. 'We're not in year two.'

Nelly picks up her sunglasses and car keys. 'We need to leave immediately. I told Freddie and Lara we'd pick them up at thirteen-hundred hours, so we don't have much time if we're going to... Come on, Rain! You two can cuddle all you want while we're camping.'

I follow her down the hall, almost tripping in an effort to keep up.

On our way to Doe's house, I realise why Nelly was in such a rush. After checking her blind spot and turning on to the highway, she tells me her plan. 'I need your assistance with something... sensitive. And extremely important. There are two properties between town and Foxhead Bay where Abigail may be living. If we hurry we can check them both and be back in time to pick up the others. I'd go myself, but sometimes it's necessary to have a comrade when undertaking these sorts of missions. A friend...'

So I say, 'OK.'

Nelly looks me in the eye for the first time since Christmas. She almost smiles, pulling into Does's driveway. 'I'll leave the car running.'

I rush inside.

I'm grateful Doe's at work and I don't have to make small talk. Or big talk. I still haven't told her about my visit with Mum. Even before that, since graduation, I've found myself holding back about things. Pulling away. She's done more than I ever could have asked for, and I can't expect her to keep giving. I've aged out of her care. I should give her space now. She's done enough.

There's a note on the kitchen bench next to a bag of bread rolls.

> Take these!
> They'll go stale otherwise.
> And have fun!
> – Doe

A comforting feeling I can't name settles as I read her large, looping handwriting.

For some reason I put the note in my pocket before grabbing the rolls and walking quickly to my room. I pack two pairs of bathers, another pair of shorts, three more shirts, a jacket, and the dress I bought for New Years. My other things – toothbrush and hairbrush and birth control – I already have.

I almost trip as I spill back into Nelly's passenger seat, bag rocking in my lap.

She drives faster than usual to the first stop. I think, for the first time in her life, she might even be speeding.

Our destination — a weathered white farmhouse with maroon trim that I've noticed a thousand times before — is immediately off the winding country road that leads to the Bay. There are three goats in a pen next to a dam, its raised edges bright with cracked orange clay.

Nelly stops the car and I freeze, suddenly wary. I was so excited to be back in her good graces, I hadn't thought about the reality of the 'mission'. What the fuck are we about to do? 'Eleanor... Maybe we shouldn't. What if—'

'I've planned it all out, Rain. *Every* scenario. You simply need to accompany me; I'll do all of the talking.'

I swallow. I think about arguing, then remember how her face fell when I said I wasn't going to the meeting with her.

So I step out of the car and follow her to the chipped maroon door. She opens a ripped screen and knocks four times, stepping back to wait.

Nothing.

Nelly checks her watch and sighs.

Then we hear shifting behind the door. It opens slowly, inch by inch, until a woman is visible on the other side of the screen. She's pale and puffy-faced, wearing a huge stained t-shirt and mismatched thongs. She blinks at us.

'Hello!' Nelly beams. 'Is Abigail home?'

'*Who?*' the woman whispers, looking back over her shoulder.

'Abigail. We're here to pick her up – we're going camping for New Year's. I hope she didn't forget...'

The woman pulls the door closed to conceal a crack of messy living room. 'I don't know an Abigail,' she says, quietly and insistently. 'You need to—' A wail sounds from behind her, somewhere in the living room. A baby, I realise after an instant of panic. The woman's face falls and she pinches the bridge of her nose.

'We're very sorry!' Nelly says. 'We must have the wrong address... Is this two-thirteen Bo—'

'This is two-fifteen!' she almost screams over the baby. 'Double check next time!'

The maroon door slams before we can reply.

The baby's screams grow fainter as we walk back to Nelly's car, the last echoes obscured when she starts the engine.

'At least we can eliminate that candidate,' Nelly says happily.

'I don't think we should...'

'One more stop, Rain! It's practically on the way home. There are banana chips in the glove compartment if you need a snack. Here's some water.' She passes me her bottle from the cup holder in the bottom of her door. I take a sip. Then I open the glove box and eat a few banana chips.

The next house is definitely not on the way home. It's up a sequence of winding gravel tracks and through two gates that I have to get out and open, clouds of dust bursting with each step. It's after midday by the time we get to a hand-carved wooden letterbox and roll downhill towards what looks like a hobbit hole: a huge grassy mound with windows and a door.

There are two men sitting outside. One in a sarong, the other a singlet, dirty work jeans and a baseball cap. They're both in their sixties at least.

As we get closer I realise the house is a long metal structure, a shipping container maybe, covered in plants and grass. The man in the sarong sits up in his deck chair. The man in the jeans looks at us warily, his hands on his hips.

I wait for Nelly to leave the car before moving. By the time I reach her, she's standing confidently in front of the man in the jeans. 'I apologise,' she says, without a trace of apology. 'We may have the wrong house... we're looking for Abigail?'

'No Abigail's here, sweetie,' says the man in the sarong.

'Suzie shows up sometimes, but only when I've had one too many cabernets!' He laughs, flourishing the printed fabric over his legs while the man in jeans gives Eleanor a stern look.

Nelly shifts away from him, towards the guy I'm guessing is his partner. 'I don't suppose you were at the Wooltide protest last year? You look extremely familiar.'

'I wish!' he answers. 'This one hates crowds, and I just couldn't stomach going alone.'

She gives me a quick, piercing glance. 'Yes. It's difficult when our loved ones have different priorities.'

Nelly barely got me to the protest last year. I didn't see how I would be helpful. I *wasn't* helpful. I just stood around and chanted a little, Nelly's screams drowning me out as we marched through the streets.

I wish I could be political like her. I try. But no one listens, and when they do, they respond to you like you're a toddler, lecturing you on *the way things are* until you're drowning in their bullshit and just give up. Nelly says if everyone would fight, we could change things. That makes me feel even worse.

I distract myself by looking at the bright orange flowers on a huge native Christmas tree. Moodjar, Doe calls them.

'The flowers mean heat's coming,' says the man in the jeans.

'They're beautiful,' I tell him, noticing his kind eyes and a crooked scar above his top lip.

'Yeah,' he says. 'It's an amazing plant. Clever. Resourceful.'

'My friend says the spirits of the dead camp on its branches.'

He raises his brows thoughtfully. 'All the more reason to give it a good prune.'

The man in the sarong laughs so loudly we turn around. Nelly's not usually funny on purpose, but judging by the delight on her face, she's in on the joke. 'Scathing!' says the man. 'You are an absolute *hound*, aren't you? You should go into politics.'

'Oh, I'm considering it!' Nelly beams. 'I'm starting with a foundation in law.'

'A lawyer! *La-dee-dah!*'

The man in the jeans groans, speaking under his breath so that I can barely hear it. 'Just what the world needs.'

I laugh and Nelly wheels around, checks her smartwatch and jumps. 'Rain! Why didn't you tell me the time! I'm so sorry,' she says, bending to shake the man's hand. 'It was excellent to meet you, but my friend and I...'

'We'd better go and find the right address,' I say. 'Thank you. Your house is beautiful.'

'Come by anytime!' says the man in the sarong. As we drive away, he calls out, 'Stay late enough and you might meet Suzie!'

Erik is waiting in the garage when we pull up, bags stacked like Tetris blocks in the back of his car. He's sweating. 'I thought you said one?' he asks his sister.

'I had an extremely personal emergency, Erik! And we're only... twenty-seven minutes late. After you completely deserted me the other day, you should be thankful I'm coming! In fact, I might just stay at home where I can access running water.'

'Jesus, Nelly! Let's just go, yeah?'

We pick up Lara and Freddie, squeezing their things into every inch of space the car has left before leaving the Bay. Freddie's backpack ends up across our laps, and Nelly squeezes an Esky between her legs in the front passenger seat. The bulk of the extra bag forces Freddie's face against the glass, but he says he can handle it for twenty minutes. With Lara's warm arm on mine, and buckles digging into my stomach, I focus on Erik's hands moving across the steering wheel. The way he flicks the indicator. The spark in his sunglasses when he looks into the rear-vision mirror.

Through the window, pastures spread then are slowly devoured by bush, trees becoming taller. Then thinner. Then drier. The dirt by the roadside is rockier and sandier and everything feels warmer somehow. We turn onto an ungraded road and, rattling like pebbles, drive for what feels like another twenty minutes. Freddie's head cracks against the glass a few times. Nelly reaches back, trying to stabilise him by gripping his shoulder, but it doesn't really work. Erik apologises every time the car lurches over a hole on the progressively bumpier track. He gets out when the sand gets thicker – does something to the tyres – and we drive as far as we can on the cloudy earth before he finally pulls up over a clump of dried branches between two peeling trees.

We spill out of the car and onto the track – a scribble of grey sand and crushed branches in the dense bush. 'The walk's pretty hard,' Erik says as he clips the front of my backpack. 'Tell us if you need a break?'

'I'll be fine.' I smile. I like walking. I'm still nowhere near getting my licence, so I walk for hours every day just to get around.

'It really is quite gruelling,' Nelly adds, strapping a CamelBak to her front and sipping from the long straw. 'You're going to want to hydrate before we begin. You all should.' She takes another long sip while she watches us. Nelly's the only one with a bag of fluid rigged up to her body. The rest of us drink from our bottles before zipping them back into each other's bags.

Then we start up the track.

The air is tight under the salty canopy – a forbidding smell, stinging with pollen and thousands of invisible creatures, closing around us like a soft, buzzing mesh. The track didn't look steep, but it feels it; a slow incline made more difficult by the sand and roots and ants' nests. My backpack is an anvil, tilting. I start to sweat in places I didn't realise *could* sweat. My earlobes. My ankles. My eyelids. It feels like the inside of my body is sweating.

If I fall, Lara might be able to support my weight. But then she'd fall back on to Nelly, who would probably step out of the way and let us both roll to our deaths.

I wish Erik would stop looking back. 'Just a little bit further,' he says.

I say something in a breathy grunt. It's meant to be, 'OK,' but it comes out more like, 'Kehh...'

Freddie's the first one into the sandy clearing. He breaks through the lower branches and sighs with relief before his body thuds onto the dry leaves. I find the energy to push my legs through the last few steps, wrestling out of my backpack. I drop, face up and panting. Patches of light spread through the grey-green treetops as something breaks through them with a snap. A cockatoo maybe. I can just hear water over my panting, and the hard breathing of the others. We breathe like one big wounded animal.

When I sit up, at least a minute after everyone else, Lara's tugging her shirt off, stripping down to a sporty blue bikini. She's still slick with sweat, but she's smiling with the serenity of an athlete. 'Coming in?' she asks us, massaging the ridges cut into her shoulders by her backpack straps.

'Are you going to the beach?' I ask, dreading another walk so soon.

Lara looks over her shoulder. 'We're *at* the beach.'

I follow her gaze through two trees reaching across for each other in a clumsy arch – the ocean is just there. A narrow strip of white sand, then bright, gleaming turquoise.

． ． ．

There are golden droplets of water in Erik's eyelashes. 'Are you gunna come in?' He grins, leaning back and swimming softly.

The small lagoon is outlined by keyholes of ancient coral. Tall cliffs wrap their pale rocky arms around the blue, so that it feels like the whole place is tucking you in. Wrapped in bush and rock and water, we're only visible from above, or from the ocean. We're the doorway in the cliffs.

Erik told me there are seahorses and starfish here. When the tide's right you can walk across the reef and find them. Nelly says they used to be everywhere – like the schools of fish so big they looked like whales, and flocks of seabirds so dark they blocked the sun – but people don't remember it. Our baseline's shifted.

Even so, it's the most beautiful place I've ever seen.

The water feels sacred. Like nothing bad has ever or could ever happen here.

I smile at Erik with what might look like confidence and his shoulders shrug underwater. 'Take your time. The view's pretty nice from here.'

No one sees the way his gaze drips over my body, or the way I blush.

Lara, Nelly, and Freddie are all underwater.

Thatch arrives in the usual way: all of a sudden, making too much noise. The motor of his dad's dinghy growls through the opening in the cliffs, which have started to glow shell-pink in the afternoon light. He's towering at the very back of the boat, one arm bent to steer while a delicate shape I know is Carissa sits in front.

'*Finally*,' Nelly says, squinting towards the boat and leaning forward off her towel.

'Are they late?' asks Freddie.

Nelly shakes her head. 'Not *technically*.'

Unpacking the boat in the shallows, I wonder if we need this much for two nights. We take out two tents, six sleeping bags, boxes of food, an Esky full of alcohol, camping chairs, fishing rods, a tarp wrapped around a portable stove, and a huge orange dry-bag. Nelly says it contains things that 'absolutely cannot be compromised', which turns out to be lights, an emergency radio, a first-aid kit, and a fire extinguisher. Eleanor Everson does not fuck around with protocol. Once we're back at the clearing and everything's laid out across the papery leaves, I help Nelly roll out the tarp. And I'm sweating again.

'Is it getting hotter?' I ask no one in particular.

'Fucken oath,' says Thatch, passing a thin metallic rod through the top of the canvas.

'Must be after four by now,' Erik mumbles. He finds the rod on the other side, pulling it down through a khaki strap. He takes a long sip from his bottle, wiping the shine from his forehead.

Nelly checks her smartwatch. 'Sixteen-hundred and thirty-five hours, to be exact. And *no one* is going back in the water until camp is completely operational. There is no way I'm setting this up in the dark. No way, Thatcher. Don't make me remind you *all* of the promises you made that night at the oval when I agreed to do this.'

Lara drops into an angry squat and swats a fly from her face. 'It's *definitely* getting hotter,' she says.

Monitored by a huffy Eleanor, we set up camp. Thatch and Erik put up the two tents inside the treeline while Freddie hangs lights and sets up the generator. Carissa and I lay out the tarp, pegging it deep into the sand and placing heavy rocks in the corners. Lara hauls over a stump from the scrub and levels it on the ocean side of the blue plastic sheet.

Nelly sets the butane stove on top, then steps back, appraising. 'Carissa – would you place a larger rock on your corner, please? You haven't got anywhere *near* enough weight there. The wind is going to come straight through here tonight.'

Carissa looks confusedly at her corner. There are more rocks there than anywhere else and I think Nelly knows it. Trying not to roll my eyes, I pick up a chunk of limestone from under a driftwood branch and place it with the others.

'Done!' cries Lara. She sprints towards the water before Nelly can stop her.

'ARE YOUS GOIN' *SWIMMIN*'?' Thatch screams through the trees an instant after the splash. 'Hurry up and peg it in, dickhead!'

Erik growls back, '*I fucking am!*' as Freddie appears through the trees, pulling a black t-shirt over his head. He nudges Nelly on his way past and she finally relaxes. She tugs her tank top off, thanking us for our hard work before sprinting into the water.

I follow, shedding fabric as I run, the sun bright and the water holier than baptism.

For the next hour or so I'm the happiest I've ever been. I know I am, as it's happening, floating on my back as the sun gets weaker, listening to Erik tell Thatch about black holes. Freddie's smoking his peace-pipe on the rocks, near where Nelly's reading, and Carissa and Lara have gone to get the Esky. I think I feel safe.

'... But how come they *know* about it? There's no actual proof or nothing.'

'There's a shit-tonne of proof, Thatcher,' Erik says for the second time. 'They've been observing them since the seventies. There's evidence. Pictures, like X-Rays.'

'Now I know you're bullshitting! X-Rays're for *bones* and shit. It doesn't make any fucken sense, mate. Stars can't just eat themselves.'

'It's not... It doesn't *eat* itself, Thatch. It's about gravity. It pulls so hard, the light can't escape.'

'*What* pulls so hard?'

'Fucking *gravity*.'

'But gravity *can't* pull, mate. It doesn't have *arms*. It's all – *in the bloody air* and that.'

'It fucking pulls! You'd *feel* it pulling if it was stronger. And easing, if it was weaker. In a black hole, there's so much pull, it's fatal – even to light. The energy's pressed into a really tiny space, and that's what makes it collapse. Vanish, kind of. But not really.'

'... Sounds like you don't know what the fuck you're talkin' about.' Thatch splashes Erik in the face then heads for shore, shovelfuls of water flying from his hands.

Erik's still sort of annoyed, but also trying not to laugh – it's a paradoxical state that only Michael Thatcher can bring out in people.

Gentle orange waves kiss his arms as I swim into them, and they wrap tightly around me.

It's suddenly dark. None of us can be bothered actually cooking any of the food we brought. Instead of using the little butane stove, we cluster around a huge Tupperware container full of spring rolls from Carissa's mum's freezer. They're still just cold enough to make me shiver.

Erik passes me his jacket.

'D'ya know what we should do?' says Thatch, taking in the circle of faces. 'We should turn all the lights off and go lie on them rocks. Stargaze for a bit. Y'can show me some black holes, mate!'

'I can't *show* you one, Thatcher.'

'Told ya they weren't real. You coming or not?'

Erik mumbles something about gravity, standing up with the rest of us.

Nelly holds a huge yellow torch as she leads us over the rocks, reminding everyone constantly to watch where they tread across the flat stretch of crumbling stone, which is covered in shells and sharp rocks hiding between blades of bunny-tail grass.

None of us thought to bring a towel, so we lay across the limestone debris. There's almost no moon tonight — just a weak curve of white amidst thousands of ecstatic stars.

Nelly starts to talk about Abigail, telling the others about the possible locations on her list, and I sort of tune out. It's not because I don't like Abigail. I don't, but I still don't want her to suffer. I just have too many other things drenching my mind. My mum. My dad. I try to focus on the fragment of moon and my friends' voices and forget about it all, but the darker thoughts tip-toe back in, like thieves over creaking floorboards.

The others are still talking, their words pluming and disappearing in the darkness. I hear the word 'meth' a few times. Someone says, 'It's not Abigail.'

I close my eyes and feel the shine of the stars.

My mum's hair used to shine. Half of it's gone now. It'll never grow back. I wonder if the police or hospital will call *me*, when she dies, or if they'll just go ahead and cremate her. Would I need to organise a funeral? Who would even go? I'm so scared she'll die and at the same time ... part of me wants her to.

I want it to be over. For her, for me. I could visit her grave and only remember the good things. Pretend everything was different.

I wonder if my dad was buried somewhere, or if they just burned him. Who did the burning? His parents? I wonder where they live. If they're alive.

Nelly's talking, about bikies I think. 'They are *not* good blokes, Thatcher! Do you have *any* idea how organised these outfits are, or how many people have suffered under the—'

'Shooting star!' yells Lara.

I don't see it in time.

When Carissa asks who needs to go to the bathroom, I say I do. I'm not lying. I've had three cans of beer since dinner, plus a few glasses of water. Nelly keeps reminding everyone to 'hydrate'.

So Carissa and I crunch back down the rocks towards a patch of scrub at the top of a rocky rise that's been designated a bathroom. Carissa goes first. I stare up, not wanting to miss another shooting star, and reach into Erik's jacket pockets, my fingers brushing a square of metal. His phone. I check the time – 10:46 – and realise he has one bar of reception up here on the hill an instant before the phone buzzes.

A message on his lock screen. From Lucy.

Starting at the top of my head, my whole body is slowly coated in a sick wave of fear. I enter his passcode, knowing I'm crossing some sort of line, and open his chat with Lucy, reading just what I can see.

Last week, Her:

I hope you like the fruit x

The 'x' is a hot little knife in my stomach.

He's written back.

Yeah. Thanks heaps

Lucy again:

> See u soon I hope. I always
> have the best time with u ;)

My whole body is in my heart, thumping blood and dread, because I can see, there, in the top corner of the evil, digital, soft-edged box that Erik liked it. He liked her message.

Now there's a new one.

> Srsly E, let's hook up. No
> strings like always 🤍

I'm aware of blood in my head. Throbbing blue-hot. A light pain spreads from the base of my neck through my skull and into my eyes. My vision sort of blurs and I stumble.

'Are you OK?' asks Carissa, appearing from the other side of the toilet-bush.

I'd forgotten she was here. I'd forgotten *I* was here. I shove Erik's phone back into his pocket and say, 'No. What? Oh. Yeah. Just a headache, from the sun. I should have listened to Nelly.'

'*For every millilitre of alcohol, you should be ingesting* at least *the same quantity of H2o!*' Carissa imitates, then giggles. 'It's nice though, isn't it? No parents! You're used to it, but for me it's nice. Oh, god! I'm so sorry Rain. I didn't mean that you were...' Her hands move to cover her mouth, then hover in the air. 'I just meant that you're *allowed* to... I've gone insane. It's the drinking. Or, maybe the freedom?'

'Umm...'

'*Sorry*, you need to go!' She turns and walks a few steps, looking out at the water.

I squat. I was busting a minute ago, now nothing. Carissa's going to think I'm pooing. And my boyfriend is going to cheat on me with Hot Lucy. Fuck. My brain throbs and I almost black-out, leaning forward to catch myself, wrist jarring on the rocks. Then a warm stream of urine cascades down, ricocheting onto Erik's jacket. Fuck. I scramble back, losing my treading and falling arse-first onto the ground.

'I'm sorry!' says Carissa, after peeking around the bush to check on me.

Fuck.

I brush the sand from my skin and pull my underwear up, then my shorts, with arms I can barely feel. Then I slide Erik's probably scratched phone back in his pocket.

Should it feel like this? This happens to people all the time. Erik and Abigail used to cheat on each other constantly. But she'd turn up to school and throw her hair back like she didn't care.

I feel like my whole body is about to implode. Some strange gravity is pushing me back into myself.

Carissa's tipsy giggles are an anchor. Something solid to hold on to while we creep back through the scrub and over the rocks to the others, waves of dread crashing. I try to breathe. To be normal. Good.

Freddie and Erik stand on the far rocks, a tiny orange ball that must be Freddie's pipe moving between them. Thatch and Lara are arm-wrestling. It looks like he's letting her use both arms, which seems to be making things more or less even. Nelly seems to be acting as a sort of referee.

Erik and Freddie start walking and we reach the others at the same time. He's smiling at me, I know, but I can't look at him. I can't speak to him. I swivel. 'Forgot the painkillers,' I say, hurrying back up the steep rise, my thong catching on the rocks and snapping. 'Fuck.' I breathe, trying to force the strap back through.

Lara rushes over, snatching one of the lanterns from her towel. 'I'll come too! I need chips.'

'Grab another six pack or two, eh?' Thatch says. 'No one's piking early on the first night. And get that trail mix Simpo's mum made, with the crispy choccies in it!'

I shove the piece of rubber through the hole, slipping my toes into the thong and speeding back towards camp. At least it's Lara who decided to come with me. She's steady. Nice. I see her all the time, usually with Jenny. I think this is the first time we've ever hung out without her best friend laughing at her side.

'Thatch told me you saw your mum the other day. We're all here for you, if you want to talk.'

'It's OK. I've come to terms with… everything. It was fine.'

She focuses the wide yellow beam of the torch over the tarpaulin, above the Esky. 'Still rough though,' she says, taking out two six-packs. 'Is there something else? You seem distracted. It's all good, if you don't wanna—'

'Lucy.'

'Buckingham? What did she… Aah. Erik? Yeah.'

'He really liked her, didn't he?'

Lara nods slowly and I feel the truth like anaesthesia, numbing my whole body. 'All the boys did. She was like, the *ultimate*. When Erik lost his V's to her it was the biggest thing. I remember how loud it was when they got on the bus the Monday after. Alf wouldn't leave the curb for about five minutes, waiting for all the boys to stop screaming. But it was stupid. It was different to the way he likes you. He *loves* you.'

I'm rummaging through the first aid kit, but I've forgotten what I'm looking for. Lara pops open a bag of chips and I flinch. She crunches. Swallows hard. 'Look, Rain. I've known Erik for a long time. Our whole lives. It's nice to see him with someone who really loves him. Who listens to him, you know? Makes him laugh. Everyone can see you guys are obsessed with each other. Don't worry about Lucy.'

I swallow two pain killers, along with the rest of my water. I try to say, 'Thank you,' but something catches in my throat.

Lara lets us walk back in silence.

Halfway to the others, their voices become clearer. Then I hear 'truth or dare' and almost turn and run. If it wasn't so dark, and if I weren't afraid my thong would break again, I might.

I settle myself between Erik and Nelly, staring out into the blackness. He holds my hand and I barely register it. I pretend to laugh at the game, but I couldn't care less. Each turns ticks by, humourless.

Dare: Lara does a flip off the rocks into the water.

Dare: Freddie swims to the boat and back, naked.

Truth: Nelly tells us all about Nathaniel Holt's third nipple.

Dare: Thatch eats a live clam.

Truth: I rank all of the teachers in the maths department according to who I'd 'most like to root'.

Dare: Carissa does an interpretive dance.

'Truth or dare, Erik?' Carissa chirps, hair loose and cheeks glowing with a rebellious pride I've never seen before.

'Truth.'

'What's your favourite song?'

'That's a shit bloody question, Simpo!' Thatch says. 'You've gotta ask somethin' a bit spicier – like what's the most drugs you ever did or who's the first girl ya went down on. Shit like that.'

'Sorry,' Carissa says, throwing her arms around Thatch's neck before swivelling back around. In a low, silly imitation of her boyfriend, she says, *'Who's the first girl ya went down on?'*

She laughs, then stops. Then she gives me a desperately sorry look.

Erik coughs.

I imagine Lucy leaning back onto silk pillows and opening her legs. Or Abigail, glossy as always, moaning ecstatically.

'Uhm...' says Erik, puffing out his cheeks and staring up at the sky. 'Lara, I think.'

A drum strikes in my brain.

Lara.

Why not Lara? Of course, Lara. I never even asked. I didn't think to ask. I try to smile, but I think I'm grimacing. I can feel them all looking at me.

'It was just one night,' Erik says. 'We weren't—'

'He did a shit job, if it makes you feel better,' Lara interrupts. 'And we were drunk.'

'It was the first time I'd done it!'

I breathe, deeply, trying again to smile.

'I'm so sorry, Rain!' Carissa says. 'That was a very awkward question for me to ask.' She elbows Michael in the stomach and he winces for half a second. 'You should have let me ask about his favourite song.'

'I didn't know you were gunna ask *that*, did I? Fucken hell, Simpo!'

'It's fine,' I hear myself say. 'It was ages ago. These things happen.'

Erik pushes his hair flat across his scalp and smiles at me sheepishly.

I look down at my arms. I'm spinning in the air a little way away, a planet on the verge of collapse.

. . .

In my sleeping bag, I turn away from him. A few minutes later he rolls over too, his back pressing into mine, his body firm, his breaths heavy.

I feel cold. Separate. Unreachable. To stop from drifting into a familiar blackness, I remind myself that I exist.

I am camping. I am lying in a tent in the scrub by a beautiful cove with my best friends. Nelly is here, wearing an eye mask and earplugs, lying on her back with her arms at her side. Thatch is snoring, his top arm obscuring most of Carissa's torso, and she is saying something in a soft, panicked voice. Erik is next to me. He is the love of my life.

Shadows of branches move in the starlight above us.

A rustle, then a crashing weight.

Someone yelling, 'Good Morning!'

A scream, high and clear.

'*What the fuck?*' Erik's voice, syrupy with sleep.

'Wakey wakey, hands off snakeys!' A happy, chirping voice from the middle of the tent. Clancy. My eyes open in a gritty squint as he falls, flat on his face. Then the face is upside down, sandy freckles and a huge grin.

Thatch is holding Clancy by the ankle, dangling him an inch or two above the tent floor. 'What the fuck're you doin'?' Thatch asks a squirming Clancy while rubbing his eyes with his free hand.

'Mum had to work early! She dropped us at the track when it was still dark, didn't she, Zac?' Clancy makes a wiggly, unsuccessful attempt at escape.

'Yep! Had to get up at four to post the edit, Erik. It's pretty good,' I hadn't noticed Zac in the doorway of the tent.

'People are *frothing*, mate!' says Clancy, barely flinching when Thatch drops him on his back. He wriggles until his face is right in front of Erik's. In front of mine. 'We only had a minute to check, but it's blowing up. Everyone's saying you're the next big thing. *Capable. Stylish. Instinctive.* Zac's account's got heaps of new followers, hey Zaccy? We can try to get reception and show ya, if you want? Or you can save it, like a surprise. I couldn't wait if I was you. Did I tell ya Maddi Carlisle's gunna have viewing parties for all your events next year? It's gunna be—'

'Would you SHUT UP!' Nelly rips off her mask and her earplugs in one surge, her spine so poker-straight it seems violent. 'This is absolutely *ridiculous*.'

Zac and Clancy both shrink, smiling like quokkas.

'Sorry, Nelly,' Clancy chirrups.

Zac examines the tent zipper guiltily as he speaks. 'We should've waited.'

'Well you *didn't*. And now we're *up*. Go and light the stove, would you? I need to caffeinate immediately. There was a stick in my back *all* night, and you really need to be tested for sleep apnoea, Thatcher, because your snoring is concerning on a *medical* level.'

Thatch looks around for defence, beseeching, but no one argues.

Clancy and Zac scramble out of the tent, laughing under their breaths and elbowing each other.

The rest of us follow them solemnly, afraid we'll set Eleanor off again. We sit on the tarp waiting for the kettle to boil, a sleepy cluster of flannelette shorts, nylon, and skin, as the cove lights up. Lara appears, rubbing her eyes and scratching sandfly bites. 'Freddie's still asleep. He woke up when we heard the scream, listened for a second, said "Not yet," and went back down.'

'Fair enough,' Erik says. 'Is it even six yet?'

'Zero-six-thirteen,' says Nelly.

'You know it takes longer to add the zero?'

Nelly looks at Erik like she's about to kick him.

'Where should me n' Zaccy put our stuff?' Clancy asks. 'The big tent or the little one?'

'The little one,' says Nelly, staring at the kettle. 'I don't want you screaming and waking me up in the morning or drinking too much and wetting your sleeping bags.'

Thatch laughs.

Carissa looks shyly over at me. 'How did you sleep?'

I stare at the kettle. 'OK, I guess. The ground was soft.'

'Would you like to go for a quick walk with me? We might see a starfish.'

'Maybe after?' I gesture at the butane stove, cups waiting patiently beside it.

Carissa nods, her foot bobbing cheerfully.

I drink my tea slowly, accepting a bowl of cereal when Erik passes it to me. When I've finished that, I go with Carissa up the beach, walking over a cluster of rocks to where a group of small bright pools are scattered, streamers of seaweed washed up overnight forming broken borders at their edges. We sit on the damp stone.

'I want to apologise *properly*,' Carissa says. 'I should never have said that to Erik. It made things awkward for you. It was the last thing you needed, with your mum.'

'You don't need to apologise. It doesn't bother me. It was... funny.'

We're quiet for a while, both swishing our fingers through the pool. I see a tiny brown octopus. A cuttlefish bone. The claw of a small pink crab.

Carissa lifts her face up to the morning-bright sky and it seems like she's going to say something else, before our names sound across the sand. She throws some seaweed back into the pool and stands up. 'We'll chat later, OK? Don't forget.'

The others are setting up a game of cricket when we get back. I would have been better off staying at the rock pool – my team might have stood a chance.

At least Erik and I are on opposing sides. He fields, a mango dripping lazily from one hand, juice running up his arm as the other hand hangs free, waiting for the possibility of a ball. I swing my bat wildly and knock my own wicket off its stumps.

Nelly calls out, 'Excellent try, Rain!' as I walk away from the fallen sticks to wait in the shallows, where I watch Nelly and Freddie make up for my lack of runs, pelting again and again between the two sets of sticks.

I do a little better with fielding. I even catch the ball when Carissa hits it softy towards me.

'OUT!'

'Is it true you don't even have to go to private study if you don't want to?' Clancy asks.

Erik shakes his head, rinsing lettuce carefully with water from his bottle. 'They do the roll and everything.'

'But ya don't have to *do* anything? They won't tell you off if you just sit there?'

'Not really.'

'Don't tell him that!' Nelly snaps, prodding her brother's shoulder with the tongs she's using to cook our lunch. 'It's not true, Clancy. You must be productive during your study periods. If you aren't, you'll end up falling behind. *Failing*. Is that what you want?'

'I failed year eleven!' booms Thatch. 'It wasn't that bad. I got my certs and stuff in year twelve, plus a heaps hot girlfriend.' He winks at Carissa, who beams.

Nelly rolls her eyes.

'Pass me the bowl?' Erik's voice, so close I startle. 'Sorry. I didn't mean to... Are you OK?'

'I'm good. Everything's good. These onions are just really strong.' I wave a slice through the air like I'm proving it.

He knows something's wrong; I can tell by the knot in his jaw. He's waiting for me to open up.

When Nelly tells us the sausages are ready, we all move to our logs and tree stumps and camp chairs, and somehow, even though we're in something like a circle, it feels like Erik's at the middle of it all. He's the one everyone loves the most.

I force down bites of sausage, bread, tomato sauce, and salad, like tiny meteors. They're heavy in my throat and I drink more beer, cicadas like a machine, grinding as we chew. Behind them, the lick of turquoise ocean on peach-pink sand.

Clancy swats a fly. A branch falls in the bush.

I jolt when, with scarlet seeds bursting from his full mouth, Thatch yells, 'I helped grow these tomatoes in Simpo's garden! Did the mulch heaps good, Emong said. And he's a bloody *dirt doctor*.'

'Soil scientist,' Carissa murmurs.

'They're fine,' Nelly says. 'I prefer—'

'Who wants dessert?' Freddie asks. 'I made some rocky road.' Without waiting for anyone to answer, he gets up and walks unhurried to his tent and back, returning with a round blue tin — decorated with a snowy Christmas scene – which he hands to Nelly. She opens it sceptically, revealing slices of chocolate and marshmallow. Freddie smiles watching her. Then he says, 'I made them myself,' in a voice like a wink.

Nelly's tongue sucks a little tutting sound through her front teeth. 'I'm not sure...'

'Up to you.' He shrugs.

Nelly contemplates, staring down at her fingers. 'Someone will have to stay sober, in case of an emergency. Someone with their *licence*.'

'I will,' says Erik. 'No worries.'

Nelly takes out a small slice. 'It's melted. You should really have placed the tin in the Esky, Freddie.' She eats the chocolate square in two bites, wiping her fingers on Erik's towel before passing the tin to Thatch, who's next to her in the circle.

'What are they?' Carissa asks, leaning over him to look inside the tin.

'*Mushies*,' Thatch says. 'Magic ones. Ya don't have to have any if you don't want.' He bites through most of the piece he pulled out. 'How 'bout a bitea mine?' He holds it out to her and she nibbles the corner, before taking the tin and passing it to Erik, who passes it to me. I think he expects me to pass it along. To Lara. So that she can take something they've probably taken a bunch before, when they were partying and hooking up and having fun with their friends and their alive parents.

'You don't have to—'

I take the smallest piece I can see and place it whole into my mouth.

This is normal. This is what people do. Fun people. *I can do this.* It actually tastes good. Warm. There's a deeper earthy flavour below the sweetness, but it's barely there. Under my teeth, tiny pieces of leathery mushroom; raspberry jellies pucker.

I'm doing it. It's done. All I have to do now is be OK.

Lara takes one piece and gives another one to Zac and Clancy. '*Share it,*' she says. 'And don't snitch.'

Then the tin is back in Freddie's hand. He eats two, then slouches and stares as Nelly climbs into the hammock, one arm and one leg hanging out, face hidden. The breeze is hot and dry, playing feathery peppermint trees like thousands of tiny wind chimes.

I wait for something to happen. For it to strike.

Zac and Clancy start rolling around on the sand, which is normal for them.

Nelly starts to laugh. Thatch joins her, then Lara, then Erik. I like watching him laugh more than almost anything. But the light makes me squint. The light shining from his body. He's luminescent. Like someone rubbed the sun into his skin. I stare and he looks down, grinning and squeezing my hand.

My hand.

Down there in his.

I almost scream.

My hand is grey. Pieces of it are flaking off onto the sand like ashes. I pull away, drawing it up to my face, too scared to scream.

But up close, it's normal. More tanned than usual, a little sandy, a scar, nails too short.

'Are you OK? Rain?'

I keep staring at my hand because I can't look at him. I can't look at any of them.

Thatch screams from across the circle, 'You're gunna be fine, Spooks! Just stay chilled, orright? You're gunna be fine!'

More distantly, Lara yells, 'Drop the octopus, Clancy!'

Nelly and Freddie are still laughing.

I half-close my eyes and try to drift away. From this place. My friends. Him. Myself.

But Erik's hand is on my shoulder. He's taking my hand. We're walking to a patch of soft soft-shaded sand, tufts of grass breaking softly to the surface, bullrushes framing the little bed in grey and brown. A small bee lands on a tiny native violet, and I could swear its stripes are blue. I watch it swaying in the hot breeze.

Erik's fingertips brush over mine and he asks, slowly, 'How do you feel?'

He's babysitting me. Oh, fuck. Is this what he thinks of me? That I'm some vulnerable little kid who doesn't know anything about drugs or sex or surfing?

'I'm here,' he says. 'Don't worry.'

The light has changed. It jabs at me from between the shadows.

'Don't worry.'

In the corners of my vision, the trees are bleeding a dark sludge. Crying it, like strips of papery melaleuca. I can smell the blackness and the pain.

'I'll tell you a story,' says Erik. 'If you want?' When I don't answer, because I can't answer, he starts anyway. 'Once upon a time...'

A shape starts creeping from behind the trees. A shadow come to life, hunched and dripping dark bile.

I close my eyes. I don't know I'm shaking until I feel him, holding me, trying to make it stop. I take a sudden, gasping breath and keep shaking against him.

'Are you OK? Sorry. I'm shit at this.'

I shiver.

'Are you cold?'

'No... It's so hot.'

'Let's go to the water. Come on.'

Resting my face on the sun-warm skin under his shoulder blade, where the black things can't come, we walk into the humming ocean.

I plant myself in the wet sand where the water is only a foot deep.

The lagoon fills with sudden, hot wind.

I'm rubbing fistfulls of sand into my skin when Erik takes hold of my wrist. 'Your arms are getting red,' he says, pulling me up and into deeper water.

I lay back, floating, him next to me with a hand under my neck. There is one cloud in the sky, breathing in exact rhythm with me. I ask the cloud if I'm going to be OK, and he answers, 'You'll be fine. You're going to feel everything, really big, for a while. Not forever. Just remember you're with me. Just float.'

Not the cloud speaking. Erik. Erik Everson. He's holding me the way a mum would hold an infant at a swimming lesson. Cradling me into deeper water, a thin membrane of blue separating the skin of my back and the palms of his hands. He tells me he's 'just going to get the sand off' then starts gently splashing my cheeks and my forehead.

I close my eyes to the touch.

'Are you real?' someone asks.

Erik laughs. 'Yeah. I'm real, Rain. I'm here.'

I open my eyes. 'For how long?'

He looks at me, sort of frowning. His brows pinch hard. Confused. He swallows. Thoughtful. 'As long as you want.'

For an instant, his light expands and I'm enveloped in it. The sun swallows me up. As long as I want. Forever, then. But no. That's not right. That's impossible.

Something is caught in my chest. It heaves and releases.

I haven't cried in years. Not since the first week in the group home. That's why I don't realise what it is at first. That, and the mushrooms, and the ocean on my cheeks. 'I'm not crying,' I say.

'Sshhh…' Erik says. 'It's OK. It's just the shrooms.'

Flapping like a seal, I roll out of his arms, landing jaggedly on tiny hillscapes of sand and steadying myself with a flurry of splashes. 'Not just the mushrooms. It's *you*. I can't keep you. You're too… Everyone can see… And I get it. I get it.'

He pulls me to him, my face into his wet chest, and rests his chin on the top of my head. 'Shh…' I keep sobbing as he guides me back through the water and across the beach. Helps me take my shorts off. My shirt. Wraps a towel around me. It's soft and big and it smells like him.

I lie down with my head on his lap.

He waves flies away.

I close my eyes and listen to the trees.

PART 5

NELLY

I am tremendously focused.

I'm quite sure I can feel the microscopic bubbles of atoms in the sand under my palm. I wonder how many are touching me. Hundreds? Thousands? I wish I had phone reception. I could look it up. How many sand grains can exist side by side in one square metre, without stacking up? Then I'd measure my hand, roughly – then do simple division to determine the number. I could also determine the number of microplastics in the same amount of sand. Tiny polymer tumours scratching their way into the fabric of our planet.

I wonder if psilocybin will grow naturally in the future. I wonder if the planet will be able to sustain it. More than likely, some corrupt individual will popularise factory-grown, plastic-laced psilocybin, which will be delivered to our doors by drone.

Not now, Eleanor.

You're on holiday.

Rather than ruminate on plastic, I try to recall the details of an article I read a few nights ago. *Corrupted: Predatory Hierar-*

chies in Motorcycle Clubs and Their Impact on Youth. It discussed the use of vulnerable under-age youth as fall-boys. Apparently, the gangs groom young men, addict them, then cajole them into making and/or selling drugs for the outfit. Sometimes the boys aren't aware the bikies are involved at all, due to the recruitment of middle-men (two or three, usually) who prey upon at-risk youth.

Classic gang behaviour.

It's sickening to think it could happen here, especially when the need for community has never been greater.

I forwarded the article to Rain, who *still* hasn't read it. I'd discuss it with her now, but I'm fairly certain she's asleep on my brother's lap. Perhaps it was a mistake for her to eat the rocky road. I didn't think she would. Then, suddenly, a piece was in her mouth and she was chewing.

Speaking of which.

I'm beginning to feel hungry.

I should go and get a mango from the Esky. A mango sounds absolutely delicious. I wonder if I could convince someone *else* to get it for me... perhaps if they felt like one too. If I could subconsciously implant the desire in them, I wouldn't have to request at all. I'd be offered.

I announce, 'Mango.'

The laughter that ensues is quite possibly the most sustained communal giggling fit I've ever witnessed. It builds slowly at first, with multiple crescendos.

It doesn't stop.

This must be the longest I've ever laughed. Except, perhaps, when Dad used to play Octopus Legs with us. *I should remind Erik. We should all play Octopus Legs. Tonight!*

Originally invented by my brother, the game involved us tucking two spare pairs of pyjama pants into our hems so that we each had eight 'tentacles'. Then we would all try to steal each other's legs. It was essentially flag football with pyjama bottoms. Dad would only ever let us win on our birthday and Christmas.

We haven't played Octopus legs in at least six years.

Quite suddenly, all of us are out of breath.

'The mushies work,' Freddie rasps from the roots of a wide peppermint tree.

It brings on another cataclysmic fit.

I'm still spasming with occasional giggles when Erik arrives.

'Hey, dude!' says Clancy, grinning at my brother while hanging by his knees from a branch that does not appear strong enough to hold him. I'd forgotten he and Zac were up there. He lets go of the branch, twisting in the air but failing in rotating his body. He lands on his back in the sand and bounces up like a rubber ball. I feel the reverberations in every molecule of my body. Zac follows, more carefully, and both sprint into the water.

Lara sighs. 'I'd better not have to go save those little shits.'

Thatch laughs and I notice Carissa has moved to sit on his lap. How very *petite* of her. I watch as Thatch whispers in her ear. She giggles adolescently and he stands, letting her fall onto the tarpaulin, which she scrunches carelessly upon landing. 'We're just gunna go for a walk. See yas in a bit.'

I don't know why they'd bother with such a useless charade. They should simply inform us they're going to have *intercourse* and save everyone the trouble of questioning why they haven't returned. It's basic safety protocol. When I tell Lara this, she sighs as if *I'm* the one being ridiculous. She picks up her hairbrush and begins to work it through my matted locks. 'Do you mind?' she asks. 'You've got the nicest hair.'

I shake my head, letting the strands fall back. Freddie's eyes are locked onto my face in a mildly transfixed way. He's not supposed to look at me like that – not when other people are around. He's clearly forgotten about the confidentiality clause of our relationship: Under no circumstances should either of us give any indication of a romantic or sexual relationship in the presence of others. We've discussed it at least six times.

The hairbrush Lara is holding comes to a sudden standstill. I'm about to ask her why she's stopped when she asks, 'Did you guys hear that?' From behind the trees emerges a crunching, smacking sound. 'Are those little shits playing Fight Club on the rocks? NOT ON MUSHIES!' Lara yells, dropping the hairbrush and racing through the scrub to the lagoon.

With uncharacteristic enthusiasm, Freddie shifts onto his knees so that his chin hovers in the air above my head, picking up the hairbrush. He doesn't say anything, which is pleasant. Freddie's verbal self-control is one of the things I appreciate most about him. I also appreciate his long eyelashes, the way his skateboard wheels scrape on the road when he stops too abruptly, and the fact that when we stand facing each other, our eyes are perfectly level.

He's hopeless at brushing hair, of course. I have to reprimand him almost immediately and school him on the importance of *beginning at the bottom*. He slowly improves. After some minutes, I can run my fingers through the strands again.

I say, 'Thank you.'

He shuffles diagonally, tarp crunching under his knees, before placing his free hand on the small of my back. Sensing my muscles tense, and quite possibly noticing me glance towards the others, his hand retreats almost immediately to his side. 'Does it matter if they see? It could be the first time.'

'Freddie,' I begin, organising my thoughts into a legitimate reason. 'If everyone sees, they'll assume something is going to happen. Something *traditional*, or *permanent*. Perhaps later we could go for a walk together, under the guise of collecting fire-wood, and...'

He nods. 'Perhaps. Yeah. Perhaps, Nelly.'

I respond to a graze on his left knee rather than to his face. 'We need to be mature about things. *Rational*. It's not that I don't—'

'I love you.' Freddie's expression is unblinkingly severe. I would assume anger, if it weren't for the words that just left his mouth.

I love you.

Freddie thinks he loves me?

Sweet Freddie with his distant eyes and overdue assignments.

He leans slightly away from me. 'You didn't know, did you? It's pretty obvious. Must be one of the only obvious things you've ever missed.'

Obvious?

It's ridiculous.

Love?

Love is chemicals spurred on by genetics and social conditioning. Freddie doesn't *love* me. He simply needs to be reasoned with. 'I think you may have had a little too much to smoke. The combination of that, the psilocybin, and the alcohol can lead to—'

'I've loved you since the second time we had sex. You came over in that shirt with the bows and told me everything you thought was wrong with Lenin's approach to reform. You said he was infantile to presume the best in people, and you kept tugging the little bows on your shirt tighter.'

I remember the night vividly. It was absolutely *stifling* in there. His room was lit by the nonsensical combination of a lava lamp and three tacky neon signs. I told him to leave the window open and he leaned across his bed, black hair fanning pleasantly across his eyes. *Lo Fi beats to study and chill out to* was playing in the background.

He said, 'I didn't think you were coming over tonight.'

I replied, 'I couldn't sleep.'

The corner of his mouth inclined, but he didn't laugh or attempt a witty remark. He kissed me lightly, and quickly, over and over again. He knows I'm squeamish about saliva.

We were supposed to stop after exams. We agreed that our physical relationship was simply a byproduct of our academic chemistry, and that neither of us was looking for anything serious. In the end, Freddie's scabbed elbows and lack of wit were too much to resist, I suppose. He's never become possessive, or attempted to initiate a more serious relationship. He has continued, resolutely, to be the same Freddie I have known and appreciated since I was four years old.

Until now.

'No, you don't!' I suddenly respond.

'I *do*,' Freddie insists. 'You don't have to love me back.' He shrugs, before taking a long drink from his bottle.

I wet my lips with my tongue. They're definitely chapped. Freddie's are red at the edges, like painful lip liner. I appreciate his lips. I enjoy where they sit in relation to his other features. I enjoy Freddie a lot. Wetting my lips again briefly, I say, 'We can continue to have sex.'

'Fuck, Nelly!' he laughs, shaking his head. 'Nah. No, thanks. Things have changed now that I've said it. It's why I tried not to for so long.' He smiles before finally looking away.

'I really do wish I could...'

What, Eleanor? *Love* him? Want to be his *girlfriend?* Support the concept of *monogamy* despite all its *outdated, patriarchal entrapments?*

Freddie holds out a hand to me. 'Friends?'

I shake it firmly.

Uncomfortable with the new tension between us and the resulting queasiness in my stomach, I tell him, 'I need to reapply my lip balm.'

He's already leaning back, taking his pipe from his pocket.

I'm expecting the tent to be empty, so I frown at the sight of Carissa. 'Hello,' I say curtly.

'Hi!' Carissa responds.

What on earth am I supposed to do now? I was *going* to lie flat on my sleeping bag and digest what just occurred between Freddie and me. Try to determine where I went wrong, and what this horrible feeling is in the centre of my chest. I won't be able to think with *Carissa* watching me.

I dig through my backpack. I may as well reapply some lip balm while I'm here. Carissa hums over the music emitting from her phone and I direct a slightly annoyed look at her. 'I thought you and Thatch were off consorting behind a bush somewhere.'

She stops, brow pinching in confusion. 'Why would you think that?' When I continue to rummage through my bag, she inspects my face with something like challenge in her large brown eyes. 'Have I done something to offend you, Eleanor?'

Don't tell me the 0.002 grams of mushrooms she ingested have unlocked some inner boldness. I take a moment to compose myself. 'I don't know *what* you're talking about. I simply didn't expect you to be here, and I was merely commenting on it. I *thought* that you and Thatch would want to spend time together before you break up.'

Carissa blinks. 'We have been. I just came in to change out of my bathers.'

I don't respond. She didn't ask me a question, so there's no need. I zip the little stick of lip-balm back into my toiletries bag.

'So,' Carissa says, smiling unflappably and pulling half of her hair back. 'Do you have any New Year's resolutions?'

I laugh. 'Of course not. They're statistically doomed for failure. I prefer to review my goals, time-lines, and action plans regularly throughout the year. Why? Do *you* have resolutions?'

'Oh. I was thinking, just to have fun.'

'Well, I suppose your new single life in a highly populated city will provide plenty of opportunities for fun. Meanwhile, the rest of us will have to console your *ex*-boyfriend.'

'Why are you always so mean to me?' She blinks, as if also surprising herself.

'*What?*'

'I used to really look up to you. And you were nice when I first started coming to the club. But since Michael and I got together, you've had a problem with me. You've had a problem with *him*. And I'm starting to think it's because—'

'What are you implying?'

'You know.'

I repack my bag briskly, considering possible responses, all of which are flimsy. Finally, I say, 'It's not at all what you're suggesting. I simply question your commitment to the cause.'

'The eco-club? School's over, Eleanor.'

'Climate Action! Greater climate action in the wider community! It seems as if I'm the only one who hasn't been completely fabricating my commitment to a greener future. Not one of you attended the meeting. Not to mention Thatch's career ambitions. Does he have any idea how much carbon emissions are produced by a mine like the one his dad works on? Next it'll be an oil rig! And you, moving across the country when there are perfectly good courses available closer to home. I suppose you'll be back on the holidays, flying in and out of the state like a self-centred celebrity. There is such a thing as unethical air-travel, Carissa.'

I unzip the tent, slightly aggressively, rezipping it before she can reply.

The sun is beginning to set as I approach the towel where Rain is still sleeping. Erik is perched beside her, leaning on one elbow and wiping her cheek. I slump down next to him. 'Carissa has an anger problem. She's absolutely out of control.'

'What?'

'She acts so *demure*. It's a lie, Erik. Complete fiction.'

'I dunno what you're talking about, Nelly. I've got other shit to deal with.'

'Oh, yes! You and everyone else, apparently. You're all too busy to consider the feelings of your family and friends, or the Greenland ice sheet, or the Boreal forests.'

I watch Erik's eyes glaze over, quite literally witnessing the moment his cognitive dissonance engages. I am so *sick* of seeing the same expression on everyone I know, day in and day out. My fists clench as I stare out at the northern horizon, in the direction of the Wooltide gas well. People care more about the towels they own or the beers they drink or the lip gloss they wear than the unfolding planetary emergency. And the most frustrating part of all is that I'm no better. I'm distracted by pancakes and friendships and well-toned *fluffing* outlaws. I bought the bathers I'm wearing off the rack at the surf shop knowing full-well they were made from synthetic materials. I applied a toxic spray tan to even out the tone of my skin. I bought plastic razors because I didn't have time to order new blades before the trip. Complete, myopic vanity. I am a vain person.

Well, not any longer.

No more, Eleanor.

'I'm throwing away my makeup,' I advise Erik, even though

he's not listening. 'I'm throwing away my razors. I'm sick of it, Erik. All this distraction. I'm not doing it any more.'

'Nel.' He sighs, patronisingly. 'Can this wait till we get home?'

I take a deep, steadying breath, suppressing tears of rage. 'You're supposed to listen to me. You're supposed to be the one person I can talk to. You have an obligation as my twin to support me and help me when I need you. I understand you think there's nothing you can do about fossil fuels. There's nothing *I* can do about fossil fuels. We've lost. The psychopaths are in charge and they couldn't care less about global tipping points. But you should at least listen to me about *some* things. I'm telling you I'm radically changing my approach to consumption and aesthetics! And all summer, I've been telling you about Abigail. *Don't look at me like that!* It's *important*. Your ex-girlfriend has practically been abducted by a man who consorts with bikies and Frank Decker, and now... Now... *Fluff*... Hold on... Yes. Of course. It's so *obvious*...'

Erik releases another exasperated sigh before stroking Rain's hair lightly. 'What's so obvious?' he asks, in a tone that suggests obligation rather than interest.

'It's just like the article said. Harrison's not just friends with the bikies because of what he does. He does what he does because of the bikies. He and Frank. What if they're... Oh, no, Erik. They could be producing *product* out there. There could be very real danger, aside from Harrison, in that house. Abigail's house!'

Before he can answer, Rain's eyes snap open.

PART 6

RAIN

Black sap bodies peel off trees and ooze towards me, sprouting legs and teeth, as noxious smoke twists down from the canopy to sting my skin. I try to take a breath, but there's no air. Just choking darkness. The closest monster, distorted, obsidian, reaches out a tarry arm. It's stroking, sticking. I try to pull back from it but I can't move – still can't breathe.

Until I look up. Straight up at the indigo sky.

I suck desperately and my lungs fill with sacred sea breeze.

And it disappears. The darkness, the smoke, the creature.

Erik is here. Still golden, the sky singing above him, sun in his pores and a white breeze in his hair. He's as much a part of this place as the glittering sand and the glow of the water. There's salt in his eyelashes.

He says, 'You're alright...'

'You're perfectly *fine*, Rain,' Nelly says. She's sitting at my other side, sparkling too. 'I'm glad you're awake, actually. I need help cooking, and there are a number of things I need to talk to you about immediately, or as soon as your cognition improves.

How is your head, by the way? You must be extremely dehydrated from all of that crying. Sit up. *Come on.* Erik will get you something from the first-aid kit; I'm sure you have a headache.'

After forcibly medicating and hydrating me, Nelly tugs me by the hand to the tarpaulin, ordering me to bring the Esky and the grocery bag. I tell her I'm not hungry and she says there's no way she's letting everyone celebrate the new year without lining their stomachs first. Projecting like a drill-sergeant, she manages to rally some of the others – Erik, Thatch, Lara and Freddie – to help us. Zac and Clancy are running in the distance, naked, with their dicks in their hands, kicking sand into the air.

Everyone except me is glowing. They're paper lanterns, speaking and bumping into each other, dancing and laughing. Erik is the brightest. When Nelly shoves a can of pineapple in his hands, he steps back and sparks fly. She tuts, seemingly unaware of the glittering beads of flame raining down on her. She adjusts the angle of a packet of chicken wings, aligning it with the positioning of the butane stove.

Carissa shows up, already dressed in red tassels. It sort of looks like a flapper dress. We all agreed to dress up tonight. 'It might be our last chance for a real party!' someone said. Carissa nailed the brief. She looks fucking incredible.

Music is playing from the speaker hanging off the branch of a tree. Erik is stirring a huge bowl of punch filled with bottles of orange juice, sparkling wine, and honey-coloured rum, chunks of pineapple darting like goldfish in the wake of his wooden spoon. I smile at the familiarity of him. The way his brows knit, then soften.

'*Lucy,*' someone whispers in my ear. I swivel as something black crosses the sky – an oily, winged creature – and I duck.

No one notices except Nelly. 'Come over here and make yourself useful,' she says.

I kneel next to her, in front of the burner, staring at the circular mirror of oil in the centre of the pan. It's so pretty.

'Stop crying,' Nelly says. 'You'll dehydrate yourself again.'

I brush the moisture from my cheek and stare at the pan. The oil is hypnotising. Nelly takes a chicken wing from the stove, its little tendons stretching and folding in the glossy marinade. There are tiny hairs on the wing where the smallest feathers were plucked. She drops it into the pan and it hisses with alarm. This plucked piece of a creature, making one last unnoticed protest. I barely have time to turn away from the food before the frothy beer is leaving my body and dripping from the leaves of a creeper.

'Are you *sick*?' Nelly accuses, shielding the barbeque with her hand. She throws a roll of paper towel at my leg and I wipe my mouth.

Am I sick?

I peer back at the chicken, just for an instant, and immediately force down another surge of vomit. I can't look at the stove. Can't look at the wing. 'I can't eat that.'

'What are you *talking* about? You bought it! It's been consistently refrigerated since we—'

'I can't eat it. I can't eat meat anymore. I'm sorry.'

'Well, you could have waited until the end of the trip! I admire you working to reduce your carbon footprint, but we didn't *prepare* for vegetarianism!'

'The punch is vegetarian!' Erik calls from behind me.

Nelly tuts. 'Am I the *only* one who takes micronutrients seriously? She needs to make sure she obtains the necessary B12 and iron requirements, especially under her current stressors.'

I take a huge sip of water, swish it around in my mouth, and spit into the bushes. Then I drink. The water is sad about something.

Soundlessly, Carissa appears, a hand on my back. 'Would you like a lemonade for your stomach?'

I look down at my beer and shrug. 'I still have half left.'

Pulling me away slightly, she whispers, 'I'm so excited to tell you, Rain. I know you've just been sick, but I can't wait another minute! I—'

In the depths of the bush, something huge and black lunges forward and I'm falling, flat on my back, staring at a canopy of slender rustling leaves and a violet sky.

'Oh my god!' Carissa gasps. 'Are you alright?' She takes one of my hands and helps me up.

I try to laugh. 'Yeah. I thought I saw a... an animal. So weird.'

'Oh. What I was saying, before that happened, was...' I watch a black mouse scuttle across the sand towards me. It sniffs. Then turns and runs away. Carissa sighs heavily. 'Forget it. Maybe later.'

'I'm sorry. I keep zoning out. I think I'm just... high?'

Is high the right word? Or is that just for weed? But I've heard it used for other stuff too. Not everything. Mum used to call heroin her 'medicine'.

'Rain? You're doing it again! It's been so hard to speak to you lately.' Her eyes are glistening, and a single black tear melts lazily down her cheek.

'Fuck. Shit. I have been hard to speak to. I'm really sorry, Carissa. I'm just going through some stuff.'

'I know! It's just that...' Her voice drops to a whisper so low, it's just another peppermint leaf in the breeze. I barely make out the words: 'I lost my... Michael and I had...' She glows brighter and the tear is gone. Evaporated. In a clear voice, she says, 'Sex.'

Nelly appears like Nosferatu. 'If everyone's finished their

public *sex-clamations*, there are vegetables that need to be chopped.'

'*One minute, Eleanor,*' Carissa snaps.

Nelly's face reddens. She wheels around, back to the stove, and drops the tongs into the middle of the sizzling pan.

My hands are still wrapped tightly around Carissa's, where they landed when she said 'sex'.

I smile at her. Then we move away from the trees, back to the group on the tarp.

As soon as we're within arm's reach, Thatch pulls his girlfriend into a bone-breaking hug, and I go to Nelly's side. She's staring at the tongs, jaw clenched, brain ticking. I turn off the stove. Flick the tongs out with a fork before rinsing them in the dish tub and drying them with the blue and white tea-towel Lara brought.

No one speaks.

Not even Thatch.

Then Zac and Clancy arrive, sand caked in their hair.

'Are those spicy?' Clancy asks, pointing to the chicken wings. 'I can't handle spicy. Makes my tongue swell up. Mum usually does me some honey soy ones when they have spicy.'

'They're not spicy,' Erik says, patting Clancy on the shoulder.

Lara, looking her cousin up and down, adds, 'Go for a swim before dinner.'

Nelly, lips still pursed, takes the tongs from me and turns the chicken.

Unhurried and half-smiling, Erik pours everyone a punch, leaving himself for last. There's no fruit left, but he doesn't say anything about it. He smiles at me, then his sister, then Thatch, shining happiness. We sit on the tarp while Nelly cooks, washing veggies under our water bottles and cutting them with a steak knife on a plastic board.

The food is bright. Nothing darkens or oozes. It's a little too bright, but if I close my eyes it's OK. Blindly, I eat cauliflower, cucumber, heirloom tomatoes, a crushed bread roll, a Rice-Krispies Treat and a handful of gummy snakes. Towards the end of the meal, I realise how I must look. Not wanting to seem like a lunatic, I open my eyes and it's just gummy snakes and I almost can't eat them. They stare at me. The pink and green one winks.

'Are you OK?' Erik asks, luminous.

I close my eyes and bite down on the lolly.

A little while later, two minutes, or thirty, Lara suggests getting ready.

I don't want to. I want to bury myself in the wet sand.

But when Nelly and Carissa both stand up, I have to follow them.

In the tent, I take the things I'll need from my backpack, my hands turning from tanned to white to pink to ash, while Nelly tells us all she's 'deprioritising commercially-driven beauty standards'. 'Does anyone want this?' she asks, holding out a small rectangular bag full of make-up.

Lara takes it. 'Lots of epiphanies happening today,' she mumbles.

Carissa laughs.

I slowly unfold my dress, the silk slipping coolly over my fingers. I cry a little, then stop. I can stop now.

'Is that a nightgown?' Nelly asks.

'I don't think so,' I say, gazing at the shimmering lace, the slight tear in the hem that meant I could buy it from Kathy for half-an-hour's wages.

'It's nice,' says Carissa, trying on a tiara in front of the camera on her phone.

Nelly does most of my make-up after watching me attempt it myself, insisting I'm too 'slow and transient' to handle the job. I don't argue. It feels nice, the brushing and dabbing and occasional fanning, even when she startles me with sharp movements or frustrated sighs. It takes a long time. I keep my eyes closed as she moves the brush to the top of my forehead, base of my chin, collarbones, cleavage. A cool dust over my cheeks; a dewy spray to set everything.

She shuffles back on her knees, and I open my eyes to her nodding. She doesn't tell me it looks nice. All she says is, 'No more weeping, Douglass.'

I try my best. There's still a heaviness in my chest and a looming darkness in the corners of the tent, but my eyes stay dry. I get dressed, pulling the clean dress over my sandy body.

Lara holds her phone out when we're done, and we all look into it and say, 'Happy New Year!'

Carissa adds, 'Best New Year's ever!' which almost makes me cry again.

Before now, my best New Year's ever was last year. We drank champagne at the oval and lay on a stretch of blue-grey beach. I went home to Nelly and Erik's house, to his room, and I realised why they call it *making love*. It had always seemed stupid before that; one of those outdated phrases forgotten by everyone except Mormons and the Amish. I'd never say it out loud, but I realised that night why some people do.

My worst New Year's ever was in the group home. A girl named Leilani held a box-cutter against my throat and told me to give her back her pillow. I told her it was my pillow, and she pressed the blade harder, until I felt it break my skin. So I let her take my pillow.

Now I'm here.

I follow Lara out of the tent. Carissa and Nelly march ahead of us like speed-walkers in a race. I watch my feet. Now that it's dark, I'm terrified. What if the monsters come out at night? What if everything is worse? What if it sucks me up and I disappear into the void, becoming a monster, haunting a different world? I don't want to look up.

But I do.

And it's so beautiful.

Tearful starlight spreads across the sand, up the rocks, and over the tiny waves at the shore, landing with loving finality on Erik. He's wearing a white-collared shirt, holding up the dark, clear sky. For what feels like all night – like multiple nights with days and light discarded – all there is, is that stretch of auroral sand and him. And sometimes the others, buzzing and hazy at the edges. I dance easily. Slowly. The trees have finally stopped bleeding and shadows disappear in the dark. I don't feel like crying anymore.

A high voice yells, 'It's eleven-fifty-eight!'. Clancy is screaming and spinning, and it feels, in the air, like there are more people here. Hundreds of people. Instead of the usual tight constriction – the otherness that comes over me when I'm in a group – I feel like we're all drops of water in the same wave.

'Twenty nine...' someone says.

A hand thuds against my back, a loud voice joining in. 'Twenty eight...'

Everyone is counting down now.

The stars burn.

Thatch and Carissa kiss. I hear it. Like ice cream. Erik holds my hand tightly, a grin on the number *three*. Over his shoulder Freddie slips his fingers through Nelly's. Zac is circling Lara like a baby magpie looking for handouts. Is that Clancy, up the tree again?

Erik laughs, then his lips press against mine, beams of silver, gold, white, lapping across my tongue, into my throat, and through my lungs, lifting me up like helium into the cooling sky.

We break apart when someone hits the ground. Clancy.

Freddie's arm falls from Nelly's shoulders and Lara's lips leave Zac's cheek.

Erik tugs my hand and we drift over a trickle of granite, through a copse of shining melaleuca and onto a sandy mattress studded with soft patches of grass.

I take his shirt off. He tries to pull my dress over my head but it clings in places, my thighs wet from wading through the ocean. So he pulls harder, until it floats off my body and flies over his shoulder, landing in the reeds.

The sliver of moon is a melting icy-pole, dripping across our skin.

Erik presses one of my hands into the sand so deeply I feel the ocean trickle up to stroke my fingers.

I dream I'm at the bottom of a cave. It's mostly dark except for a sharp slanted beam of light – a knife of gold in the blackness. That strip of life is warm and budding with moss. I stand on the wet ground, eating bugs off the walls and watching the spear of light sparkle wetly on the cave wall.

When I wake up, the inside of the tent thunders with life. Breathing and stirring and snoring. I close my eyes, hoping to go back to the cave, where there was nothing to be afraid of, nothing to explain, nothing to hide. But it's gone.

I lift Erik's hand from where it rests on my stomach and roll off my sleeping mat, unzipping the tent slowly before slipping out, alone, into the silver morning.

By the time I get back from the toilet, the others are awake.

We eat beans on toast and go for one last swim then pack up lazily, scrunching and cramming clothes and toiletries into our packs. Thatch lies on top of the huge, sandy, poorly folded tent, while Erik and Lara attempt to zip it closed.

We don't bother cleaning the beans from the pots before shoving them into a bag and throwing the bag onto Thatch's dad's dinghy, where we say a rushed goodbye to him and Carissa – a bundle of exhausted, sunburnt bodies clustered like limpets around the little boat.

'Do you have a lift to the party?' Carissa asks me. Shit. Her going-away party. It's today. Apparently it was the only day her pastor could make it. *Shit.* She reads my thoughts. Or maybe my face. 'You can just pop by... or, if you need to stay home, I understand.'

'I'll be there. Thatch is driving me. Right?'

'Yeah, orright. But you owe me a—'

'She doesn't owe you anything, Michael.' Carissa grins, the tip of her tongue nuzzling at her front teeth.

The walk takes twice as long as it did on the way here, despite being a cooler day and mostly downhill. No one has any urgency left in their muscles. Freddie, who's in front, keeps stopping to stare at banksia flowers, balls of melting sap and peeling bark. Down the line, we all do the same. 'Did you guys see that?' he keeps asking. Nelly keeps saying, 'Yes,' on every-one's behalf. I direct my eyes at the ground because, every now and then, black shapes still move behind the trees.

Clancy's mum is waiting for him and Zac on the track, parked on the sandy rise behind Erik's four-wheel-drive. She talks to Lara while we load the car, and beeps her horn when she drives away. Zac and Clancy's hands dangle out of the windows as we follow them — until one of their wrists hits a branch with a loud snap and they both retract inside.

I close my eyes, my head bumping along next to Freddie's.

I wonder, watching Erik's competent hands navigate the wheel along the rough track, whether Lara loved him. Or even Lucy. Maybe they still do. It's hard not to.

At Doe's house, he pounces out of the driver's seat and opens my door, taking my backpack and my hand. He's a balloon, pulling my heavy body along, dropping my bag next to the *welcome* mat and leaning on the timber frame of the veran-dah. 'I'd better not come in,' he says, nodding towards the car.

I try to answer, but fear drips like tar down my throat, stop-ping like a plug in the centre of my chest.

After a few seconds, he says, 'I'll call you later.'

I clear my throat. 'I'll be at Carissa's. And Marli's home tonight. I might not have time.'

'Oh. OK. We can get coffee before you start tomorrow?'

I feel a tear paint a path down my dirty cheek.

He shifts on the balls of his feet, the muscles in his forehead tightening as he looks back at the car, then at me. 'I can stay. I'll just go tell—'

'It's nothing. Just an aftershock. I think I need some... time to myself.'

'Some time to yourself?' he echoes. 'As in...'

I keep crying. Warm, unsteady brooks running down my cheeks and falling onto the colourful mat. 'I don't know.'

Erik steps back like I've taken out a handgun. 'You don't know when you'll be free, or you don't know if... Are you saying you—'

The car horn beeps and he looks back again, towards Nelly, who's leaning across from the passenger's side.

At the same instant, Doe calls my name from inside.

'Rain...?' Erik says.

Another surge of blackness crashes in my chest and I shake my head.

He's too whole, too hopeful. I turn away from him and open the door.

He's still standing there when I close it.

As soon as I'm inside, my whole body breaks.

Doe catches me. Literally. She catches my crying, limp body. Dirty and bruised, shoulders starting to peel. 'Oh, *darl*,' she says, pulling me against her chest and squeezing, tight.

There's so much strength to her. So much softness.

Carissa's house is resonant. Even before Thatch and I have left his dad's car, the voices and colours and textures are too much. I try to shut it out, distance myself, but I can't. Not anymore. Everything feels heavier now.

I walk behind Thatch, pulled along by his confidence, past the other cars, through the open door and into the front room that Carissa and I are never allowed to sit in, past the good sofa covered in its plastic sheet. I almost brush up against a figurine of Jesus, pain painted lushly on his twisted face, as the bright pop music gets louder and louder.

Maybe I shouldn't have come. It's hard to stop my shoulders curling forward when I see all the people. The singing, laughing, normal people.

Carissa bursts into view wearing a yellow dress like a

boiled lolly. She hugs Thatch tightly, then holds him at arms length, taking him in with affectionate amusement; he's wearing a collared shirt buttoned to his throat and he's tried to smooth his hair down with something that looks like cooking oil. In the car, he told me didn't even wash it or brush it – just wet it in the shower and put what he called 'hair lotion' in. I offered to try and fix it, but he told me it was 'bloody perfect'.

Carissa beams at him. After making sure her mum isn't watching, she unfastens the top button of his shirt, kisses his cheek, and pulls us into the crowd.

'You'll have to meet my cousins later!' she smiles, pointing at a knot of girls a little older than us, party dresses swishing with effortless rhythm. 'They're not really my cousins, but we–' A kid, around seven or eight, knocks her off balance. He's running fast, holding a basketball to his chest. Thatch tugs her out of the way as a stream of little bodies follow the first, screaming and laughing louder than I ever have, most of them waving iced cookies. Carissa's mum weaves through the narrow track formed by the kids, a huge plate full of the same vivid treats resting in her hands. With a commanding look, she makes Thatch and I take one each before moving towards a bunch of straight-laced people who must be from Carissa's church. I recognise one of them — an old white guy who walks like a cartoon frog. The pastor. He came to her house once to pick up a box of oranges. I almost startle when I see my old Literature teacher Miss K standing next to him, a red-haired toddler on her hip. I didn't realise she'd be here.

'Is that your guys's English teacher with the little Ranga?'

'*Thatcher*,' I say, in a tone that's become habitual.

'Yeah?'

'You can't just call people whatever the fuck—'

'It's offensive,' Carissa cuts in, gently. 'It's based on the word orangutan. Do you see now? You can't compare people to apes based on the colour of their hair.'

Thatch wipes his hand across his wet head, then smears the excess oil across his shirt. 'Well, I didn't bloody know that.'

Carissa smiles. 'It *is* Miss K – Mum invited *all* my teachers, but thankfully only she showed up.'

Our old Literature teacher must have heard her name; almost instantly, she passes the toddler to a woman who, judging by her hair, must be its mother, and strides over to us. She wraps me in a patchouli hug which makes me feel like we're breaking a rule. 'How are you?' she asks, sincerely.

I have to hold my tongue. Literally, clamp it down with my teeth, because, for an instant, I want so badly to tell her about the mushrooms. About uni, and my mum, and my probably-dead dad, and my pop, and Lucy, and Lara, and Erik. I almost do. Then I say, 'Things have been really fun. We went away for New Year's. Camping.'

Miss K's eyes linger on my false smile and she pushes her frizzy hair back over her wooden earrings. 'And you're still going to Uni this year? Visual Arts, wasn't it?'

'Yeah. I'll be living in the city with Eleanor. Her parents' friends – the Bells – have a townhouse near Uni we're going to rent. It's only one bus away from the campus.'

'As in *Shire President* Bell? Wow. I bet it's a swanky house. And you got your scholarship?'

'A partial one. They cut some of the funding. But I've been working, so I should be OK for the first semester.'

'Better than a smack round the head with a wet fish!' says Thatch, crumbs on his chin. 'That's what my dad used to say when I was a kid. If I didn't like my dinner or something, he'd go – *"It's better than a smack round the head with a wet fish!"*' He takes another bite of his cookie, before adding, 'How ya goin' anyway, Miss?'

Miss K's fighting back a laugh. 'Good, Michael. Tell me about your plans for the next few years. You won't be smothering people's seats in Vaseline, I hope?'

'Nah, Miss...' Thatch says, guiltily. 'Haven't done that since year nine. I've got a job now – starting on Monday. *Brickie's labourer*. But my dad reckons he'll be able to get me something on the mines soon.'

'You'll be making more than I do!' she laughs.

'That's the plan.' Thatch winks.

Carissa nudges him in the ribs but the teacher keeps laughing. 'Enjoy your party!' she tells Carissa, hugging her for what I guess is the second time today.

'You too!' Carissa smiles, pulling us towards the food.

A huge gingham tablecloth has been thrown over the dining table with around seventy different dishes crammed on top of it. Whole fish with glossy, staring eyes, bowls of rice, chicken adobo, satiny noodles and the supple pink bodies of octopuses. In the centre, the curve of its tail pointing accusingly towards the ceiling, is a roasted pig.

Bile rises in my throat.

Fuck.

Not now.

I can't do this now.

Sour vomit and tears scratch at my throat, my face, my eyes, burrowing through me, out of me, as the room swells and my chest catches.

It's happening again.

Why is it happening again?

I thought it was over.

The drugs are out of my system... aren't they?

A black puddle swells below the belly of the dead pig. It grows, flooding the gingham and oozing over the rest of the food, dripping over the edges and onto the floor, splashing invisibly across the black straps of my sandals. I stifle a scream, elbowing past Thatch, knocking a tender sheet of pork from his hand as I plough through the crowd to the bathroom.

Thank *fuck* it's empty.

I lock the door with trembling fingers as my breakfast splatters into Tala's pristine basin. *Shit.* Turning on the cold tap, hard, I vomit again, again, again, gasping soundlessly between each spasm. Whitney Houston sings through the door, powerful and free: 'Oh, *I wanna dance with somebody. I wanna feel the heat. Yeah, I wanna dance with somebody.*'

Stomach empty, I stoop over the mess, trying to ignore the back smoke twisting around the ashen figure in the mirror. I can't look at it. I won't.

Hunched, I sip from my cupped hands until the taste has mostly disappeared. I clean the sink with wads of toilet paper, rinsing and wiping, rinsing and wiping. I open the window above the bathtub and reach for a spray bottle I know is filled with homemade orange-oil. My reflection smouldering in the corner of my eyes, I focus hard on a cross-stitch of Jesus hanging above the toilet. I tell him, 'I'm sorry,' and I spray him in the face.

The song changes.

I force myself to leave the bathroom.

Thatch is still at the table, head-and-shoulders the tallest person in the room. Carissa, down by his bicep, is looking at something through the laughter. Looking at me. Her smile falters, then she weaves her way over. I wipe my cheeks and my chin again with the back of my wrist.

'The pig...?' she whispers.

I nod, guiltily. Rejecting food is about as sinful as rejecting the holy spirit in this house.

But Carissa smiles. 'Meet me at the bench.'

Calmed by her voice, I navigate an awkward path through

the bodies, out the laundry door and into the little orchard on the south side of the property.

It's better here. A dry breeze tiptoes through the bare fruit trees, the music is soft and distant, and no one else is here. The bench seat, made of weathered wood, sits nestled under the biggest pear tree. When the tree blossoms in spring, it's mythical. We'd sit here for hours last year, writing or reading or drawing or talking, gazing up at a thousand milky flowers.

'You still trippin, Spooks?' Thatch cannons from out of nowhere.

I jump and he laughs, squeezing onto the bench next to me as Carissa settles onto his lap. She hands me a plate of rice, noodles, spring-rolls. Looking at the food, a tiny knife of hunger stabs at me. I guess my stomach is empty.

Thatch and I start to eat.

He finishes first, but only just. Then he lifts Carissa like a bottle of milk, putting her back down on the seat before telling us, in a gruff, workman-like voice, 'I'm gunna check on the tomatoes. Make sure the aphids aren't gettin' to 'em.'

He's giving us a chance to talk.

Thatch is a fucking sweetheart sometimes.

I chew my last few scoops of rice slowly, watching him rake his hands through the soft dirt of a distant garden bed, lifting a handful to his face. For a second I think he's going to eat it. Then I realise he's sniffing. He lets the dirt fall and wipes his fingers across the oil stain on his shirt.

'Shit!' I say, spinning to face Carissa. 'I've barely spoken to you about it. You and Thatch. The... Was it...?'

Her smile is luminous. 'It was perfect,' she sighs. 'He was so careful, Rain. I'm so happy it happened. But now...'

'You have to leave.'

She nods. 'It's the most amazing course, and my brothers will be close by. But after last night, I never want to be away from him. I want to grow old and turn into trees together, like Baucus and Philemon, and just sit on a hill together for the rest of time. But instead I'm *leaving*. Do you think I'm doing the right thing?'

I sigh. 'I've never known you to do anything but the right thing. It's going to be amazing for you. Thatch is...' At the moment, Thatch is pulling weeds from the tomato bed, crushing them in his hands and dropping them in a little pile. 'He'll always be your first.'

She looks at him blissfully, the way she does when she's writing something good. Then she says, 'What's a *franga*?'

I almost choke. I put my plate down on the ground and adjust my position on the bench, crossing my legs. 'It's slang. For condom. Why?'

She lets out a tiny chirp of laughter before swivelling to check for grown-ups. 'Michael said he put the... *franga*... in his pocket afterwards. He said he didn't want to choke a dolphin.'

I stare at Thatch's back. He's still squatting in the dirt pulling weeds, a group of flies resting on his shoulders. 'He's really an environmentalist, at the end of the day.'

Carissa's laugh is a bellchime and Thatch's head whips around. 'You guys talking about me?' he calls, reaching the bench in about four massive strides.

'None of your business,' says Carissa, accepting him onto her lap with a pained grunt. 'You have to come and visit me,' she strains, invisible under his weight. 'Both of you.'

'I will,' I say, leaning backwards to look into her eyes. 'You're... You were my first friend here. I hadn't spoken to anyone except teachers my whole first week until that day in the library.'

She takes my hand and she leans back, her face reddening with the strain of Thatch's body. 'I'm so glad you asked me where the printer was.'

Tala appears a few metres away, on the other side of a raspberry bush, and Thatch jumps to a stand like a loitering soldier in front of his commanding officer. Tala gives him the sort of look that means *yeah, you'd better stand up*, then directs her eyeline at her daughter. 'Your lola is on the phone, Nak!' With that, she turns and walks back into the house.

Carissa follows. Then Thatch and I.

The next few hours hurry past, mostly thanks to the karaoke. I've never been in a room with so many good singers, even when we'd stay with my mum's friends, who were almost always musicians. Mum was always disappointed that I couldn't hold a tune. I think, maybe, I did it to spite her. But Carissa's voice is sweet and clear. She sings alone and with her mum and with her dad. Mariah Carey and Ed Sheeran and Dolly Parton. Thatch screams his way through a rendition of *Flame Trees* as I eat cremè caramel and mango ice-cream, sweet and cold and silky on my raw throat. He finishes on a guttural, aggressive note, dropping the microphone too hard on the rug, walking back to us proudly as the feedback shrieks.

Thatch keeps eating dessert during the speeches. He only puts his plate down when Carissa picks up the microphone, pausing to choke back sobs as she says goodbye to us all. Thatch's own eyes glisten with moisture. He nods and smiles and wipes it away with his too-short sleeve.

After that, Carissa opens presents, thanking and hugging everyone separately. She cries when she sees my painting. I cry, too.

Most of the young families leave after that.

Then the church friends.

Then some of the cousins.

Then Miss K. She hugs us again, and it's a little less strange this time. 'Thank you for being such amazing students. You'll pop in, won't you? Say hello to the twins for me. And don't let

Eleanor do too many practice essays next year.' Thatch hugs her too, knocking her breath out. I think he's happy a teacher agrees with him about Nelly's practice essays.

When it's just us left, and the families who are staying, Carissa tries her best at a cavalier smile. Thatch's mouth opens a little, but he doesn't say anything. I swallow, then hug her again. It feels like she's holding her breath. I don't breathe either, out of solidarity. We stand there as one unbreathing pillar for as long as I can hold on. Alone together one last time.

I leave them, watching my feet all the way through the house, out the door, down the garden path, to Thatch's dad's ute. I open both of its unlocked doors, feeling a gust of hot air leave the cab.

After about ten minutes, Thatch is with me.

He grabs the heavy driver's door and thrusts it backwards and forwards a few times, trying to fan cooler air through the car. There's a blank expression on his face. In a voice so croaky and soft I barely recognise it, he says, 'Fucken boiling.'

I say, 'Yeah.'

'Better get the car back to Dad. He's goin' south today. Fishin'.'

I nod, climbing into the passenger seat.

When we hit actual tarmac again, he turns on the radio. Paul Kelly, I think. Blanketed in static. He nods for a while, before saying, 'Simpo was my first ever girlfriend.'

He winds the window down the last few inches, wiping his face roughly and clearing his throat.

Doe's watering the base of a jacaranda tree when I get home, lilac origami browning on the ground below it. 'How was the party?' she asks.

'It was... good.'

'Chicken curry for tea tonight?'

'Oh... I'm a vegetarian now, I think. I can make my own dinner.'

'Chickpea curry, then. There's a tin in there somewhere. You can get started while I finish this.' She flicks the hose, detaching a few more papery petals from a low-hanging branch.

I'm grateful for the slow, simple chore of making dinner. Chopping. Stirring. The sound of chickens through the kitchen window and Marli walking in just before we eat. Usually she skips or dances through the house, but today she walks with an unrecognisable weight. She doesn't call me 'Raindrop' or 'Sis'. Just my name, in a low, tired voice.

Across the dining table, she prods at her chickpeas and barely looks at me or her mum. I don't think it's helping that the curry I made looks and tastes like the glue used in primary school art classes.

'How's Emma?' Doe asks, chewing a little too enthusiastically.

Marli shrugs. 'You tell me.'

She and her girlfriend moved in together when they started uni, thinking it would be this big adventure; the next step in their relationship. But their timetables clash and they're both working part time.

'Oh, love. I'm sure next year will be better.'

'I told you at Christmas, Mum. I don't even know if we'll be able to *afford* housing next year. The landlord's putting the rent up. It's fucked.' She picks a green bean out of her bowl, chewing off the end. 'What's new with you guys, anyway? Any updates?'

Doe rises from her chair. 'Excuse me, girls. I don't know about you, but these things go straight through me... be back in a tick.' It couldn't be more obvious what she's doing, but Marli, unusually, doesn't seem to notice. She tips her spoon and the bean falls dismally back into the liquid.

'Everything's good,' I say. Then, in a quick, low breath, I add, 'Except for the mushrooms.'

Marli looks up from her bowl for the first time. 'What?'

'I did mushrooms last night. The magic kind... The drug.'

'*Fuck*,' Marli says. 'I didn't think you were into that scene.'

'Neither did I. But...' I can't seem to keep things in with Marli. I shouldn't vent to her now, when she's going through her own shit, but, selfishly, I do. I tell her about everything. The dark, tarry shapes. The messages from Lucy. The black hole in my chest. 'Everything feels so heavy. I feel *so* heavy. I don't think I can hold onto it any more. Any of it. I don't think I can keep him.' I feel the now familiar prickle of tears. 'Everyone else wants him, and he's going to be away half of the year, and I'm just... Maybe Thatch and Carissa got it right. If it's going to end soon, why delay the inevitable?'

She sighs. 'I don't know, Rain. It's not easy. Everything just gets harder. I *live* with my girlfriend and it's still so fucking hard. I don't know if there's anything happening with Erik and Lucy – it was just a message. But if you're going your separate ways... maybe it's better to end things now.'

I nod, feeling the black sludge drip from the ceiling onto my shoulders, under my skin and through my blood. I didn't expect this reaction from her. Optimistic, vibrant Marli is telling me to give up. I feel my face blanch.

'Look,' she adds. 'I'm having a really crap day and I don't want to project my own shit onto you. You know I like Erik. He's nice, and he seems honest. Remember when I got that bubble-gum lipstick and I wouldn't stop wearing it every day, and I had it on my teeth that time and he came up and whispered, "There's a bit of pink there..."? That shit was really nice and really fucking honest. But yeah. He's also a *guy*. Maybe just take a break or something. Think about things.'

'Yeah. No... Thanks, Marli. I will.' I put a chickpea in my mouth and chew for a long time before swallowing. 'I'm sorry about the curry. Maybe I needed to add more salt?'

'I don't think salt's the problem.' She holds up her spoon, letting the pale gravy glug back into the bowl, a piece of carrot diving suicidally at the last moment with a sad plop. 'So,' Marli continues. 'Are you going to book in and see someone? About the hallucinations?'

'Yeah. I should. I will. Please don't tell your mum, though. I don't want to worry her.'

Giving up, Marli pushes her bowl away. 'I won't tell Mum. But you have to actually go. And you have to watch a movie with me tonight. My choice.'

Marli sets up her projector outside, the image fluttering across a white sheet hung between the lemon tree and the chook pen. To make up for my inedible dinner, we pour huge bowls of cereal and crunch through the first ten-minutes. Because of all the crunching, it takes me a few scenes to realise why Marli chose the movie; administering cathartic therapy sessions through film is one of her go-to tactics, and the not-so-subtle story about a traumatised foster kid (Matt Damon) and his insightful, if inappropriate therapist (Robin Williams) is a little on the nose.

'It's not your fault,' Williams says.

I have to clench my teeth to stop from crying.

Marli stares at the screen innocently.

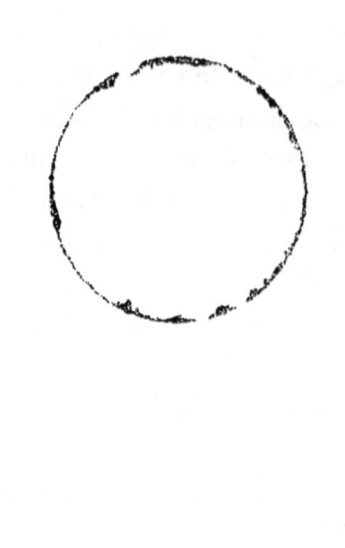

PART 7

THATCH

If Erik's gunna be in a shitty mood all day he can fuck off. *I'm* the one who just broke up with his chick, and *he's* the one bloody acting like it.

I was pretty sad last night. My dad left the sec I got home from the party cause he wanted to get to the fishing spot before dark. Fair enough. But now my *best mate* hasn't even asked me about it. I had to sit at my place alone all night, heaps sad. It was real quiet and smelt like old milk and the only thing to eat was a bag of grated cheese. I had a bit of a cry. Then I ate a fair bit of the cheese straight outa the bag and looked at flights to go see Carissa, but they were heaps expensive, so it'd take me a while to save. Even if I got there I'd have no cash to spend and nothing to do except get in her grill and probly piss off her brothers and her new mates.

So I gave up on that and watched a bit of porn n' TikTok.

Now I've decided. I'm not gunna be sad. I'm gunna be happy. I had a heaps hot, heaps nice girlfriend and we're still mates. And once I've got a job I'm gunna make heaps of cash and get heaps of chicks and when Simpo's done with her Uni stuff maybe we'll get married and have heaps of kids. Probly not. Ya never know, but.

I told Erik about my plan to be heaps happy this morning, but he wasn't even bloody listening. It's a top-tier day and he keeps checkin' his phone goin' heaps quiet bitin' his lip. I'd reckon he was nervous about his trip if I didn't know how bloody moody he gets when somethin's up with him n' Spooks.

It's just the four of us here at the beach – me, Erik, Lara n' Nelly. Jenny's still in Bali, Zac n' Clancy're still sunburnt from New Year's and Freddie reckons he's gotta help his mum with some shelves. I reckon he's full of shit. He's gettin' stoned in his room or seein' the secret girlfriend he won't tell us about.

So I'm stuck here with Nelly readin' her book, Erik sulkin' on his bloody phone, and Lara hoggin' the only goggles. They're *her* goggles I spose, but still.

To make Erik feel better, I go – 'She'll talk to ya tomorrow, mate. *Forty-eight hours.* That's the rule.'

Nelly chimes in to tell me I'm wrong as bloody usual. 'That applies to *missing persons*, Thatcher, not romantic relationships. Rain is trying to metabolise her first psychedelic experience following a lifetime of trauma. She'll take as much time as she needs.'

'Yeah. She's been through some shit, that's for sure. But she'd better hurry it up if she wants to see ya before ya leave, mate.'

'Five days!' Lara says, stompin' back up from the water. She flicks her goggles so the water flies off of it onto our hot skin and Nelly moans like she likes it. Like the chick did on my phone last night.

'Get a bloody room,' I tell her.

'With the goggles?'

'Yeah. If ya want. Or Lara. You're single and she's single and yous're both into chicks.'

'I'm not into chicks!' says Lara.

Nelly says, 'That is inappropriate verging on harassment, Thatcher. You have no right to comment on Lara and my sexual suitability for one another, even if—'

'*I'm not—*'

'Fucken *harrassment*? You're off your head, Nel. I was just sayin' if you wanna get a girlfriend, you needa—'

'I don't want a girlfriend! I don't want any sort of relationship. No offence, Lara.' For some fucken reason, Lara rolls her eyes and heads back for the water with the only bloody goggles. Nelly keeps talkin' like nothing happened. 'Is it so difficult for you to believe that a girl – a woman – can enjoy having sex without wanting to tie herself to one particular person?'

Erik looks up from his phone finally and goes – 'Stop talking about sex, Eleanor.'

'*Excuse* me?' Nelly says in her heaps scary slow voice. 'You and Rain have intercourse inches from my head every weekend, with just a wall between us, and I'm not *permitted* to discuss my views with close friends?'

'Not very mature of ya, Erik. I'm disappointed, mate.'

'Shut up, Thatcher.'

'Get off your bloody phone and I might! Tell Hot Lucy to call ya later.'

'Fuck off,' Erik says. 'I'm not talking to Hot Lu— *Lucy*.'

'Yeah right. You're tellin' me she hasn't tried to hook up since she's been in town?'

Erik doesn't move a muscle.

Nelly drops her book. 'She has, hasn't she?'

'She just messaged. Once or twice. To be polite.'

'Have you considered *blocking* her?' Nelly says.

'That's a bit bloody extreme!' I tell her.

Erik looks at the water, real hard. Then he gets up. 'I'm gunna go check on Freddie or something. See ya later.' He grabs his shirt and his towel and legs it up the beach. He doesn't ask me if *I* wanna go to Freddie's. And it's my last bloody day off before work and I'm fucken devo that the cutest chick that's ever wanted a bar of me had to leave – the least he could do is ask me to come too. Have a bit of bloke time.

I'm considering runnin' after him when I hear a massive roar over the hill and two fat motorbikes come rollin' over. Harleys I reckon. The bikies park on the verge near the public dunnies, take their helmets off and look past us at the water. It's the same blokes from the pub – the younger one with the dog foot on his face and the older one with the dead eyes and the beard. I wonder if they're gunna go swimming. They've both got jeans on but, so probly not. Then the older one's pointing, right at me. The younger one does a bit of a smile and they start heading over.

Lara gets back at the same time, pressing her hand on a jellyfish sting. 'Are they coming to us?' she whispers.

'I think so,' Nelly whispers back.

Then the two blokes're next to us, lookin' down. 'Hey, mate,' says the young one. He looks at Nelly and does a bit of a nod. 'Nice day for it.'

The older bloke just stares.

'Yeah,' I tell 'em. 'Yous gunna go for a swim, or...?'

The young bloke cracks up a bit. 'Nah. I wish. Just meeting a mate before we head back into town. You guys should come. We're having a barbie. Plenty of drinks and food.'

'What kinda food?'

He cracks up again, then answers me like he's not sure I'm serious. 'I dunno exactly, chief. Left it with some of the younger guys. It'll be good though.' He gives the girls a wink. A pretty good one.

Nelly's interested. She's got that face she gets when she wants to be a bloody rebel. I give her a *be careful* sorta look, but before it can land, she says, 'OK.'

I spose we're goin' to a fucken bikie party then.

It turns out the address they gave us is for a pretty big holiday house in Mooney River – not the nicest one, but decent – near the weir. I sorta wish I'd had a shower like Nelly and Lara instead of just goin' on my phone. I'm feelin' salty now.

'Honestly, if you didn't want to come, you didn't have to,' Nelly says, jumping out of the car before Lara's even turned off the engine.

Lara slams her door a bit, putting her keys in her pocket. 'I'm just saying, I'm not getting myself killed by bikies for you. If this is sketchy, I'm gone.'

'*Please*. I don't think Sam would be stupid enough to harm two attractive, white, middle-class, teenage girls. Imagine the publicity!'

'*Sam...?*' Lara says, 'You're on first-name basis with the bikies now? Head Girl my arse. You've got a thing for him don't you? *Sam?*'

'Nah. No way,' I accidentally say out loud. 'Nel's not into tattoos.'

'We're here for research purposes only,' Nelly says, smoothing down the front bit of her top. 'I want to find out what this *organisation* is doing in our town.'

Lara looks at me and I give her a shrug.

We go after Nelly, who's walking like she's in the bloody Olympics, up to the curb. There's two blokes there, in their vests, with the logos and everything. It's pretty fucken gnarly. The blokes aren't, but. They're just average blokes – one weasely fella with a goatee and one real little one that looks like he couldn't knock out a flea.

'How ya goin'? I say. The goatee bloke nods and we walk past 'em and into the place.

We go up the path and there's another two bikies standin' outside the front door. I get wondering if they've *gotta* stand there, like if they've been posted there to keep a lookout in case of cops. These two could be brothers, both big and hectic looking but with clean beards and city haircuts. I nod to 'em and they nod back.

Nelly says, 'Good afternoon.' I just about crack up.

'You guys Pup's mates?' one of the blokes asks. The other one says, 'Come through.'

And we're in. In the fucken midst of it.

Here we bloody go...

But it's not much.

I expected a rager with Jack Daniels fountains and naked chicks but it's just a normal barbie with a couple more tough dudes. There's a bunch of chicks but most of 'em are older.

Pup comes walkin' in from the backyard and spots us. 'Ya made it!' he calls out. He gives the girls a quick hug with one arm and shakes my hand like we're good mates, giving me a pat on the shoulder. 'I'll get you guys a beer, eh?'

I say, 'Cheers.'

'Just a fizzy please,' says Lara.

Sam winks. 'Righto, Skipper.' He's a pretty fucken cool bloke, Sam. I can see why chicks'd like him. Tough. Real chill.

Doesn't seem to stop Nelly saying whatever the fuck pops into her head. She looks him dead in the eye and goes – 'Beer gives me digestive issues.'

Pup doesn't even blink. 'We wouldn't want that,' he says. 'We've got some wine and stuff out the back – come through.'

So we go out the back and it's still pretty normal – there's no bike ramps or chicks with rings through their nipples. Just pasta salad out of plastic containers, garlic bread in alfoil, garden salad, snags and chicken skewers. I have a couple while I'm lookin' round.

Pup talks to us for a bit. I ask him if him and the other blokes are gunna move here for good and he says, 'Nah. Just here for a few weeks sorting out some business. Back to the city after that.'

'*I'm* moving to the city soon,' Nelly says.

He nods and gives her cup a quick *cheers* with his beer. Then his phone must go off cause he grabs it outa his pocket and has a bit of a look. Something on there pisses him off. He's stopped smilin' and now he's lookin' pretty fucken scary. He puts his phone back hard in his pocket, goes, 'I'll catch you guys later,' and walks straight over to some blokes at the fence. He says something to 'em, then goes inside, leaving the blokes at the fence lookin' heaps worried.

I reckon I might know this one bloke at the fence, but his back's turned. The way he's standing's heaps familiar — tight shoulders, a bit of a forward lean. It's no one from the Bay or school. Doesn't look like he surfs. Maybe I know him from footy. 'Oi...' I ask the girls. 'Where do I know that bloke from?'

Lara turns quick and then splutters a bit, so Coke goes on her chin. 'Are you serious?'

Nelly has a look. 'Honestly, Thatcher. You don't recognise the person you pummelled last weekend? That's *Harrison*.' She says his name heaps quiet, like a hiss.

She's right, but. It fucken *is* Harrison. The shithouse haircut shoulda given him away.

Nelly gasps and I look where she's looking, to the back door. *Abigail's* coming outa the house. She looks pretty much the same as always – a bit paler for sure, and skinnier. There's something sorta uncomfy about the way she walks. Heaps more careful than she used to.

'Abigail!' Nelly calls out.

Abs turns round. She doesn't say nothing. Not even a bloody wave. She just goes over to her piss-weak boyfriend and says something in his ear. He looks at us, his arm round her shoulders, like a cuddle, but a bit higher than normal.

Nelly marches right over there. I chuck my snag on the table and follow, getting there just as she starts having a go. 'Don't pretend you didn't hear me, Abigail Marie Brown. You know as well as I do that we need to have a conversation, for the sake of our friendship.'

Harrison pulls Abs closer, his arm tight, almost round her neck.

Abs goes – 'What do you want, Eleanor?'

Nelly's gobsmacked, so I go – 'How ya doin', Abs?'

Fucken Harrison answers, 'She's fine.'

I fight down what I wanna say, which is *No thanks to you, dickhead.*

I should fucken smash him again. But I dont wanna start shit at a bikie party.

So instead of rippin' Harrison off Abigail and decking him, I go – 'I reckon we have a fresh start, eh? Let bygongs be bygongs.' I stretch out my hand and Harrison shakes it as hard as he can. His hands're like little crayfish claws. It doesn't really hurt what he's doin', cause he's a bloody pussy. But it's still a bit fucked — pincin' a guy like that when he's being a good bloke.

Nelly's going to Abigail, 'Where on earth have you been?'

'Nowhere,' Abs says, having a look at her fingernails. 'Just living my life.' Her fingernails're a bit more dodgy than usual, now I get a good look at them. Two're missing – the thumb on one hand and the pointer on the other.

Nelly makes a confused sound. 'I-I've... We've all been

trying to call you. Messaging you. What's going on? We thought you were—'

'I told you she's fine,' Harrison says.

Abigail smiles, but not like she used to. 'What's the big deal? We're not in high school anymore. People move on.'

Lara's with us now, holding my sausage. 'Abigail! Hey! Come have a chat with us? Catch up. We've got heaps to—'

Harrison does a massive sniff, like an angry nose-blow, backwards.

'You guys should go,' Abigail says. 'I don't know what you're doing here.'

Nelly crosses her arms and leans back a bit, like she used to in her arguing competitions. 'We were *invited*. I had no idea I'd be seeing you, for the first time since graduation.'

'I don't have to call you every day and check in, Eleanor. For fuck's sake. Just give up. Move on with your life. You guys aren't my parents.'

'But your *parents* don't even know where you are! I spoke to *Bianca* the other day and—'

'Don't talk to my sister. Don't talk to anyone in my family. Just leave me alone. I'm fine.'

'They're just jealous,' Harrison says to Abs, talking into her neck.

'Let's go home,' Abigail whispers.

They're outa there quicker than a rat up a drainpipe. Abs grabs her bag and Harrison shakes a couple guys hands, softer than he shaked mine, and they're gone.

And me n' Nelly n' Lara are just standin' there with our dicks in our hands.

I go to say that out loud, cause I reckon it'd get a bit of a rise out of Nelly, but she looks too devo for me to do it. Like the time she tried to do CPR on a bat using a rolled up bit of paper to blow through, but the bat wouldn't come back alive. She couldn't handle it. She couldn't handle that she couldn't save it. That was one of the first times I ever went to the Everson house. The fucken bat'd probly been dead a full day before Nelly found it. Good thing she used the rolled up bit of paper.

'...Should we go too?' Lara says.

Nelly stares for a sec, then nods.

I run to grab another snag.

When me and Nel get back to her empty house, she says, 'I suppose Mum and Erik are off doing something preferable to this. *Typical.*' She looks round, grabs a newspaper from next to the fruit bowl and starts goin' through it real fast.

I grab some chips and fancy salsa from the pantry and eat 'em over the sink and Nelly keeps tearing through pages like they've just rooted her boyfriend. Not that she'd ever have a boyfriend. She told me she never would. 'Unbelievable...' she goes, half under her breath. 'The town is crawling with them and there isn't a single mention.'

I dunno what she's talkin' about. The salsa's good, but. It's green coloured, not red, and it's got heaps of little seeds in it. Green tomatoes? That was a book Mum used to read me about some bloke that didn't want green tomatoes and ham but this fucken nutter wouldn't leave him alone till he tried them. And then at the end the bloke realises he *does* bloody like the tomatoes and he should've been eatin' 'em this whole fucken time. Maybe it was eggs, now I think about it. Tomatoes sounds better, but.

'You're dripping that on the floor, Thatcher!' Nelly screams at me outa the blue.

I bend down and wipe up the blob of salsa off the hardwood with my thumb then smear it on my boardies.

'*Thatcher!*'

'What? It'll wash right out when I go for a swim! It's just green tomatoes and that. Organic.'

'Just because it's *organic*, doesn't mean you can smear it all over yourself! You're behaving like an absolute—'

We hear the crunch of tires and spot Anita's car through the front window. A sec later, she comes in the house. With Hot fucken Lucy. They're wearing tight gym clothes and I've gotta focus real hard to just look at their faces. 'I ran into Lucy at pilates!' Anita says, putting her keys and her water bottle on the bench.

Lucy's doing a *massive* smile. Through all her teeth, she goes – 'Such a crazy coincidence! I didn't even know your mum took that class. And then she just insisted I pop by to say hello.' She glances down the hall, heaps casual.

'It's a pity Erik isn't home to say hello,' Nelly says.

Nita says, 'Drink, Lucy? Coconut water? Lychee juice? I've got a local sparkling here leftover from Christmas.'

'*Should* we?' Lucy laughs.

'I'll add a dash of lychee juice.' Anita winks. A *heaps* fucken good one.

'That's not very good post-workout nutrition, Mum. You should really—'

'Eleanor...' Nelly's mum goes to tell her something, then zips her mouth. She looks up at the ceiling. Then she pops the cork on her fizzy wine. 'Will you two be having any?'

I go to say yeah, but Nelly gives me a look that tells me to shut up. 'No. We won't be.'

'You guys aren't going out tonight or anything?' Lucy asks.

Nelly ignores her, so I say, 'Nah. I've gotta go to work tomorrow.'

'We've had an extremely tiring day, and we'd both like to relax before the new week.'

'What did you do today that was so tiring? I thought you went to the beach?'

'Yeah!' I say. 'And we went to a bikie–'

'Bike ride,' Nelly says. 'We enjoyed a bike ride through the pine plantations. BMX. My bike was blue and Thatch's was orange.'

Anita looks us up and down. Nelly in her little skirt and sandals. Me in my boardies and thongs. 'You two have been riding BMXs in the pine forest?'

'Well, we didn't wear this! They have onsite facilities for people to shower and change after the bike rides.'

'They? Who's they?'

'The owners.'

'Of what?'

'Ah... I believe they're called Forest Speed Racing.'

Anita takes a big sip of her drink. Then another one. 'Forest Speed Racing...' she says, doing a bit of a nod. 'What about you, Lucy? How was your day?'

'It was good! I took Polly for a walk on the beach first thing and helped Mum around the house. Then Dad showed me some of the programs he used at the agency. You know, Eleanor, I actually thought you two were about to say something about *bikies* earlier. Not bike riding. Because of the other night, remember? It's so strange... I keep seeing them everywhere. The Devil's Rangers. I went with Dad last month to show one of them a property! It's a huge place, with two stand-alone dwellings and a shed that could easily be converted into a third. It went really well for my first showing! My dad was *really* impressed.'

Nelly's eyes just about pop out of her head. 'What *guy*? Which property? Did they *purchase* it? Why?'

'I'm not really supposed to... There are confidentiality clauses. I don't want to be unprofessional.'

'Of course,' says Nelly. 'I hardly care anyway. It's just that *Erik* mentioned he might be interested in exploring property development in the future. The distant future. And I'm sure he'd appreciate the information on local sales. But it hardly matters to me.'

'Well, you didn't hear it from me... But it was that young guy with the tattoos, and a super scary one with a beard. The weirdest part was, they weren't even the buyers.'

'What do you mean, not *the buyers*?'

From behind Lucy, Anita throws her arms in the air and mouths, *Rude*, to Nel, who flat-out ignores her, waiting for Lucy to answer.

Lucy goes – 'Oh, it happens all the time! People will bring a friend along, or a parent. Never bikies, but I don't like to pry into other people's business. It's just that, you notice when the people are bikies.'

'Well, who was the buyer?'

'A local guy. Creepy. Frank, I think. Decker.'

Nelly goes real still. She drops the newspaper down. '*Where?* What is the address? Is it the turn off after—'

'Eleanor!' Anita says, pouring a bit of a top-up. 'That's not an appropriate question.'

'I would tell you! But my parents would be really mad. Sorry...'

'Don't apologise, Lucy,' says Anita, holding out the bottle. 'Would you like a top-up?'

Nelly gives her mum a look like she's gunna punch her. She grabs me by the elbow and pulls me all the way outa the kitchen, down the hall into her room.

She pushes the door closed behind me and I have a bit of a wobble, but I get my balance back pretty quick.

Nelly's walking from side to side. '*Conniving... Duplicitous... Lascivious.*'

I feel like fish and chips. Maybe an icy-pole after. Frosty Fruits. 'Wanna go get Tilda's?' I say.

Nelly stops muttering massive words to herself and nods. 'Of course. I'll buy. As soon as we've run a brief errand...'

Brian Decker's place is a couple streets back from mine, right on the edge of town. There's no doormat out the front or nothing – just some hunks of Styrofoam and a bit of bone that looks like lamb shank and a crusty old dummy.

'Nah...' I say, when we get to the door.

Nelly puts her hands on her hips and starts whispering heaps hard at me like a teacher in a test. '*Don't you see?* It's a *lead*! Frank Decker. He's connected to it all. And Brian is his *nephew*. He could have important information leading to Abigail's whereabouts! Harrison and Abigail *must* be renting one of the houses on the property. How else would Frank and Harrison ever become affiliated, if not through their mutual connection to the bikies? Think about it... If they're manufacturing, they would want to be located out of town, and they'd need someone there at all times, someone who isn't a Devil's Ranger, in case the place were ever raided or—'

'Fucken hell, Nelly. We're not the bloody cops. It's none of our—'

'It's *Abigail*, Thatcher.' She looks at me, massive blue eyes, dry lips starting to shake. 'We need to at least *try*.'

I crack pretty easy.

I always crack when Nelly's about to cry.

I kick the dummy outa the way then knock hard three times on the door.

There's a bit of yelling inside. Screaming kids, then a lady goes, 'QUIET THE FUCK DOWN!' at the top of her lungs and they quiet down a bit and the door opens a crack. Brian's grandma peers through like she's expecting the cops. I know her from the time she picked up Brian from primary school cause he set a roll of dunny paper on fire, and from the time she was at the bottle-o yelling at the bloke behind the counter cause they'd run outa their special casks of red.

I've never seen her up close but. Her hair's a weird purply-black colour with grey at the top and she's got massive matching purple sacks under her eyes. 'Yeah?' she asks, in a real gravelly voice.

Nelly's stock still, frog in her throat, so I go, 'G'day, Mrs Decker. I'm Michael Thatcher.'

A little kid shows up under her legs. He's got yellow hair and shit all over his face. 'Back in the house,' Decker's grandma says, pushing his little head behind her legs. '*Miss*.'

'Miss what?'

'Miss *Decker*,' she tells me. 'Not everyone's gotta be married.' She hawks some spit, then swallows it.

'I couldn't agree more!' Nelly pipes up. 'Marriage is an archaic institution, existing only to perpetuate the indentured servitude of women.' She stretches out her hand for a shake, but Decker's gran doesn't take it. 'We're Brian's friends from school. We were hoping to—'

Decker's grandma turns over her shoulder and screams, 'BRIAAAN!' so loud I reckon her lungs might pop out. Her and the little yellow haired kid go back inside.

A sec later Brian rocks up. He gets to us and steps back two times like he's scared I'm gunna take a swing. 'I didn't take your fricken drinks,' he says.

'Whadya mean? From the oval? Have you been goin' in there and takin' shit outa the—'

'It's *alright*, Brian...' Nelly says over me. She uses a voice I only hear every now and then, when she's tryna get me to wash my hair or join one of her bloody clubs. She talks to Brian like that – real soft and nice. 'We just wanted to chat. We were catching up and we thought that we'd stop by.'

'Yous've never come over before,' Brian says.

'Well, no,' says Nelly. 'But people change. We're all getting older and—'

'It's cause of my new mates.' Brian does a bit of a smile.

Nelly goes real still. '*What* new mates?'

Brian picks at a spot of brick next to the door and shrugs.

'She asked you a question!' I say, pissed off cause there's a fly on my face. Brian freezes and Nel gives me a look. 'Sorry,' I say, even though I'm not. 'This fly's just pissin' me off. Let us in and you can come to the oval.'

Brian sniffs. 'When?'

'Whenever.'

'And ya won't kick me out?'

'Nah. Not if you're bein' a good bloke.'

'Have I gotta put the drinks back?'

'What fucken drinks? Have you been in there—'

'No.' Nelly says. 'No, you don't. But you need to follow the rules of the oval, and contribute. We run things communally, in a fair and equitable manner. As long as you respect that, you can come whenever you'd like.'

'Yous better not be lying,' Decker says. He turns round and we follow him into his shit house. There's a couple more kids in here as well as the yellow haired one from before, all runnin' round in a circle with a weird song playing on a beat-up old tablet on the floor. One of em's got a pizza crust hangin' out of his mouth. It looks like a pretty old crust. Decker's gran couldn't give a shit. She's next to the kitchen window sippin' out of a coffee mug, red stains all round the outside of her mouth. The hall's got pencil all up the walls like a trail pointing out the way to Brian's shit room at the very back of the house.

These old houses sometimes have little rooms off them –

closed in verandahs where you can store stuff or hang out when it's hot. They're not usually bedrooms, but. The walls're too thin and spiders and stuff get in real easy. In Brian's 'room' there's not even any screen on the window – he must get heaps of flies when it's hot.

The saddest thing's not the actual room. It's how he's *decorated* it. His mattress looks even shittier than mine and he's got no sheet on the bed. Even *I've* got a fucken sheet on the bed. There's a massive drawing of a horse on the wall but its eyes're way too far back and its neck's heaps too short. Thing looks more like a crocodile. Then he's got this bookshelf with no books on it. Just a couple magazines and a comic with a were-wolf on the front. There's heaps of other weird shit, like a homemade candle and a plastic sword and a scratched-up shoebox and a massive cup and straw shaped like Darth Vader. The straw's red, so it looks a bit like one'a those laser swords from the movie.

Brian sits on the floor and picks up the werewolf comic and pretends to give it a read then puts it back down on the dirty shelf. 'If yous're tricking, I'll tell my mates. I've got mates now. If yous do anything, they'll come after ya.'

'Are you referring to your uncle's friends from the Devil's Rangers?' Nelly asks him, moving a crumpled-up shopping bag and sitting down too.

'Not just Uncle Frank's mates. Mine too. Why're you sticking your nose in anyway? It's none of your business what they're doin'. Free country. Just stay outa their way. Stay outa *our* way.' He smiles, his eyes flicking up like he's tryna get a rise.

She does the soft voice again. 'Brian, you need to be reason-able. What could they possibly want from someone your age, in your situation?'

'You don't fricken get it, do ya? *You* and *him*, and your

fricken brother. Yous don't know what they're like. They're nice. Real proper guys and good mates. They got me chips and drinks and didn't even ask for nothing back. Said they're gunna let me hang with 'em soon. When I'm ready.'

'Do you mean join the club? The Rangers?' Nelly asks.

Brian shrugs and picks up the Darth Vader cup. He holds it up like it's heaps fucken pricey, lookin' down through the straw.

Nelly makes a sorta fed-up noise in her throat. 'You need to listen to us, Brian. There are much better people for you to be consorting with.'

'Dunno what consorting means. *Snob* word.'

Nelly does a quick sigh. 'We're just worried about you. We're here because we care, and we don't want anyone ruining what we have here. There have been certain cases, where criminal enterprises come to small towns specifically to prey on unstable youths... convince them to do certain things.'

'They're not using me. Uncle Frank's known 'em for *ages*.'

'But *Brian*... Your uncle may not be the best example for you either. We heard he bought a new house and we—'

'How'd ya hear that? Sposed to be a secret.'

Nelly blinks. 'It doesn't matter. We need to know where it is, and if our friend and her boyfriend are there. You remember Abigail? She might be in trouble.'

'She's not in trouble. Saw her the other day. Uncle Frank got me Hendo's in Bandler Beach and we went to see the new place.'

'So he *is* renting it to them? And it's near Bandler Beach? Is it the property on Balai Road, after the fire trail?'

'Dunno road names.' He shrugs. He picks up his comic again, flipping through it to a page with heaps of blood splatters and big words in hectic white writing. Nelly waits for him to talk. I can tell it's taking all her effort not to say nothing. When

Decker opens his mouth again all he says is, 'Wanna play Werewolves for a bit?'

I crack up. I try hold it in, but it sorta sprays outa me unexpected.

Decker's whole body gets angry. His little fists go tight and his face gets real red and ratty. 'I fricken *knew* yous were tricking me!' he says, standing up. 'Yous don't want me comin' to the oval. You're gunna get me like always. Push me out.' He takes a step forward and Nelly stands too, backing away. 'Get fricken lost then! I've got mates that're heaps better fighters. And they've got other shit to fight with, other than their hands. Shit to *kill* with. I'm not scared of *yous*.'

'Brian,' Nelly says in her soft shampoo voice. 'We promise you we weren't going to trick you. We only want to—'

He spits on her. Right on her skirt.

He wipes his mouth, lookin' just as surprised as us.

All I see's red. My neck goes hot and my legs go hot and I push him heaps harder than I mean to.

He flies.

His back curls and hits the wall, right where his crocodile horse is. It gets all crunched up, and I'm pretty sure there's a hole in the wall behind. He tries to sit up, holdin' his ribs, then Nelly's draggin' me out. The same song's playin' again and the kids're still dancin'. Decker's gran must've gone out the back cause we don't see her.

Nelly hauls me all the way to the road and right down his street till we're on the corner. I'm even hotter now. Boiling. My head and my belly and my throat. I wanna turn round and go back and smash him. I wanna kick the streetlights and punch the stop sign.

But I don't wanna scare Nelly. So I squeeze my fists shut and my eyes and my jaw and try thinking of something else. Dirt. The beach. Lamingtons. Mum's jewellery box.

We're pretty much back at Nelly's place before the hot feeling's gone from my neck. She doesn't talk the whole way and neither do I. Not till we're at her driveway. Then I say, 'That was fucked.'

Nelly whispers, 'Yes.'

I stop and check her skirt where the spit was. You can't see nothing – just a patch that's a bit darker. I bend down and rub it for a sec, till you can't even tell. 'There ya go,' I tell her. 'Can't even see where he got ya.'

Nelly starts doin' the face she does before she cries. Tight shaky lips and upwards eyebrows, looking all round. 'Thatcher... You really sh—'

'He fucken *spat* on you, Nel. He's lucky I didn't *kill* him. Don't worry about Decker anymore orright? Don't worry about Abs or the bikies. I don't want you gettin' hurt. Just bloody drop it.'

Nelly stops in a bit of shade so I've gotta walk back a few steps when I see she's not next to me. She grabs me. Hugs me real tight for heaps longer than she usually does. She's not a big hugger, Nel. But she's huggin' me tight and her face is smooshed into my shirt. I hold her head and her back and she says something into me.

'What?' I ask the top of her head.

She looks up. There's a bit of space between our heads, but not much. I feel a bit guilty for a sec, having her so close, but then remember I don't have a girlfriend. But *then* I remember Nelly'd never hug me like *that*. Nelly said she'd never hook up with anyone who didn't do ATAR or who didn't brush their teeth every single bloody day or anyone who didn't read the news. But the way she's looking at me now, I almost reckon she would. I almost reckon she *wants* to.

'I wish the world wasn't so *awful*,' she says. She hugs me for a bit longer but she doesn't say nothing after that.

It's just about dark by the time I get home.

Dad's still down south with Snapper so no one's done the dishes or swept up or nothing.

I'm heaps knackered but I've gotta stay up and get my stuff ready for work. I'm heaps hungry too. Nel didn't feel like gettin' Tilda's — not after all the shit happened at Decker's place — and I couldn't be fucked goin' by myself. I find some oats in the back of the cupboard and make a massive pot of porridge. I tip about half a bag of sugar on top, then I eat it outa the pot, laying down on the couch. It's a heaps boring dinner, but it fills me up.

I reckon I'll just play a bit of X-Box.

Then I'll get all my stuff ready for my first day of work as a brickies-bloody-labourer.

Tomorrow's a big fucken day.

Someone's ringin' me.

I go to roll over and answer it. I'm not in my bed but. I'm on the couch. So I roll right down onto the ground and knock my knee real hard on the table. I hold it tight in both my hands and roll onto my back, hissing like a fucken python. It's not too bad, but.

Where the fuck's my phone?

I grab all around me and on the ground and in my pockets – all through the couch. The phone stops ringin' then starts again. Then I feel the corner of it, right under the middle cushion. A lawn-mower starts goin' off outside and I finally get my hand round my screen to see who's callin'.

Rodney.

Why the fuck's he callin' me in the middle of the night?

And why's that arsehole got their mower on?

Then it bloody hits me.

I smash down on the green button and go – 'Rodney?'

'Where are ya? I'm out the front.'

'Just on the dunny. I was *busting*. But I'll be off in one sec.'

'Well hurry up, mate! The boss is waiting.'

He hangs up and I run round the house for a sec tryna figure shit out. I'm still in the boardies I wore yesterday. They've got salsa and dirt on 'em but they'll have to do. I chuck on the first shirt I find on the ground – one of Dad's that's a bit small for me and has a couple holes in the shoulder. It smells clean but. Erik's socks are sittin' on top of my boots, ready to go, and I tug em on – I'll do the laces later.

What the fuck else is there?

Lunch.

I grab my school bag out of habit from the floor in my room, chuck in the rest of the grated cheese and a two-litre bottle of orange fizzy from the cupboard. The gloves Nelly got me are up on the bench – I chuck them in on top of the fizzy and the cheese and run outside to Rodney's old ute.

'You gunna lock the house?' he asks me, leaning out the window.

I just about fall flat on my face trying to turn round while

I'm running but manage not to stack it. I go back in the house, grab the keys from inside, go back out, lock the fucken door and pelt to Rodney's car. The back's probly still open but I reckon it'll be right. Nothing bad's happened yet.

Rodney gives me a look like I'm fucken nutters when I get in his car. He has a good squiz at my shorts and my hair and my face while he's pullin' down the street. Then he goes – 'Might wanna rub that sleep out your eyes before you meet the boss.'

I reckon I've got most of the sleep outa my eyes by the time we get there and I do up my laces and fix my hair a bit. I didn't get to brush my teeth or nothing, so I swish a bit of orange fizzy in my mouth and swallow it, then I give my teeth a rub on the bottom of Dad's shirt.

The site's right in the middle of town – a new slab where they knocked down a little wood house. I remember it cause it had a little circle window up the top and a massive tree out front with a tire-swing on it. That's all gone now. There's just a big dirty slab that Rodney reckons they're gunna turn into units. He tells me not to talk to the boss about how I liked the tyre swing or the little window, cause he might get pissed off.

The boss's name's Max. He's got a sunburnt bald head and he shakes my hand hard. He seems orright. And he's got a heaps cool dog called Red that just sits in the shade, tongue wagging all over the place, not giving a shit.

'You got any experience on site?' Max asks after just about breaking my hand.

'A bit,' I tell him. 'I did two weeks work experience for school. Got my white card and all that. Did a bit of landscaping over summer for my girlfriend's dad. Just shovelling and shit. Shovelling and *that*. Sorry.'

'Swear all you want, mate. Just get the job done. If the trial goes well and Rodney tells me you pulled your weight, I'll get your bank details this arvo and we'll see you tomorrow.'

I nod like I know what the fuck's goin' on. What's a bloody *trial*? Am I sposed to work all fucken day and not even get *paid* for it?

There's not even any time to ask Rodney before we're unpacking the boss's truck and gettin' started. Once the mixer and all the bags and tools and shit are out of there, some other guys rock up to help out. Max n' Red hit the road. Must be good to be the boss and fuck off whenever you want.

I'm a while off that.

My first job of the day's to run wheelbarrows choker-block full of sand from a massive pile next to the road down to where the cement mixer is at the side of the slab. The empty barrow weighs about three tonnes on its own and the front wheel's a dud, so it's bloody hard. I'd be fucked without the gloves Nelly got me. I do four or five wheelbarrows till Rodney tells me it's enough. Then he makes me stand there and watch him mix the cement. He calls it 'mud' and he goes on and on like a fucken science teacher about how you've gotta get the amounts of sand and water just right or else the whole batch of mud'll be fucked. He shows me for a bit, then watches while I do some, talkin' in his best bloody teacher voice.

I'm knackered by smoko.

I sit on a stack of bricks next to some bloke from Brazil or Italy or somewhere – I'm shit with accents – and all he wants to talk about is how I should never trust a woman even if she seems heaps nice upfront. He says that's how he ended up here. I dunno if he means Australia or workin' as a labourer. 'All women are vampires,' he says, doin' a sorta slurp noise.

I go to make a joke about how I wouldn't mind gettin' sucked off by a chick vampire, but the bloke's so pissed off I don't bother. 'Want a sip of my fizzy?' I say instead.

He looks at me like I've just offered him a crack pipe then shakes his head and says he has to make a phone call.

'Just a quick one,' says Rodney.

I've barely stopped sweating by the time I'm back at it, runnin' wheelbarrows full of bricks back and forth from the pile out the front to Rodney and the other brickies. I stack 'em up next to each of the guys, twelve at a time, then go runnin' back for more.

Rodney screams out, 'More mud!' and I've gotta cart piles of cement back and forth to all the brickies and dump it in piles next to the bricks while the sun smacks me in the face.

I'm fucken starving by lunch. Probly the most hungry I've ever been. I take out the cheese and start pouring it into my mouth. It's heaps chalky and a bit melted and it clags up my mouth. I drink the last few sips of my fizzy and Rodney tells me, 'You shouldn't drink that shit.' He makes me fill the empty bottle up at the tap. Then, when I get back, he gives me a stack of his Vegemite crackers.

He's a good bloke, Rodney.

I watch him grind bricks for a bit after lunch. He measures 'em, does a score line, then cuts through with the grinder. I get to have a coupla goes after he shows me, which is pretty sick.

Then I've gotta run barrows of bricks and mud for a couple more boiling-hot hours.

The bloke from Brazil or Italy keeps havin' a go tellin' me the 'The mix is too dry!' but in his accent it sounds like '*da meex ees too dry!*'

I didn't fucken mix it, I wanna tell him. But for all I know he's just sayin' it to get a rise — see if I'll keep my mouth shut or not. It's hard fucken work.

And I'm not even gettin' *paid*.

I just about have a word to Red about it when he gets back, but Max won't stop barkin', so I keep my bloody mouth shut and help the other blokes pack up.

Before we leave, Rodney tells the boss I did a heaps good job. 'The best kid we've had for ages,' Rodney says, stoked.

He'd *wanna* be stoked.

I worked my arse off.

'Reckon you could drop me off at the Everson's instead of my place?' I ask him. 'I needa borrow a water bottle for tomorrow. This thing's cooked.' I wave my dented fizzy bottle round for proof.

'No worries, mate,' says Rodney. 'No difference to me.' Then he starts talkin' about Erik and the swell the other day and I zone till we get to my place. 'Set an alarm tomorrow, mate!' Rodney says through his open window.

I give him a salute, then start crunchin' down the gravel to Erik's door.

It opens pretty much in my face.

It's not Erik, but. Or Anita, or Nel.

It's Hot Lucy.

She does a bit of a smile and wipes her hand over her mouth.

'What're you doin' here?' I ask her.

Erik shows up, pushing back his hair. The top bit of his boardies is open and the white string's dangling in two lines. As soon as he sees me, he starts strugglin' to do it up, fingers slippin' all over the place. It reminds me of my dad trying to roll a ciggie when he's pissed. He looks at me once, real quick, eyes like a dog in trouble, then back down to the string.

'What's goin' on?' I say. He keeps fumblin' with the strings, so I turn round and say to Hot Lucy – 'That's pretty fucken rude what you did.'

She doesn't look as hot all pissed off with the sun shinin' right on her face. 'Erik's a big boy,' she says. 'He can be with whoever he likes.'

'So you hooked up with him? Yous hooked up?'

From a bit further inside, Erik says, 'Fuck.'

Lucy moves her sunnies down off her head to her eyes and pushes past me, up the drive.

I think about yellin' after her. Callin' her a fuckwit or a skank. I don't, but.

By the time I close the door behind her, Erik's nowhere.

The garage and the TV room and the kitchen and the deck and the old trophy room Anita's made into a yoga room are all empty. I go to check *his* room but his door's closed and I don't reckon I should push my way in. Not just yet. I'll give the dickhead a bit of space. So I go to the freezer and have a bit of cookies n' cream while I wait. The brain freeze is pretty bad, but I push through till It's just about gone. Then I have some butter on bread. Then the rest of the chips from yesterday.

I grab a beer outa the fridge and have a nice long shower – get all the dirt and sweat and cement off me. I'm fucken filthy. I even use some of Nelly's shampoo and that. I get real clean, drinkin' the beer in about three sips just before I turn the water off.

The towel's heaps soft. I rub it all over my sore skin and my sore muscles and go to Anita's room and get a pair of footy shorts and a singlet from a bag in the closet chock-full of Andy's old stuff. Erik's shit's too small for me.

Once I'm a bit more clean and full and dressed, I go to Erik's room. I knock a couple times but he doesn't say nothing so I open the door. He's looking out the window, leaning his forehead against it, his arms drooping down. His phone's in one hand.

'What happened?'

He starts to say something but his voice's too high and he stops straight away.

I sit on his bed and wait for a bit, sorta wishing I'd cracked another beer. 'Wanna talk about it?'

'No,' he croaks out, lower than normal now.

'Just a coupla things then. First of all, you're a bit of a dick-head for that, mate. Didn't you learn anything from Abs? Just be single if you wanna root around. Rain's goin' through it bad with her mum bein' batshit and her dad bein' dead without you goin' and rooting Hot-Fucken—'

'What?'

'... Huh?'

'*What* about her dad?'

'Bloody hell!' I say, throwin' my arms up in the air. 'Now I'M the fuckwit cause I broke my bloody—'

'Her dad's dead?'

I wanna be pissed off. But now I'm looking at him, he's a bit of a wreck. He looks worse than he did after getting pummeled by that wave the other day. Heaps more scared.

'I had to promise her I wouldn't tell ya, but I've fucked that up haven't I?'

He stares at me. 'You didn't fuck up, Thatch. I did.'

I chuck myself down on his bed, cause I dunno how long he's gunna stand there like a dickhead and I've had a big fucken day. 'Hot bloody Lucy, eh? I gotta say, I didn't see it comin' this time. Yous rooted, then?'

He shakes his head.

I mull it over for a sec. 'Blowie?'

He shakes his head again.

'Well, what the fuck else is there? She give you a handy?'

He looks like he's gunna spew. He does a quick nod then shakes his head and says, 'I dunno...'

'Well, start from the bloody beginning, mate.'

So Erik pinches the top of his nose like it's bleeding and closes his eyes. 'She said her mum wanted to borrow a spanner.'

'Lucy's mum?'

'Who the fuck else's mum would it be?'

'Don't get angry at *me*! *I* didn't cheat on your bloody girlfriend.'

He sits on the floor, then goes dead-still and dead-quiet again.

'Tell me what happened, ya little wanker.'

So he tells the hardwood in front of his face what happened. 'Lucy came over to borrow a spanner...' he says. 'We went to the garage. It took a few minutes, cause everything got moved, after dad. I didn't know if we still had one.'

'Had what?'

'A spanner.'

'Oh. Then she grabbed your—'

'We were talking. That's it. Then she asked me about Rain. I told her I hadn't heard from her in a couple of days. Lucy was almost mad about it. She said, I should be with someone who supports me. My career. She said, if she was my girlfriend, she wouldn't be able to get enough of me. She said my hair was getting long. She touched it. And then... I dunno.'

'She gave you a wristy. You blew your load. Most boring story in the world, mate.'

'No!'

'I thought you said you—'

'I didn't... finish.'

'Hah! Didn't know that was even bloody possible. What's the point?'

He picks up his thong and hurls it across the room at the door. It's a pretty shit throw. Erik never could bowl for shit. Then he says, to the floor, 'She's never going to forgive me. And Nelly... And *Mum*...'

I get up off the bed even though I'm fucken knackered and give him a bit of a pat on the back. 'She'll forgive ya. It might take a sec, but she will. She fucken loves ya.'

. . .

When I get back to my place, I get everything perfectly bloody organised for the morning. My gloves and one of dad's big-brimmed hats, my boots and a different pair of Erik's socks, the two sangas I made at Erik's house, and some banana bread and the water-bottle he gave me. I even chuck a load of laundry on and hang up some work clothes. They'll be dry by the morning for sure.

Before I go to sleep I send Erik a quick message.

Hang in there mate

PART 8

ERIK

I have to take the picture down.

The one of us. At the ball. Last year.

I can feel the glossy waves of her dress under my hands. See the light in her hair and the crinkle in her nose. Hear her saying my name.

What did you do, Erik?

My memories from yesterday are like a shitty movie I'd never watch. Some actor I don't recognise doing things I'd never do. Saying things I'd never say. 'I need to tell you something... Please let me explain... It'll never happen again...'

I almost couldn't tell her at all. She was so beautiful, standing in the garden, the sky cracking red and purple through the trees. My mouth got dry and I had to choke the words out.

Rain made a sound. A low, soft, *oogh*. Then she cried. Her tears were heavy, but her face barely moved. She was distant. Resigned. It was like watching someone mourn something that'd happened a while ago. Like she was remembering it.

I told her I'd love her forever.

She wiped her eyes. In a quick exhale, like a ghost from the shadows, she said, '*Go.*'

I went home.

When I got there, Nelly threw a bottle of perfume at me, and some highlighters. She told me I'd ruined everything and I could go fluff myself. She told me to get out of her room before she screamed. She was already screaming. So I left.

Now I've got to take the picture down.

The old canteen's like a shell someone trod on. Broken. Deserted. I lie on the concrete and try not to look at anything that reminds me of Rain – the demolished walls or the scratched up roof or my own arms. I close my eyes, but that's worse.

When Freddie walks in I'm hunched in a sandy corner, staring at a bottle top. He sits, taking out a stick of alfoil and his little red pipe.

'How much?' I ask him.

He says, 'Yeah, right.'

He pats me on the back when he passes the pipe.

Thank fuck for Freddie.

The weed makes everything seem further away. The look on Rain's face. The rubbery feeling of Lucy's mouth on mine. The way I knew, in every cell, that I didn't want to do it. The way I did it anyway.

Then a jolt of panic crashes through me.

I reach for the pipe but Freddie puts his hand on my arm. Back still slumped against the wall, he says, 'Let's go to the beach first.'

'Too busy.'

'Jumprock? The tide's right. If you can handle the cliffs.'

I squeeze the foil closed on the rest of his weed and stand up, slipping it into my pocket. 'Yeah. I can handle it.'

I step off and the limestone crumbles under my toes, falling off the edge with me, down into the secret blue, shimmering cold. If Rain were here, she'd be scared to jump. I'd have to coach her through it. Hold her hand. And she'd only do it once.

Freddie and I end up at Thatch's. It's empty, cooler than the oval. His back door's open.

We make a bong out of an old Powerade bottle and pass it back and forth until my eyes feel like they're bleeding.

Freddie says, 'I heard about you and Rain.'

The first time I ever kissed her was in this house. On Thatch's bed, on the other side of that wall. 'Yeah. It's over, I think.'

'She might give you another shot?' Freddies says. 'You guys've been together for ages. You're good together.'

I nod. I need to change the fucking subject. 'You still seeing that girl you met at Leavers?'

'Nah. She didn't really want anything serious. It was good while it lasted.'

We don't talk for a while. I pass him the bong and he passes it back. Four more times, until there are only a few crumbs left in the foil. The smoke moves thick through my muscles and my head. I lie on Thatch's couch and finally stop thinking. Freddie puts on a cartoon with bright-coloured animals on an island and I watch it through mostly closed eyes, trying to focus on the story.

'Want to go get some food from Tilda's?'

'Nah. I'm good.'

He puts on his sunnies and tells me he'll 'be right back.'

I message Thatch.

I message Nelly too. Tell her I'm sorry.

I've only got a few days left with her, then I'm gone. For months. She'll be in the city with Rain after that. I might not even be allowed in the house. I'll just be the deadshit brother that cheats on his girlfriend and fucks everyone's life up.

My hand moves like a habit to my phone. My chat with Rain. I scroll upwards. Backwards.

This morning:

> I'll love you forever
> I'm so sorry

Last night:

> I'll come to town. To your
> window. Just write back

Call not connected

> I'm sorry. I love you so much

Call not connected

> Can I call you?

My bleeding eyes keep moving upwards, to the day before camping.

The morning before we left for the cove.

Rain:

> Don't forget your snorkel

My phone buzzes in my hand and hope surges through me like blackcurrant syrup.

It's not her, though.

It's Lucy.

> Everything OK? Let me
> know if u need me xx

I tap on the picture above the message, hit *Unfollow* then *Block*.

Too late, Erik.

Too fucking late.

Freddie gets back and I try to eat some of his hot chips. They taste like warm leaves.

Then Thatch comes home covered in dirt and sweat, smiling wide when he sees us. 'Yous better've saved me some!' he says, grabbing the paper package off the table in front of me.

Freddie puts something else on TV. A documentary about a guy who saw aliens. I close my eyes and it's kind of real. The aliens. They're slimy and cold. They've done something to me – taken something from me. But I can't remember what.

When I wake up, the TV's off and there's a blanket covering my legs and a mug of water on the coffee table. I drink it in two swallows, mouth full of cotton and eyes half-closed, Thatch's alarm going off in the next room. It's early. Five-thirty.

I make us instant coffee. He downs his in three huge sips and tells me I should've added more sugar and milk. 'And it was too fucken *hot.*'

I tell him to fuck off. Then I ask if he wants me to make him anything for lunch.

'Nah. The guys always get burgers on Wednesday from the food truck down by the river. I'm gunna have to scab off Rodney, but. All Dad's cash is gone and I don't get paid till next fucken *week.*'

'I'll put a hundred in your account. For letting me stay.'

He says, 'You're such a fucken show off,' but he doesn't tell me not to put the money in, so I transfer it just after he goes. Then I do his dishes.

Wrist deep in soapy water, I can't call Rain again.

You have to stop calling her, Erik.

But it's like muscle memory. As soon as I've dried my hands, I'm trying again.

Only this time there's no dial-tone. Instead, an AI voice says, 'Your call could not be connected. Please check the number and try again.'

I try again.

The same thing.

It must be something to do with the reception here.

Thatch's Wi-Fi.

It'll work at home.

. . .

Nelly's yelling at me before the front door's fully open. 'Look who decided to show up! Thatch tells me you've been smoking yourself silly with Freddie. Don't get me started on him, supplying you when he knows you're emotionally vulnerable. Come on. I need your help. If you're not too *stoned*.'

I follow her into her room. She starts rummaging around in her closet and I sit in her desk chair. Lower the seat down so my knees are tucked up like a spider's. I straighten them out again, then say, 'I'm sorry, Nelly. I know I said it already, but I'm really sorry.'

Nelly turns around and rolls her eyes.

'There's something wrong with Rain's phone. I need you to call and make sure she's—'

'She's perfectly *fine*, Erik. I spoke to her ten minutes ago. She's getting ready to go to work, despite the fact that she can barely string a sentence together. You can't get through to her because she blocked your number.'

It feels like the chair's lifting up off the ground. 'Is she...' I say, swallowing. 'Is she OK?'

'Of course not! She's absolutely devastated. She's practically an *orphan* and her boyfriend just *betrayed* her. And that's not to mention the imaginary *sludge monsters* she's been seeing everywhere since New Year's!'

I thought I knew how this conversation was going to go. Nelly'd yell at me for a while, then she'd stop. I'd ask why Rain's phone wasn't working and she'd tell me. Then I'd ask her what to do. How to fix it. And she'd tell me. But now she's talking about... 'What?'

'*Sludge monsters.*' She says it slowly, like I'm an idiot. 'Black oozing figures that crawl from the shadows. She's been hallucinating, obviously. I knew she shouldn't have taken those mushrooms. It was completely the wrong time and place. You should have stopped her. You should have—'

'It was her choice! I didn't know she'd been... seeing things. I didn't know. Why didn't she tell me, if she was... I should have stopped her. You're right. Is she OK now? Is she...'

'It's none of your business! Don't lean back on my chair like that; you'll damage the mechanism. And don't *sigh*. You did this to yourself. If you're going to sulk you can do it in your own room. I'm extremely busy.'

'What do I do, Nelly? I need someone to tell me. I need you to tell me how to make it better.'

I notice her softening a little bit. Her crossed arms loosening. 'There's no way to make it better, brother. Not immediately. For now, we can pack for your trip. Mum baked a cake last night to process her emotions – you know how fond she is of Rain. I tried to tell her that monogamy is imperfect in homo-sapiens, but she still felt the need to break out the expensive cooking chocolate. We can pack for your trip, and we can have a slice of cake for breakfast.'

I'm shaking my head before I realise. I clear my throat. 'I don't feel like packing right now. Or cake. I forgot, actually. I have to go into town. Pick up a new board.'

Nelly studies my face. 'Listen to me, Erik. If you see Rain, it will only make matters—'

I get up so quickly the chair spins.

The main street's busy, so I park behind the supermarket. There are buckets of flowers outside the doors. Yellow and white and purple, wrapped in brown paper. Maybe I should buy some for Rain.

Dad used to buy Mum flowers all the time.

I leave them in their buckets, turning left onto the main street.

When I see her shop I walk faster.

Then I'm under the sign, outside, looking in expecting magic, like a kid that just shook a slow-globe.

And there she is. Inside. Holding a dress on a hanger, reaching to put it back on a hook. No customers. Just Rain, stepping back from the hanger, letting her heels drop. A sign saying *Closed* hangs in the centre of the door above another sign with opening hours. 9:00-4:30.

I check my phone. Five minutes till she opens. Then I knock. Hold my breath. She turns. Freezes. We stare at each other through that closed door for what feels like half my life. Then she walks towards me.

The click of a lock. A tinkling bell.

Nothing between us but empty air and silence.

Say something, Erik.

'Can we talk? For a minute. Please?'

She presses her lips together, letting a long breath out through her nose. Then she opens the door a little bit wider. Lets me in. Locks it behind me.

I follow her into a little beige room at the back of the shop and she stops next to a stack of boxes. Waits.

'I love you.' The words leave my mouth weak and watery, soaking into the chips in the paint and the open cardboard boxes and down into the drain of the little sink in the corner. I should have thought of something else – something better. I had the whole drive here to think. 'What happened with Lucy was the worst thing I've ever done. It was so empty, it's almost a joke. I'm almost glad it happ—'

She slaps me hard across my cheek. Her hand drops and she stares at it for a second, like it moved without her permission. 'Fuck,' she says. 'I'm sorry.'

'Don't be!' I pull my hand away from the place she slapped, to show her it's OK. My cheek's buzzing hot and my eye feels like it's watering a little bit. It feels good. 'You can do it again, if you want?'

She moves back and leans uncomfortably against the sink, arms crossing, lips tight. So tired and scared that I want to save her. From me. From the version of me that did this to her. Her voice splinters. 'Why are you here, Erik?'

'I... You blocked me before I could... You have to let me try to explain. Lucy didn't—'

'Did you come to my work to talk about *her*?'

'It wasn't what you think! It wasn't... I didn't...' I almost say *cum*, then stop myself. I move a little bit closer. Just half a step. 'I was an idiot. Selfish. So fucking stupid. But we're *each other's*. You and me. I'd stop everything for you – the tour, everything. I'd come to the city, if you wanted.'

'You hate the city.'

'Who gives a shit? I love *you*.' I reach out and touch her wrist, just above the place where her hand disappears into her other arm. Still crossed tight, I notice the jade and silver bracelet. She's wearing it. She didn't throw it out or give it away. It's there, on her skin. 'Tell me what you want, Rain. Please. I'll do it. It's *done*.'

Slowly her arms loosen. I catch her hands as they fall, soft like petals. 'I want you to go overseas. Go and win. Have fun. I'll have Nelly, and Marli, and I'll be studying, and I won't make it awkward if you come to visit. I'll give you and Nelly the place to yourselves. And one day, maybe we can be... friends.'

She makes a little noise in the bottom of her throat – like the shadow of a cry. Then she reaches for her wrist with her left hand, unhooking the little bracelet and letting it drop into her palm. She holds it out to me. Green tears on a silver chain.

'No. I gave it to you. It's yours.' But she keeps her hand stretched out and her eyes fill up with tears. She swallows.

Looks at me like I'm hurting her. So I hold out my hand, not knowing what else to do, and the tiny chain falls into it. Warm and light. I close my fingers around it. Put it carefully into my pocket. 'I'll keep it for you,' I tell her. 'I'll keep it until you want it back.'

I reach out for her then. I can't help it. I pull her into me as her chest jolts — a little sob — and her arms drift up my back and rest on my shoulder blades, not gripping, but there.

Her. Us. Me.

I kiss the top of her head, my heart pushing at my ribs like it wants to leave my body and stay with her. Tilting her face up, I can see the wetness rimming her eyes, her pink-flushed cheeks, the curve of her bottom lip.

She pulls away like I'm on fire.

Too much.

You shouldn't have tried to kiss her, Erik.

Blinking into a distant kind of focus, she pushes past me, back into the shop. I follow her, watching her flip the sign in the glass so that the word *closed* faces us instead of the road. She opens the door slowly and the sounds of the morning come into sharp focus. 'I'll see you, Erik,' she says without looking at me.

'Yeah...' I say, walking out into the heat and the noise. 'See ya, Rain.'

When I get home, Mum's in my room. My big suitcase is on the bed and there are some clothes, folded, next to it. 'I couldn't find your carry-on. Do you want to take it, or will you have enough room with your backpack and your...' Her voice changes when she looks up. I must look bad. I bring the back of my hand to my eyes and she rushes to me. 'Oh, my *baby boy*.'

I lift my shoulders, trying to shrug, but something catches in my chest and I gasp, 'I ruined it, Mum.'

She reaches up to cradle my head, bringing it down onto her shoulder. She says, 'Shh...' and that makes me cry more than I did in the car. I'm such a fucking idiot. Mum pats my back for a minute, until I calm down. Pull away. 'Come on, baby,' she says. 'Let's go into the kitchen.'

She cuts me a big piece of chocolate cake. Pours a full glass of milk. I haven't had a glass of milk in about ten years, but it tastes good. Cold.

Nelly gets home as I'm finishing it, slamming the door and calling out something about the nerve of adolescents today. Apparently some kids were throwing rocks at seagulls and wouldn't stop when she yelled at them. 'Every second person on this planet is either a *literal* criminal, or morally bankrupt. Is there any cake left, Mum? I'd like an *extremely* small piece.'

'And you'd like *me* to get it for you?'

'Well... yes.' Nelly nods.

'Yes what, Eleanor?'

My sister rolls her eyes. 'Yes *please*, obviously. Manners aren't my highest priority at the moment, Mum. I've just been abused by a cluster of degenerate children. Did *Erik* have to use *manners* in order for you to bring him a—'

'Give it a rest, Nelly!'

'I will *not,* Erik! I'll have you know—'

Mum slams the cake knife on the bench and picks up her car keys. She stomps through the kitchen, to the front door, and slides on her sandals.

'Where are you going?' Nelly asks.

'Away!' Mum calls back. 'You'll have to cut your own cake. And sort your own dinner. And put the bins out.'

Nelly waits for the door to close before saying, 'That was completely unprovoked.' She gets up and slices herself a little piece of cake, eating it at the bench.

'Where do you think Mum's gone?' I ask.

'Probably to *blow some glass*,' says my sister, slicing off another bit. She eats that second one pretty fast and cuts a third. Then she takes out the Greek yoghurt and piles a few dollops on.

'Try cutting a normal piece to begin with. And have ice-cream, not yoghurt.'

Nelly points the chocolatey knife at me, waving it around like a teacher's white-board marker. 'Protein, Erik! Perhaps you'd understand if you prioritised your own macronutrients. How many pies did you eat last week? Twenty-four? Not to mention the carpet of beer cans you and Thatch have been scattering around the Bay. Drink your milk and mind your own business.'

I fight back the urge to tell her to stop lecturing me. Have a slow sip of milk instead.

She puts the knife down. Pushes the cake away. 'I've *almost* mounted enough intelligence to approach the police. All I need now is hard evidence; what I've heard from Lucy, Brian, and a particularly gossipy worker for the State Archives would all still be considered speculation.'

'What are you talking about?'

'I conducted some light *espionage* when you were off with Freddie yesterday, and I managed to locate the property Lucy told us about. The one Frank Decker purchased for the Devil's Rangers. It's definitely the right one – there was a red sticker that said *sold*. It looks like the house is a little way back on the property, past some large sheds. I didn't quite have the nerve to open the gate and drive in. I want to make sure Abigail's there first. It's too late to take the drone out *now* — visibility would be awful — so I'm going to go back first thing in the morning and see if I can't spot something recognisably *hers*. Abigail's. Once I know for sure she's there, we can make plans for her retrieval.' Nelly smiles like she's just closed a debate.

Her expression changes to confusion when I tell her she's fucking lost it.

She flushes for a second before squaring her shoulders. 'After what you did to Rain, I'm in no position to accept your judgement. You should be thankful I'm even *talking* to you.'

'So be angry at me! Don't go snooping around some random bikie den. It's dangerous. I'm not letting you—'

'*Letting* me? Believe it or not, I'm capable of deciding for myself, Erik. Unless I'm mistaken and we've stumbled back in time a few hundred years, you do *not* have jurisdiction over my actions.' She glances, just for a second, at the bench by my elbow.

I grab the car keys so fast I bruise my knuckles.

'*Give me those,*' Nelly whispers.

I stuff them in my pocket. Take another bite of cake and sip the rest of my milk. 'You can have them back tomorrow. Arvo. When it's too late to go kill yourself.'

Nelly lets out a little eruption of rage somewhere between a scream and a bark. I won't give her the keys, no matter what she says. She knows. She goes to the fridge and takes out the Greek yoghurt and blueberries, half filling a bowl.

Then she goes back to the cake and slices off a pretty big piece, cramming it on top of the blueberries.

I don't know what to do, so I go to the garage. I do my usual workout, just a lot slower. I take breaks to stare at the wall. After that, I watch some old movies of Dad's on the big TV – *Crystal Voyage* and *The Innermost Limits of Pure Fun*.

I don't see Nelly again til late, in my room, when I'm stretching on the floor before bed. She walks in smiling. That can't be good. 'I have a proposal for you,' she says. 'A *mutually beneficial* proposal.'

I let go of my knees and my feet hit the carpet, the keys I

still haven't taken out of my pocket crashing together with the motion. 'I'm going to bed, Nel. I don't want to hear it.'

'If you come with me,' she says, leaning on the wall so casually I know it's a ploy, 'Then I'll talk to Rain. I'll use my best rhetoric, Erik. I've already started brainstorming. I'm confident I can convince her to give you another chance, or at least unblock you so that you can plead your case. All you need to do is accompany me on a leisurely drive to a recently sold property, followed by a quick drone flight. If anyone finds us, we'll simply say we're doing a project for school.'

I sit up so fast my head spins. 'What?'

'We'll say we're hobbyists, testing out our new toy! What's the worst that could happen?'

'I dunno, Nelly. We get our heads bashed in with crowbars, maybe? We'd be trespassing. They're bikies. Do you know what that means? They kill people. And Harrison's tapped. Dangerous.'

'Oh, please! I'm sure the bikies won't actually *be* there. We can operate the drone from the car! We could drive away the moment we sense danger. It's foolproof. Completely risk-free!'

I laugh.

'Isn't it worth it, Erik? For another chance with her?'

I close my eyes. Swallow. Reopen them. 'One minute, Nelly. From a *distance*. We stay in the car. And if anything feels wrong, we leave. Straight away.'

My sister's smile widens. 'Get some sleep, brother. Tomorrow is an important day!'

She pretty much skips out.

I turn off the light and lay under my sheet in the blue dark, looking at every photo I have of Rain. Some of them even manage to make me smile – like the one I took of her at graduation getting the Art award, or the one we took together under her doona at Barry's house. Clips of her learning to surf. She got up a few times, but the last time she fell she hit her head on something. Her board, I think. Thatch swears it was her own knee. She had an egg-sized bump for days after.

I stare at every picture. Every video.

I try to sleep, but my whole body aches.

PART 9

NELLY

I watch diligently for kangaroos on the side of the track. It's extremely important to be vigilant during dawn and dusk, especially on back roads, and Erik doesn't seem to be watching the bush at all. He's barely spoken since I woke him up at zero-four-hundred hours, except to try to convince me that we shouldn't go through with the plan. He insisted on driving, even though I've been here once before and he hasn't, and he's veering too far to the left; there will be grey and black dirt all over the hubcaps after this. We'll have to wash the car as soon as we get home.

'It's the next gate, Erik.' Predictably, he doesn't respond. 'Park here, before that stump. *Here!*'

'I'm parking!' he replies finally, a hysterical edge in his voice. He pulls up, closer to the gate than I would have liked. The bumper may be visible from the house.

'Reverse a few inches. The bumper is vis—'

'Let's just go into town. We can go to the bookshop. Whatever you want. I'll buy you thirty-four books. Hard backs. Let's just go. This place looks fucked.'

For a moment, I'm tempted. The morning light casts eerie shadows through the canopy and dry grey dirt puffs around my shoes the second I step out of the car. I can't believe Abigail lives here. She always hated getting her shoes dirty. She'd waste half of my hand-sanitiser trying to rub off any scuff marks.

'It's far too late to turn back now,' I tell my brother sternly. 'And I'm going to have to take off from the paddock. These trees are just far too dense for the launch.'

Erik pinches his eyes closed momentarily. 'Let's just get it over with,' he says, opening the boot and extracting the drone bag. He closes the door so carefully I barely register the sound, and passes me the bag. Placing it carefully over my shoulder, I lead the way through a small section of scrub.

The debris of sticks and leaves hasn't been tended to for at least a decade. A definite fire hazard. I shove aside what looks like a rusted old tap as we move through the stretch of malnourished trees toward cleared land, arriving at a long-fallen fence. The rusted tangles of wire and flaking posts mark the separation between bush and paddock. I stop a few metres onto what once may have been grass, taking the drone from its carry bag and assembling it atop a desiccated tree stump. Weather conditions are good, considering the time of day – a rising sun at our backs and no breeze whatsoever. The powerlines are behind us, so there's no risk there. It's so early, I'm sure Harrison and Abigail will sleep through the noise; I once witnessed Abigail sleep through her alarm for three full minutes.

'We're doing this for her,' I say.

Erik nods, steadying himself.

I'm quite efficient at setting up the drone now. I've been practicing. I extend the lower arms, then the upper two. I insert the joysticks into the remote control and power it on, followed by the drone itself. They communicate immediately.

Erik flinches at the sound of the tiny grinding engine and whispers, 'Pretty sure this is illegal.'

Using the left joystick, I lift the drone into the air. As it rises to eighty metres, the treeline comes into view over an expanse of paddock, the small dam round and dark in the corner of the screen.

'Higher,' Erik pesters. I increase my altitude slightly, looking up to the small drone in the distant sky. A hundred metres. Legally, I should be thirty metres higher, but I can't see how anyone would ever know. Besides, it's difficult enough to make out details on the screen from this altitude.

An ancient tractor is decomposing on the dry grass, its shadow extending arrow-like in the direction of Abigail's presumed location. The smaller shed appears and I attempt to place it on the aerial map I researched on real-estate listings. The larger shed should be just... *yes!*

There it is, a grey square like on a maths test, its shadow a black parallelogram. Parked next to it is what appears to be a white van. I fly lower.

With a sudden, powerful wrench, Erik wrestles the controls from my hands. I attempt to fight him off but he has far too much experience with Thatch; he uses his elbows as weapons and his leg to tip me off balance, seizes the control and continues manoeuvring so that I can't take it back.

'Erik!' I crane over his arm to watch the screen as he pivots and ducks, attempting to fly the drone higher.

A figure – scraggly and somehow familiar despite the distance – steps into range, walking across the small screen, shadow following. The figure appears to point at us, or should I say, at the drone whirring above the shed, then two things happen simultaneously: a *bang* resounds in the distance and the screen blackens.

Erik drops the controls.

He looks at me with suddenly wide eyes and rushes towards the trees, fumbling in his pocket for what I assume are our car keys. I don't move. '*Come on!* We need to—'

'You need to give me those keys, mate.'

The command comes from the treeline. A Devil's Ranger, the one with the reddish beard and hollow eyes, is stepping casually over the fallen fence, illuminated by the still-rising sun. His beard glows orange and the patch on his leather vest gleams.

In his left hand is a gun.

I've only ever seen guns in films, or on the belts of police officers where they seem equally performative; more costume than prop. This gun is neither of those things. It is dark. Black. Square. Large.

It is real.

The boundaries of my vision blur and all thought leaves my mind. I had a speech planned, in the event of discovery. All trace of it has left my memory. My voice is inaccessible.

Erik steps in front of me. 'Please,' he says quietly. 'We didn't see anything. We're just...'

'Keys. And phones.' Moving closer, the man flicks the gun an inch or two upward, as if ticking a box in the air.

'Please,' Erik whispers.

'Are you deaf, kid?'

Erik shakes his head, taking the car keys and phone out of his pocket, tossing them onto the ground near the man's feet. The outlaw picks them up slowly, bending at his knees and keeping his eyes fixed on us. He rises. Then he points the gun directly at Erik's chest.

'You too,' he says, referring to me while staring at my brother. I dig through the front pocket of the drone bag and extract my mobile, tossing it on the ground the way Erik did so that the man can lower his gun and we can leave. Surely now he'll let us go. But the weapon stays where it is, its wide black eye pointing at Erik's heart.

'Passcode?' asks the bearded Ranger.

'Nineteen-fifty-two,' I say immediately, my throat dislodging at the simple request. 1952. The year Rosalind Franklin captured the first photograph of deoxyribonucleic acid.

The outlaw lifts the phone to his face, typing in the number, as arrhythmic footfalls announce the arrival of another person. Frank Decker. He is pelting towards us in a way that would normally be ridiculous – knees rising, legs turned out in a fashion reminiscent of a wooden puppet from the Seventeenth Century – but isn't under present circumstances. He's waving the crushed remains of our drone. 'I got it!' he pants, presenting the crooked piece of metal as if expecting praise.

He does not receive any. 'You left Harrison in the workshop?' the bearded bikie asks flatly, his eyes and gun still trained on my brother.

Frank's smile falters. 'No. He's on a run. I told him there had to be two of us here, but he went out anyway to get the—'

'You're telling me...' The outlaw uses his free hand to wipe the space under his nose, agitation clear in the set of his jaw. 'You left the workshop empty?'

Frank takes a step back. 'I'll go now!' he says, startled, turning and hustling back to the shed. 'I'll run!'

The bikie pauses to contemplate something before swivelling and firing his weapon. I squeeze my eyes shut and reach for Erik, clutching his side. When I look again, grey dust is still rising from the patch of soil where the bullet landed, a few metres behind Frank Decker's awkwardly sprinting form.

The bikie returns the muzzle of his gun to my brother. 'Where was I?' he asks, as if casually interrupted while conversing with a friend. He lifts my phone to his face and scrolls for a few moments. 'Eleanor Everson... Friends call you Nelly. This is your brother, Erik, and the two of you live at number 4, Beera Way, Foxhead Bay. Nice street. Big house, I bet. I know the area well. Get a lot of jobs down here.' He puts the phone in the pocket of his vest.

'Please,' Erik says. 'My sister had nothing to do with it. It's mine. The drone. I flew it. Not her.'

The man only smiles. There is something unnerving happening in his eyes. I have no words to describe what I'm observing, except that it appears as if something is missing. Something that I'm used to seeing in people's eyes is not present in his. The hairs on the back of my neck stand on end.

'*Please...*' Erik repeats, in a voice slightly higher than usual. A voice more reminiscent of his ten-year-old self.

The man releases a derisive out-breath. 'That way,' he grunts, pointing his gun through a dense patch of scrub.

Scenarios fly through my head. Episodes of television. Hostage situations. But those were all in cities in America. None of them were here. I never thought it would be possible for something like this to happen here. And now, in the face of it, I am helpless. Stupid. *Frozen.*

Erik takes my hand and pulls me forward before dropping back, just behind me, the gun now fixed on his back. My body begins shaking as we walk across the short stretch of forgotten pasture to the treeline. I'm shaking so violently I lose my grip on my brother's hand.

I look back, expecting to stop, but the bikie gestures forward and, with effortless authority, issues a command. '*In.*'

I step over a tree trunk, submerged by bush. I want to hold Erik's hand again. I want him next to me, not behind me. I need to see that he's alright. I try to tune in to his breathing, but sticks crack and a cockatoo shrieks. The outlaw's boots thud behind us and I use every piece of restraint within me not to look back; to keep going, deeper into this forbidding, parched forest.

Eventually, Erik and I arrive at a dried up creek bed. We can't walk any further. The edges are steep, pitching down towards a channel that appears to have been dry for at least two decades.

I turn. The man's gun hasn't wavered, though his face is red from walking and there are beads of sweat on his forehead. 'Go on.' he says, using the gun to point first at me, then at the ditch.

'It's OK,' Erik tells me. 'It's like the dunes. Just more sticks. Let's slide down, yeah? It's easy.'

I nod, my teeth rattling so powerfully I worry they may crack, which could compromise forensic attempts to identify me. Unless, of course, the bikies remove dental evidence from the scene. They're *organised* criminals, after all. They'll scatter our remains across the property. Throw our ashes into both dams. The police will never find us. Our friends will never see us again. Our mum. Our dad.

Erik moves past me and begins to slide down the steep, dirty embankment. He gains momentum, flying forward and crashing on his hands and knees into a nest of fallen branches. They snap one after another, the way popcorn does in the microwave.

Erik stands, pink scratches blooming on his palms and forearms. With no thought other than an instinct to be with him, I slide violently down the sandy ramp. Erik catches me before I can imitate his landing, though a sharp pain still travels from my ankles through my shins. He holds my arms tightly, staring into my eyes as if attempting to communicate telepathically. And, strangely, he succeeds. *I love you, too,* I tell him with my eyes, shaking under the steadiness of his grip.

'ON YOUR KNEES.' The Devil's Ranger's voice blasts from above, his command ricocheting up the walls of the creekbed.

I am crying. I look down as some part of me spins away. It's as if I'm levitating.

'It's OK,' Erik whispers.

I watch myself move from above. My low, yellow ponytail. My shaking body. The puff of grey sand where my knees hit the ground. I don't feel the rubble or the sticks. I'm holding onto my brother. The first person I ever held.

When I hear the bang, I wait for my body to fall.

But it doesn't.

And neither does Erik's.

I land back in my skin.

What I heard couldn't have been a gunshot. It was dull. Low. A resonant *thud*.

'Abigail?' Erik says.

And there she is. Abigail is standing over the bearded man, holding a rusted tap attached to a piece of pipe. She holds it uncertainly, the way she would have held a bat in Phys Ed, her face misshapen by surprise. 'What the fuck are you two doing here?' she asks, walking carefully around our would-be-executioner's prostrate form.

'We came to save you,' I say.

Abigail releases a peel of laughter, before clapping a hand over her mouth. When she is sure the outlaw hasn't regained consciousness, she says 'You did a shit job,' and prods him lightly with her toe. She has bare feet – almost unheard of – and is wearing a pair of faded black leggings and a cheap beige singlet; nothing like her usual style. She is extremely thin. Her hair, which she used to condition and mask and style religiously, is lifeless. Her once-clear skin is marked and faded.

With a jolt, I notice a large bruise on her chest, just above her clavicle, as well as a series of smaller marks on her upper arms. The traces of hard-pressing fingers. She attempts to hide the marks with a tilt of her neck, her free hand covering her decolletage. Her self-consciousness is unrecognisable.

After pushing ourselves up, Erik and I climb silently, digging our nails into the dirt, tugging at the roots of half-dead trees. His hands leave bloody marks on the wood and leaves. My feet slip, but somehow I don't lose any ground or any speed. Something in the very centre of me pushes upwards, and my body follows, over the ridge of crumbling dirt, onto the flat expanse of dry, crunching undergrowth.

A trace of her old attitude emerging, Abigail pushes back her hair and prods the fallen outlaw with the rusted tap. 'He's a total fuckwit, this guy. Is he dead? Did I...?'

Leaning slightly, I examine the broad black expanse of the man's back until I notice the rise and fall of breath. 'Alive,' I confirm.

Erik clears his throat. 'Our phones... They're in his...'

Abigail passes him the tap and, without flinching, yanks the man's jacket open and pulls the phones and keys from his pocket. She holds them out to Erik, who passes the tap back to her. I sense a strange energy between them. A silent acknowledgement.

Then Abigail asks, 'Should we, like, tie him up?'

I nod, brusquely, composing myself. With a slight twitch in my index finger, I take the gun from the bearded man's hand. 'Give me your shirt,' I tell Erik. I pull the scrunchie from my ponytail, and, handing it to Abigail, instruct her to, 'Tie his hands together,' while I point the gun at the man's back.

Abigail heaves his arms and his hands together, wrapping

the scrunchie twice around his wrists. It's tight. With any luck, it will cut off the circulation. I hold my hand out for Erik's shirt and realise it's still on his body; his fingers on the hem, his mouth open slightly. 'Erik!' I say, prompting him to startle and quickly take it off.

I rip it along the seam, pull the large rectangle of fabric lengthways and roll it up, before knotting it tightly around the man's ankles. I step back, examining my work.

Abigail gives the man another prod with her foot, firmer than the first. 'You guys should get out of here,' she says, covering herself with folded arms. 'There are others.'

'You're coming with us. You have to get out of here, Abigail. It's not safe for—'

'I can't just run away, Eleanor. This is where I live. Harrison's my boyfriend. I... love him.'

Bewildered, I gesture frantically at the scene around us. 'Harrison is not a safe person for you to be around. You *know* that. You have to come. Now. Immediately.'

'He loves me. He's just been through a lot. We're good, when it's working.'

The tied man lets out a heavy breath and I speak in hushed tones, despite having the gun. 'You *think* you love him. But methamphetamines have a negative impact on your—'

'I'm not using drugs! I mean... I *did* it, like, once. I didn't like it. It made me feel... dizzy. Harrison barely does it. It's not what you think. He's not a druggie.'

'He's working with them, isn't he? *Manufacturing.* Do you have any evidence? Any product we could bring in?'

'I'm not stealing from my boyfriend!'

Erik places a hand on my upper arm and I bite my tongue. When he speaks, it's in a tone much gentler than mine. 'You don't deserve this, Abigail. I know you... I'm sorry people have...

That I... You deserve a lot better than this. Come with us. Give it a week. A day. If he loves you, he can let you go for a day.'

Abigail looks back over her sagging shoulder, her arm weighed down by the pipe, towards the sheds and the house. 'All of my stuff's inside. And Doja...'

'We don't have time to—'

'He'll kill her! If he sees I'm gone, he'll—'

'Alright!' I say, flustered, gripping the gun as the bikie's fingers twitch. 'You have two minutes. Two minutes to gather... *Doja*... and whatever else you might need. Erik: Go and get the car and meet us at the front of the house.'

Erik turns and sprints through the bush, a cacophony of snaps and rustles erupting around him, while Abigail and I run back across the dry field. The gun is heavy and warm. I make sure to point it down, fingers as far from the trigger as I can manage. Abigail slows at the large shed and I match her pace as clanging and mumbling from inside become audible through the sheet-metal walls.

Frank Decker must be inside. My grip on the gun tightens. We tiptoe from the shed to the back door of the dilapidated farmhouse where I pause, raising the gun. In a voice that sounds slightly tinged with television drama, I say, 'I'll cover you.'

Abigail flies into the house and I wait, breathing heavily, sweat sticking my shirt to my underarms. Abigail appears after approximately thirty seconds, holding her curler, a brightly-coloured shopping bag bulging with clothes, and a ragdoll kitten.

I can't stand pets. The urination, the shedding, the constant drain on resources and the environment.

But there's no time to protest. Abigail holds the cat to her chest and hurries past me along the side of the house, below a dilapidated scratch of shade cloth. Something registers suddenly in my peripheral vision — movement below the crooked beams of the patio. As if some subliminal training has been activated, I turn robotically and point the gun.

At *Sam the Pup*.

He smiles. Descending lightly from the porch and striding towards us, he says, 'You're full of surprises.'

'I'll shoot you!' I answer. 'I *will*. I'm familiar with the mechanics.' I eye the gun, then his face, wondering if I'm in any way capable of pinching the trigger beneath my index finger.

Sam laughs. 'I'm sure you are, Nelly. But you've got the safety on.'

Naively, I look down. He ducks and lunges towards me, snatching the gun from my hand.

Abigail screams.

I cover my face with my arms, but Sam is retreating. 'Relax!' he says, sliding the gun into the back of his jeans. 'I'm not going to hurt you. Where are the others?'

Abigail begins to speak but I interrupt her. 'Abigail had absolutely no knowledge of our – *my* – plan to come here. I swear. I came here because I knew that she was in danger, and I had to do something, and if you shoot me because of it, well, I suppose that's a price I'm going to have to pay, but don't for a moment think that she had anything to do with it.'

Sam the Pup is still smiling, while Abigail stands immobile, clutching her kitten.

I continue my argument. 'I came here for my friend. I didn't want any trouble – it's your *colleagues* who caused the problem. As for their whereabouts: Frank is still banging around cluelessly in that shed, Harrison's out, and your friend is lying by the dried-up creek. He's bound with a shirt and a scrunchie and seems to have a concussion. If you go and help him and forget you ever saw us, I could... owe you.' The words fall with a significance I'm not sure I intended.

Sam licks his lips, then frowns. 'You knocked out *Cal*? How did you manage that?' He seems not to care a great deal. Perhaps he'd be glad to be rid of his lurking, dark-eyed comrade.

'With careful planning and ingenuity,' I respond.

'You think I'd let you three drive away after knocking down my brother in arms and getting a good hard look at the property?'

My heart drops when I realise. *Three*. He knows Erik is here.

'You know what?' Sam continues. 'I don't think you'll make any trouble, Nelly. I know where you live. Who your friends are. And this... club I'm part of... we've got a lot of connections. More than you'd think. This town's ours. The city's ours. You say anything, to anyone, and things are going to get really hard for you. And you...' He steps towards Abigail. 'If I didn't know what a unit Harrison was, I wouldn't let you go. But I know him. You stay away from guys like that from now on. Don't take his calls. You hear me? Go home to your parents and tell them to keep you inside.'

Hoisting her kitten and her bag of clothes, Abigail turns her back on the little farmhouse and rushes towards the trees. I pivot, ready to follow her, but my name sounds abruptly — *savagely* — from Sam the Pup's mouth.

I turn to face him.

The devilish glint is gone from his eyes. 'I'll see you in the city,' he breathes.

Without waiting to be dismissed, I sprint after Abigail, the car waiting for us on the dusty track, open doors and idling engine. Erik doesn't wait for us to do up our seatbelts; he speeds away, only slowing to turn onto the highway.

His hands shiver slightly on the steering wheel and his breath is still heavy. My heart pounds.

You're alive, Eleanor.

We're all alive.

We drive for at least ten minutes before Abigail speaks. 'I can't go home like this...' she says, looking down at her beige singlet while her kitten, perched on her shoulder, scratches at the headrest. She begins to dig through her bag of clothing, scattering pieces across the back seat as she fishes out a long-sleeved, high-necked shirt.

I stifle my annoyance. I suppose we all need to clean ourselves up before going home. I'm covered in sand and sweat. Erik is still shirtless, scratches and cuts over his arms and stomach.

'We'll go to Dad's house,' I say, a plan forming quickly. 'He's at work, but the spare key is on top of the utility box. We have some clothes there. Erik – we'll go to Dad's, alright? *Erik... Hello?* I need verbal confirmation that you're going to—'

Erik brakes and my body jams against the seatbelt. He indicates, sliding too quickly onto the gravel shoulder before coming to a complete stop. A small truck rolls past, flicking dust and pebbles, its horn blasting in protest along the road ahead. 'What did you do that for? If you can't respect the rules of the road, get out of the driver's seat and let me—'

'*Jesus fucking Christ*, Eleanor!' Erik's voice catches, rough and exhausted. 'That guy almost *killed* us. Why do you... Why can't you... We almost *died*. We were dead...' Another truck flies past and he loses the will to sit upright. He bends forward as if rehearsing the brace position, head on the lower half of the steering wheel and fingers twined behind his head.

We almost died.

I almost killed him.

Despising the tears collecting in the corners of my eyes, I tell him, 'We can't think about that at the moment. We need to get changed and wash off this blood and... We need to take care of Abigail, and we all need to hydrate. We can process the rest of it when we have time.'

Dazed, Erik restarts the engine, indicating back onto the highway. 'You owe me so fucking much for that, Nelly.' In a whisper, he adds, 'I *told* you...'

Dad's pathetically barren street seems (for the first time) a welcome refuge. I'm far less judgemental of the oil-stained pavement outside the garage and the lack of vegetation in any of the garden beds – less critical of his choice to leave a spare key in such an obvious location. With Erik and Abigail huddled behind me, I reach for the key, finding it with my fingers amongst the grit on top of the fuse box. No time to waste, I insert it quickly into the lock, twisting the metal and opening the door in one movement.

I am confronted by the most traumatising thing I've seen all day.

On my dad's generic grey fabric sofa, below the dim light of an uncovered bulb, is my mother. She is completely naked, lying more-or-less on her back, with her legs turned at a slight angle. My dad is penetrating her from above, his face contorted into a pained expression, his hips thrusting powerfully.

It takes me a fraction of a second to absorb all of this before my parents are immobilised by shock. I scream. Mum screams also. Erik reaches past me and slams the door. He rushes back towards the street and I hear him mutter, '*What the fuck?*'

I make out a similar sentence in my dad's voice from the other side of the door.

Abigail snorts. 'Should we...?' she asks, smirking as if holding back a laugh.

I have no idea how to reply.

Then my dad's front door opens slowly, revealing my mother. She's fully dressed, thank god, though her cheeks and chest still show signs of physical exertion. 'You told me you were going to Bandler Beach for breakfast!' she admonishes. 'Why are you... Where is your shirt, Erik? You're *bleeding*!'

Erik steps back, avoiding eye contact.

'Whadya mean, *bleeding*?' says Dad, still pulling up his fly and attempting to cover a final strip of private flesh at his lower belly. 'What've you kids...? You've got dirt all over ya!'

'We... fell!' I answer, defiantly. 'We took the drone out to some pastures to film... Erik. Abigail and I were helping him capture some footage of the summer, for a new edit, but we fell.'

'He took his shirt off for the photo,' Abigail says, suppressing a smile. 'He thought it'd be hot to do a shirtless one.'

Mum gasps and Dad says, 'Jesus, mate. A grungy photo's not worth hurtin' yourself over. Did ya at least get some good footage before you dove into a ditch?'

Mum tuts at him. 'Come in, babies. You too, Abigail. Let's get you cleaned up.'

Once inside, Erik walks directly to the bathroom and closes the door firmly behind him.

Mum flinches slightly at the sound. 'Would you like an iced coffee, girls? Dad's got some—'

'No I would not like an *iced coffee*! I would *like* to know why I just saw the two of you fornicating wildly on that disgusting sofa!'

Mum and Dad share a guilty look.

'I'll have an iced coffee...' says Abigail.

The shower turns on in Dad's bathroom as Mum begins bustling around the kitchen, taking out glasses and a spoon. Dad retrieves a jar of freeze-dried instant coffee and a bottle of milk, which he smells covertly before passing to Mum.

Apparently there's nothing left to do but stand in the awkward silence drinking iced beverages while my brother has an *unethically* long shower. By the time he reemerges, dressed in his dirty jeans and an oversized lilac hoodie I left in the spare room, I've almost finished my drink. '*Finally*,' I say. 'Other people need showers *too*, Erik.'

'You first, Abigail,' Mum interjects. 'There are towels below the sink.'

When Abigail is gone, I whirl on my parents. 'I am absolutely appalled. I don't even know where to begin. You were supposed to be at *work*, Dad. The two of you were supposed to be getting a *divorce*. And we find you here, in the middle of the day, in the throes of sweaty, rough... It's disgusting! And to go about it in secret, like a couple of teenagers. Where's your car, Mum? I suppose you parked it around the corner, to avoid controversy?'

Erik groans, pulling the hood down over his face as he walks out into the sweltering courtyard.

'It's not the time, baby,' Mum says, stroking Doja, who has made herself comfortable in an empty fruit bowl on the kitchen bench. 'We'll have a family meeting later today and discuss everything. I understand your...'

'REPULSION?' I shriek.

'Sweet'eart,' says Dad. 'What two grown adults do in the privacy of their own—'

'Home? This isn't a home! This is a lonely little den with no character and no frying pans! You live here because you *ruined* our home.'

'Yeah... Yeah I did. I'm sorry, kiddo. I'm gunna keep doin'

my best to put it all right. I'll just ah... I'm gunna go bring the bins in.'

Dad is in the courtyard with Erik when Abigail emerges, standing a few metres from the kitchen bench on the other side of the fly-screen. 'Is it all closed-in out there?' Abigail asks, plucking the cat out of the fruit bowl and holding it to her chest.

Dad nods. 'Yeah. Just watch her on the lattice by the fence there.'

Abigail and her animal join Erik and Dad and I finally have my turn in the shower, cleaning myself briskly with a bright-blue shower gel which smells vaguely of aluminium. I dress, then recite my morning affirmations in the mirror. My voice is lacklustre, the statements falling weakly from my lips.

Erik and Abigail are hovering near the door when I come out. 'Finally,' Erik says, clutching the car keys. 'Let's go.'

'We'll see you at home!' Mum calls to our exiting backs.

I walk Abigail to her front door, her sister Bianca opening it before we have a chance to knock. Abigail phoned her from the car, so she knew we were coming. The scene is emotional and I'm far to mentally fatigued to linger in the foyer with them. I leave immediately, promising to return tomorrow.

Erik drives for approximately two minutes, making three turns, and we're home.

Mum and Dad are waiting at the kitchen bench. Dad clears his throat and dry washes his hands. Mum turns and walks into the pantry.

Quite uncharacteristically, my brother is the first to speak. 'Let's get this over with, yeah?' The words buzz ominously as Erik and I seat ourselves on stools across from our parents, Mum depositing a bag of popcorn on the bench between us.

'I spose you two kids have a few *questions* about what you saw,' Dad begins.

'Yes,' I agree bitterly. 'For instance: Did you use protection, or will we have to worry about a post-separation bastard sibling?'

Erik's face pinches.

Dad looks at Mum, who answers carefully, 'You don't need to worry about *that*, Eleanor. I know it's strange, but... your dad and I have managed to... We're in a very good place at the moment, kids. I know it might be difficult to process, but—'

'So, what?' Erik laughs emptily, staring at the window opposite him. 'You forgive him? After everything.'

'Ricky. Your mum's—'

'Don't answer for her,' Erik interjects. 'And don't call me *Ricky*.'

Mum considers her response. 'We were planning to tell you, soon, that it may be a possibility that we might... reconcile. We didn't want to say anything too early, in case. But I love your dad. We've had a life together. We have both of you.'

Erik's arms tighten over my jumper.

Then Dad growls, 'I've been a *mongrel*. I don't deserve your mum, that's for fucken certain. We weren't that much older than you kids the first time I saw her. I had to beg her to give me a go, and for some reason she bloody did. Best thing that ever happened to me. Other than you two.'

'So... this is where you've been disappearing to?' I ask Mum, deducing the reason for her absences. 'You've both been lying about your whereabouts for months, have you? How irresponsible! What if there'd been an emergency?'

Mum puts down her kernel of popcorn and sighs. 'Let's give this some more time, baby. You've had a busy morning and you're not quite ready to accept the news. Dad and I will pop out to the workshop – I have some accounting to do – while the two of you think. Chat.'

'Will you two be right on your own?' Dad asks sheepishly, raising his inner eyebrows and scratching the back of his neck.

'*Please*,' I scoff. 'We're used to it these days. Try not to have *intercourse* while you're there, if it's not too much trouble.'

Mum and Dad's absence unleashes a heavy silence into the house. Despite my last words to them — the betrayal and disgust I still feel — I want badly for them both to come back. I've never felt more vulnerable than I do at this moment.

Eleanor Everson... Friends call you Nelly. This is your brother, Erik, and the two of you live at number 4, Beera Way, Foxhead Bay...

A prickling sensation runs up my arms and I begin to shake again.

It's just norepinephrine and cortisol, Eleanor. Stress hormones.

You are perfectly safe.

I launch off the stool and run to the front door, locking it.

'Nelly,' Erik says, as I dash to the back door. 'They're not going to—'

'Be quiet and check the garage!' I scream, my shaking hand fumbling on the lock. My fingers slide on the latch, hopelessly, my knees shaking as the muscles in my legs weaken. All of me weakens. I grasp the door handle as the rest of my body slides uselessly to the ground. Erik is there. As he always is. He takes my hand from the door handle and sits on the ground next to me, holding my fingers, and I gasp, 'I'm so sorry!' before losing my breath completely.

You're out of control, Eleanor.

'Shh...' he says. 'We're safe. No one's coming. We're safe.'

Through panicked inhales, I apologise again. 'I'm so... *sorry*... Erik... I shouldn't have... I was... I almost...'

I'm fairly sure I'm hyperventilating.

'It's OK, Nelly,' my brother whispers, taking my face in his hands. He strokes my fringe with his thumbs as I continue to gasp, emitting an asinine *hah-hah-hah* sound in my panic. For minutes, this goes on, until the noises finally stop and my breathing finally slows. Then he says, his gaze fixed on the hardwood beneath us, 'We found Abigail. You did. And you were right, Nelly... She needed us to do that. So... it was worth it.' He lets his hands drop before lifting his eyes.

I focus intently on them and whisper the thought I've been attempting to suppress. 'What if they're coming? What if they're coming to *kill* us? They might want to finish the—'

'Nah. They fucked up, Nelly. That guy was tapped. He clicked. Made a mistake. I think Abigail did him a favor when she knocked him out.'

I consider it. 'Yes... I suppose it wouldn't have been an approved kill... Could have attracted heat... Upset his superiors... Still, it's easy for *you* to be so confident, when you're leaving tomorrow.'

He bites his lip. 'Maybe I should put my flight off a few days.'

'Don't be ridiculous. I'll have Thatch. He can stay in your room. And I should be able to convince Rain to stay over again, once the dust has settled.'

'Yeah.' He squeezes the muscle between my thumb and index finger as my heartrate returns to normal. He lets go, before mumbling, 'I'm really gunna miss you.'

A wet cry escapes my throat.

'I love you, Nelly.'

.   .   .

Thatch arrives in a racket of slamming doors and bellows.

'You're a fucken fibber, Nel. A bloody tricker. You said ya wouldn't go after the bikies. You bloody promised. And then Erik rings me up when I'm *still at fucken work* just to tell me you've just about *got murdered*.' Thatch throws himself onto the sofa between us, concrete dust puffing. 'How's Abs then? She get back home OK?'

Erik answers, 'Yeah. She'll be OK.'

Thatch's offence drops and his tone changes to excitement. 'Nelly held the gun, ya said? Such a fucken rebel. You're a bad bloody influence, Nel. I've been sayin' it for years.'

In my exhaustion, I can't think of a counter argument. Perhaps I *am* a rebel.

A loud noise echoes through the house and I clutch Thatch's forearm. A moment later, I realise it's knocking.

The bearded man is at the door. His gun is pointed.

Pulling his arm from my grasp, Thatch rushes jovially towards the sound, announcing, 'It's for me!'

Erik and I look questioningly at one another.

Thatch re-enters the room with Rain, who must have come straight from work; she's forgotten to remove the lanyard of keys from her neck. They rattle against a light-blue crocheted blouse, which she's wearing with her plaid skirt.

'Hi,' she says. Erik stands abruptly, pulling the lilac hood off his head. He motions as if to embrace her, then backs away. Her arms are crossed, her face set in caution. 'I won't stay for long...' she says. 'Doe's just having a swim and then we're going to see Pop.'

'You can come back here afterwards,' Erik says. 'Stay. In Nelly's room, I mean.'

Rain shakes her head, eyes on the hardwood floor, and replies with a simple, 'No.'

'Do you want a Ribena?' Erik persists. 'I think there's still some cake in the kitchen if you—'

'No. I just needed to make sure you were OK. You and Nelly. I came as soon as I finished. Thatch said...'

'I'm certain he exaggerated,' I say, leaning back and crossing my left leg over my right. I provide a concise summary of our morning. Rain listens intently, a hand resting against her throat. Her pupils are dilated, glistening with what appears to be fear.

'We're perfectly fine!' I assure her.

'But they know who you are? They could come after you?' Her eyes linger on Erik.

'They won't,' I insist, as much for my own benefit as hers. 'They're not *unreasonable*... We didn't acquire any footage. We didn't steal any drugs, or money. We simply collected our friend.'

'Speaking of money,' Rain says, reaching into her bag. For a moment I think she's holding a banknote; then I realise it's a scratchcard.

'I *told* you they were habit forming. What did I say, Thatcher? It's a terrible idea for a—'

'I won,' she confesses bashfully. 'On the ticket Thatch got me for Christmas. I found it this morning in my pocket.'

Thatch whoops and punches the air. 'How much? If it's more than fifty bucks you've gotta give me half. That's the rules.'

Rain smiles crookedly. 'It's more than fifty bucks.'

'Well, how much is it then?' I press. 'We haven't got all—'

'A hundred and fifty. Thousand.' She utters the last word softly, in a tone I can only describe as *embarrassment*.

Thatch stumbles backwards.

'That's amazing!' says Erik. Hesitating for a moment, he holds up his hand in the air in front of her.

Rain slaps it softly, before moving her hand behind her

back and holding it there. She turns to Thatch. 'I want to give you half. Seventy-five.'

He shakes his head, dumbstruck. 'You're not fucken serious...'

Rain nods.

'Nah... Ya can't've read it right. Gimme a look. Show me it. Sometimes people read 'em wrong.' He holds out his palm and she deposits the card into it. Thatch examines it carefully. He looks at Erik, then at me. Then at Rain. 'It's too much, mate. Just gimme ten grand. That'd be fucken—'

'I'm giving you half,' Rain says with another timid smile. 'It's the rules.'

Thatch surges toward her. In one movement, he lifts her off her feet, holding her above his head in a tight bear hug while releasing a carnal scream unlike anything I've ever heard. He hoists her – her entire body – over his shoulder, before dropping her on the couch to land upon his concrete dust. He throws his arms in the air and lets out another scream. 'This is bloody nuts! I'm gunna get a ute! And go to Bali! And get a new board and a bottle of that French shit. Champagne. I'm gunna—'

'You're going to budget carefully and invest wisely,' I caution him.

He strides towards me, grabbing Erik's hand on the way and dragging us into a three-way-embrace. 'I'm so fucken glad yous didn't die!' he exclaims tearily into our necks.

Then he releases us, only to knock Rain down a second time, screaming something unintelligible at the top of her head. Her hair is completely ruined by the time he lets go. She pats it uselessly, her gaze moving to my brother as she slides the scratchcard carefully back into her pocket. 'Can we...?'

Erik's 'yeah!' is desperately earnest.

Naturally, as soon as the two of them have walked through

the front door, Thatch and I rush to the trophy / yoga room window, peering around Mum's protea bush to watch them. They stare at each other for a minute, somewhere between smiling and crying. Rain shrugs. Erik says something. She seems to gather herself before replying, speaking for slightly longer than he did. He moves to her and they fall into a long embrace. Ten seconds, easily. They separate when Doe's sedan appears in the driveway.

When Erik wanders back in, Thatch and I are arranged casually on the sofa, looking at him expectantly. He shakes his head, the loss written on his face. 'I'm happy for you, Thatch. I just need a second.'

Despite my carefully compiled anecdotal and statistical evidence that Rain should take Erik back, she will not concede. 'Nelly,' she says, twenty-one minutes into our phone call. 'You need to listen. I understand what you're saying. I get that it's complicated. But it's not just about Lucy. It was never going to last between me and Erik. He's too... We're too... different.'

'You're the same in the ways that matter! You're both kind and gentle and quite smart and occasionally funny. And you're in *love*.'

'You don't believe in love, Everson.'

'I believe in you and my brother, *Douglass*. I believe in *science*. Are you familiar with any studies in error-related negativity? It's been proven that neural networks adapt after mistakes, and people can *genuinely—*'

'Nelly—'

'Let me finish! I haven't even arrived at my graph. I have a graph here charting Erik's emotional wellbeing over the last two years. I'm going to email it to you now, and you'll see a clear correlation between your presence and his happiness.'

'Please.'

'We almost *died*! And my brother is still more concerned with *you* than anything else. He *hates* himself for hurting you.' I sniff angrily, fighting the emotion in my voice.

There is muffled movement on her end, suggesting a slow change of position. I hear chickens, and assume she's sitting outside on the small wooden stool by their pen.

She breathes out contemplatively. I resist moving on to my next point and wait for her to speak. 'I don't know what happened to me after I ate that rocky road. I used to be able to hold things in... It's like someone unlocked the doors and threw away the key. Everything – all the darkest things – are rushing out. Do you want to know something really pathetic?' She laughs. 'After your brother came to Doe's house and told me – after it happened – I thought I was going blind. I couldn't see properly. Literally, Eleanor. Everything blurred. The parts of my brain in charge of sight just gave up.'

'I've heard that can happen with extreme stress. You really should have called me or Doe to take you to the hospital.'

'I shouldn't have to go to the hospital because my boyfriend cheated on me! It's not normal. I'm not normal. I'm... broken. I can't be with him because I love him too much and I'm too fucked up to cope with things like a normal... like any other person.'

'With the right medication and more talk therapy, I'm sure you could maintain a loving and healthy—'

'I'm not *medicating* myself just to be with him! You need to leave it now, OK? You need to let us move on.' I scan my notes desperately for a useful rebuttal, but I know it's futile. 'I have to go help with dinner...' Rain says. 'I'll call you tomorrow.'

I blink rapidly, responding with a tight-lipped, 'Mmhmm.'

'I'm glad you're OK,' she says. Then she hangs up.

It takes me a significant amount of time to absorb my failure. When I'm certain I'm not going to cry, I leave my bedroom, knocking on Erik's slightly ajar door before entering. He and Thatch are kneeling beside his three-quarter-full suitcase. 'We heard most of it through the wall,' Erik says.

'I'm sorry. I tried my absolute hardest.'

He nods. 'Not your fault.'

Attempting to be helpful, I'm sure, Thatch adds: 'Least you're not dead in a bikie ditch! And I'm fucken rich. I can come visit you overseas! Root for ya! Life's good, mate. We're healthy and we've both got jobs and heaps of mates and food and the beach. And now you'll be free and clear for the trip, eh? Think about all the parties! All the chicks!'

Erik doesn't answer.

Shortly after that, Thatch leaves with a huge smile and a hard slap of the door-pane. 'See ya in Indo, dickhead!' he calls down the hall.

There isn't time for Erik and I to debrief; Mum arrives home a few minutes later. She hovers while I help Erik pack the remainder of his suitcase, offering us snacks and giving him reminders like: 'Don't ride on the bike paths at night,' and 'Don't drink at strangers' houses,' and 'Make sure you put sunscreen on your ears, too.' Before she goes to bed, she gives him a long, tight hug. 'I've set my alarm for five-thirty. I'll make you both a coffee and some toast before you leave for the airport.'

'Thanks, Mum,' Erik replies.

At eleven-fifteen – six hours before we need to leave the house – he locks his suitcase and board bag, and I help him drag them to the front door. I follow him back to his room and we lie down side-by-side, both staring at the ceiling.

'I've been thinking,' Erik says. 'You should call that guy. Sam. Do it when Thatch is with you. Say you're sorry or something. If they want money, I've got some saved.'

'I'm not giving an outlaw gang your *money*. You were right earlier... They've got more to lose than us. I'll tell him we're going to stay quiet. That we don't want any trouble.' We're both quiet for a few minutes. 'Did you see Dad's pubic hair? There was grey in it.'

Slowly, Erik slides a pillow over his head, groaning. Eventually he rolls onto his side, facing the wall. I know he's thinking, so I wait. 'I thought we were so different,' he mumbles. 'Me and Dad.'

'You *are* so different. Your temperaments couldn't be more opposed.' I'm about to comment on assumed differences in pubic hair, but I stop myself, stifling a laugh.

'I'm not talking about temperaments,' Erik says, rolling onto his back again and adjusting his pillow. 'I'm talking about choices. He's a cheater. I'm a cheater. It's the same thing.'

Suppressing another laugh, I say, 'You're not a *cheater*, Erik. You're a human being. A human being driven in part by animalistic impulses which you must fight to overcome. Dad is also a human being, I'll grant – but nothing like you. Really, you're much more like Mum. It's *me* who inherited Dad's desire for control and status. I'm well aware of it, and not ashamed in the slightest! You and Mum on the other hand... You only want to *love* things. I'm not sure I'm capable of that. Even with Freddie, I...'

Oh, fluffing fluff.

Now you've done it, Eleanor.

My brother's face swivels to point directly, and accusingly, at the side of my own. 'You. You're the one Freddie's been... Since *Leavers*?'

'Since *well* before Leavers.'

'For fuck's sake,' Erik mutters. 'He's one of my best friends, Nelly. You could've told me.'

'We were two consenting adults, Erik. I don't need to tell you every detail about every one of my sexual experiences.'

'Jesus, Eleanor! I don't want to know about it. Just tell me next time, if you're fucking one of my friends.' He shifts again, uncomfortably. 'You can do what you want. Just... Don't keep stuff from me. Not if it's important.'

I fold my arms across my chest, examining the bar of moonlight above the curtains. Inhaling for fortitude, I admit, 'There's just one more thing.'

He lets his head drop back dramatically before grumbling, 'Yeah?'

As casually as possible, I say, 'I know the identity of Rain's father. I've known for over a week now, but I've been speculating for months. I contacted a few music venues in the city, after exams, to ask if they had any photographs of local artists from the nineties. I claimed I was completing a project on the rise of homegrown indie music. In actual fact, I was searching for photographic evidence... And I found it, Erik. Images of Rachel Douglass. And in some of them, a young man. A contemporary. Then, when Mum and I were in the city, I met with a woman from a few of the photos named Rhonda, who still works at one of the clubs, and I found out—'

'*Stop*,' my brother says. He appears angry, which seems a severe reaction to what I would term impressive amateur detective work. 'I don't want to know. You shouldn't have done that. If Rain wanted to know, she would have... It wasn't your place, Eleanor.'

'She's my best friend! I was only trying to—'

'Stop. Stop trying. You can't fix everyone's problems. You need to wait until she's ready. Offer to help. But you can't keep forcing things, Nelly. You can't control everything all the time.'

I sigh. Perhaps he's right.

'Do you think I should tell her?'

'You kind of have to.'

I accept his advice begrudgingly, deciding aloud, 'I'll wait until after we've moved.'

He covers his face with his hands and is quiet for a long time. I begin to think he's asleep, but then he shifts onto his stomach and sighs into his pillow.

'It's going to be alright,' I say, rolling onto my side and patting his back comfortingly. 'Like Thatch said... we're alive.'

Erik exhales heavily. 'Yeah... We're alive.'

At the same moment, we both roll onto our backs.

Staring at the ceiling, I say, 'Repeat after me.'

'What?'

'I would like you to repeat what I say, after me. I'm going to take you through a series of affirmations, and you have to repeat them confidently: as if it's *already done*.'

He sighs.

'Repeat after me: I am brave.'

'Nelly...'

'*I am brave.*'

'I am brave,' he whispers.

'I am compassionate.'

'I am compassionate.'

'I am a hero.'

'I'm not—'

'Yes, you are. Now say it.'

'I'm... a hero.'

'Now all three, in a row.'

'I'm brave. I'm compassionate. I'm a hero.'

'Excellent. Now, repeat after me: I have many talents, including wave selection, aerial manoeuvres, and barrel-riding.'

'I have many talents, including wave selection...'

'Aerial manoeuvres.'

'Aerial manoeuvres, and barrel-riding.'

'I am going to dominate the competition.'

'I am going to dominate the competition.' He laughs into the dark, warm silence.

I take his hand over the sheet and squeeze it tightly, allowing my eyes to close. I know instinctively that his are closing too, and I wait for the rhythm of his breathing to slow my own.

ABOUT THE AUTHOR

Foxhead Bay is Alice Woodland's second novel — sequel to Mooney River. Alice Grew up in Western Australia and now lives with her growing family in coastal New South Wales.

Follow Alice to stay updated on more titles in the Mooney River Series ~ @alice_._woodland

www.ingramcontent.com/pod-product-compliance
Lightning Source LLC
Chambersburg PA
CBHW020912130726
47904CB00006BA/1848